'Do you think because I laugh when the courtiers try to court me?'

She didn't know how tempting she was as she stood there, her head tipped back, challenging him. Had he been young and carefree he would have been tempted to crush her in his arms and tell her that she was the most desirable woman he had ever seen—but that way lay only pain and grief, and he had been burned before.

'How can I think you anything when I do not know you?'

'I know you heard Baron de Froissart asking me what would win my heart earlier this afternoon. I gave him no reason to hope, nor have I encouraged others. It is the way of the Court to jest over such things.'

Sir Ralph bowed his head. Was it possible that she was that innocent? It hardly seemed likely. She had been wed before and must surely know her own power? Once again he felt an overwhelming desire to take her in his arms and kiss her, but crushed it ruthlessly. It was madness! She was not for him.

Dear Reader

It is a great pleasure to tell you about *The Banewulf Dynasty,* which I have written for your pleasure and mine. I have always loved the idea of knights wooing their ladies in the *courtly* way, and so my first story begins at the Court of Love in Poitiers. It was here, so the troubadours tell us, that the art of true *Romance* began. In those far-off wondrous days knights would do anything to win the heart of their lady, but no true knight would take a lady by force. Indeed, it was a matter of honour to protect, honour and adore your lady, often from afar. To suffer the pangs of unrequited love, to languish at your lady's feet, was a feeling so exquisite that a man might die of it and think himself in Paradise.

Alayne is accustomed to knights trying to win her, but none can touch her cold heart until Sir Ralph de Banewulf—who calls himself an imperfect knight, but is in truth a very perfect knight—comes into her life. She has vowed never to marry again, for her first husband was a wicked brute and no true knight. It is only through learning to love and trust again that Alayne can find happiness for herself and begin the dynasty that will live on in Stefan and Alain de Banewulf.

I hope you will have as much fun and delight in reading these as I did writing them. Please visit my website: www.lindasole.co.uk and tell me what you think of my stories. I'd love to hear from you.

Anne

Look for Stefan's story, in **A Knight of Honour**
coming in June 2005.

A PERFECT KNIGHT

Anne Herries

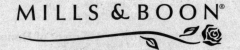

First published in Great Britain 2005
Harlequin Mills & Boon Limited,
Eton House, 18-24 Paradise Road, Richmond, Surrey TW9 1SR

© Anne Herries 2005

ISBN 0 263 84364 5

Set in Times Roman 10½ on 12 pt.
04-0405-92423

Printed and bound in Spain
by Litografia Rosés S.A., Barcelona

Anne Herries, winner of the Romantic Novelists' Association's Romance Prize 2004, lives in Cambridgeshire. After many happy years of having a holiday home in Spain she and her husband now have their second home in Norfolk. They are only just across the road from the sea, and can see it from their windows. At home and at the sea they enjoy watching the wildlife and have many visitors to their gardens, particularly squirrels. Anne loves watching their antics and spoils both them and her birds shamelessly. She also loves to see the flocks of geese and other birds flying in over the sea during the autumn, to winter in the milder climes of this country. Anne loves to write about the beauty of nature and sometimes puts a little into her books, though they are mostly about love and romance. She writes for her own enjoyment and to give pleasure to her readers.

Recent titles by the same author:

THE ABDUCTED BRIDE
CAPTIVE OF THE HAREM
THE SHEIKH
A DAMNABLE ROGUE*

*Winner of the Romantic Novelists' Association's Romance Prize

and in the Regency series
The Steepwood Scandal:

LORD RAVENSDEN'S MARRIAGE
COUNTERFEIT EARL

and in
The Elizabethan Season:

LADY IN WAITING
THE ADVENTURER'S WIFE

Chapter One

Alayne watched the shallow stream as it burbled and chuckled over boulders worn smooth by the passage of time, its waters so clear that she could see the tiny creatures that lived on the sandy bed. Behind her she could hear the laughter and chatter of the courtiers. One of the ladies was playing a lyre; others ran hither and thither screaming with mirth as they indulged in foolish games.

The sun was too warm for playing games, Alayne thought. She sighed as she trailed her fingers in the cool water of the stream. Was she growing weary of the endless pleasures offered at the Court of Love? Poitiers was often so named because of the troubadours, who sang of that fine courtly love of which many dreamed and few truly found. Sometimes Alayne believed that 'fine' love was merely a myth; she wearied of all the intrigues and found the life shallow. And yet where else could she go? There was nowhere else where she could be safe and protected as she was here.

A tiny shudder ran through her as she thought of the fate that awaited her if she were to leave the court, and she knew that she would rather waste her days in idle pleasure than be at the mercy of those who wished to control and manipulate her life. Her lovely face was sad as the memories came back to haunt her—the reasons why she had fled her home.

'Alayne! Alayne, come and join us,' one of the ladies screamed as she ran by, hotly pursued by a young knight intent on snatching the kisses he had won from her, which she now refused to pay. 'Save me from this wicked seducer, I beg you.'

Alayne smiled at their foolishness, but shook her head. She was in no mood for joining in their play; besides, she suspected that the lady fully intended to be caught once she had reached a secluded spot within the gardens. It might be nice to be kissed by a handsome lover, Alayne thought, and sighed—if only she could be as carefree and as happy as that girl!

Little though she knew it, her sadness was reflected in her lovely face and noticed by more than one knight present that day, for she was the kind of woman who attracted attention without seeking or wanting it. There was about her something that drew men to her, like moths to the flame.

Her thoughts were far away from the court at that moment, trapped in the recent unhappy past. It was almost a year since she had in desperation sought the protection of Eleanor of Aquitaine, who was a distant kinswoman of her mother's. Alayne had always admired the Queen. At the age of twenty Eleanor had taken the Cross and gone to the crusades with her husband King Louis VII of France, but that marriage had been annulled and Eleanor wed to Henry of Anjou, now Henry II of England. And there had been no one else Alayne could turn to in her distress.

'Why so thoughtful, my lady?'

Alayne glanced up as she heard the voice of the Baron

Pierre de Froissart, a little smile of welcome on her lips. He was held by most ladies of the court to be both handsome and charming, for he had a pleasant singing voice and an attractive manner.

'I do not give my thoughts so lightly, sir.' She pouted her lips at him, an unconscious teasing in her eyes that sent a fierce thrill of desire through the knight who looked down at her.

'Will you let me sit with you, lady?'

'Assuredly, sir. I am weary of my own company.'

Pierre de Froissart laughed and sat on the dry grass beside her, a look of amusement on his face. He sought her out most days, though he had never tried to court her. Alayne knew that several ladies sighed over him and gave him encouraging smiles. She suspected that he might have paid court to more than one lady, though such *affaires* were always kept secret.

It was an unspoken rule that courtly love should remain private. A troubadour approached his love in secret, offering his tributes of poems, songs, flowers or pretty trinkets. The lady would acknowledge the offering or not as she pleased. Indeed, it was the secret nature of the courtship that lent it excitement.

'Yet I think it is by your own choosing that you sit alone, lady. There are many who would court you had they the chance. You keep your admirers at a distance, I think.'

His eyes saw too much! Alayne's dark lashes veiled her eyes as she glanced down at the water, though her heart beat faster and brought a becoming colour to her creamy complexion. A blush touched her cheeks, but she did not answer him at once, for it was true that she had chosen solitude that afternoon.

She was a particularly beautiful girl, her dark hair only

partially hidden by the sheer veil she wore attached to her headdress of green and silver, her eyes a wonderful blue that made people look at her twice. Her dark lashes were long and silky; brushing her cheek as they did when she closed her eyes for a moment, their effect on men was startling and they had been mentioned in more than one poem to her beauty. She was the kind of woman that men dreamed of having in their bed, a tantalising temptress, with red lips that begged for kisses, her seeming innocence merely fanning the flames of their desire.

For the past several weeks someone had been sending her poems and small gifts of flowers. As yet her admirer had not spoken directly to her of his feelings, merely leaving his tributes where he knew she would find them on her walks or delivering them by means of a page who was sworn to silence.

'I wished to be quiet for a little…to think…' she said at last, bringing her eyes up to meet the man's suddenly.

'I would pay a forfeit for your thoughts,' de Froissart offered, as she was silent once more. 'For I do not like to see you so sad.'

'You need pay no forfeit,' Alayne replied. It was a game often played by the courtiers, and the young men tried to win kisses and more from the ladies. 'I was thinking of nothing in particular. Only that it is pleasant to sit here in the sun and yet…' A sigh escaped her and she did not go on.

'Can it be that you seek something more, Lady Alayne? Something fine and perfect, an intimacy not often met with, and seldom found in marriage…' He plucked a long stem of grass and chewed the end, his eyes watching her. The tip of her tongue moved nervously over her bottom lip, the act unconsciously sensuous and arousing fires of which she was completely unaware.

'I have no wish to marry again,' Alayne said, getting to her feet with a fluid, graceful movement. She found any talk of marriage unsettling. It was, of course, because her father, the Baron François de Robspierre, had tried to force her into a second marriage that she had sought protection from Queen Eleanor. 'Marriage is for making alliances and securing territory. Love is another matter.'

'You speak truly,' de Froissart agreed at once. She was lovely, and like many others at the court he dreamed of her, of having her as his lover. 'The intimacy of which I dream is beyond compare. To admire from afar the lady I worship is more than I could ever ask, but to know her, to share that exquisite intimacy, would indeed be heaven.'

Alayne's cheeks were heated. Was the Baron de Froissart her secret admirer? His words to her that afternoon seemed to indicate intense feeling on his part. Yet she was not sure of her own feelings. She had heard much of this perfect love from other ladies of the court, but was she ready to begin such an *affaire*? There was a part of her that longed to know the true love of which the troubadours sang so sweetly, but another that shrank from any physical contact.

'Alayne! Will you not sing for us? Her Majesty begs you come to her.'

Her thoughts took a new direction as a pretty young woman came towards them. Marguerite de Valois was a popular member of the court. She received endless tributes from her admirers, but she withheld her favours from all. Some of them had been set foolish tasks by the Courts of Love to try and win her, but she remained aloof, giving no man more than a nod in passing no matter what they did to please her.

'Willingly,' Alayne cried and went to meet her. She was glad of the interruption, for the Baron had made her uncertain, a little nervous. She liked him well enough as a friend, but any attempt at intimacy frightened her.

Marguerite glanced at her flushed face as she joined her. 'It is not for me to advise, Alayne, but I would be wary of de Froissart if I were you.'

'You do not like him? He is generally liked at court, I think.'

'As to that…' Marguerite shrugged. Her long fair hair was covered by a silver veil caught from a little cap, her green eyes thoughtful as she looked at Alayne. 'You are very beautiful, Alayne, and wealthy. There are men who would do anything to secure such a prize. I do not deny de Froissart's charm. I say only that I would not trust him.'

'You know that I do not wish to marry again?'

'I have heard that your marriage was not happy…'

'I prefer not to remember,' Alayne said, a closed look coming to her face as she forced the cruel memories back to that tiny corner of her mind where they habitually dwelt. 'My father wished me to marry again so that he could gain advantage from my widowhood for himself, but the Queen forbade it. She has given her word that I shall not be forced to marry against my will.'

'You are fortunate,' Marguerite said with a sigh. 'I shall be married when I am seventeen whether I wish it or no.'

'It is the lot of most women,' Alayne said. 'My father was furious when I sought the Queen's protection. He considers I am his property to dispose of as he wishes, but I shall not be sold again!' Tears sparkled in her lovely eyes, but she refused to let them fall. Her wedding night had been unspeakable and it was only the sudden demise of her husband, who was so many years her senior, that had saved her from further humiliation at his hands.

Marguerite pressed her hand and smiled. It was because so many women were forced into unhappy marriages that the code of courtly love had gained so much popularity in the languorous climes of Aquitaine and southern regions of France. How much sweeter the stolen kiss of a young lover than the clumsy embrace of an uncaring husband!

But the court was waiting for Alayne to sing for them. She was led to the place of honour beside the Queen's gilded throne. She smiled and curtsied respectfully to her friend and champion.

'Sing for us, Lady Alayne,' the Queen requested. 'Sing something sweet that will bring tears to our eyes and gladden our hearts.'

'Yes, your Grace,' Alayne said and, taking a lyre from one of the other ladies, began to play a haunting melody, the pure notes of her song catching the attention of all those gathered in the glade that warm afternoon in the year of Our Lord 1167.

It was a song of love unrequited, of a lover left to weep alone and die of a broken heart, and of a love so pure and tender that it touched the hearts of all those who heard it.

Her song was of a perfect knight, a man who chose death rather than bring harm to the lady he adored. But where, Alayne wondered, would she ever find such an honourable knight? She did not believe that he existed outside the songs of the troubadours.

'His Majesty bids me visit the Queen at her court in Poitiers,' Sir Ralph de Banewulf said to his cousin Harald

of Wotten as they talked that afternoon in the great hall
of Banewulf Manor. Banewulf had begun as a fortress in
the days of William the Conqueror, but a new house had
been built adjacent to the tower in more recent times for
the sake of comfort. 'I cannot refuse Henry's request,
though you know I have no love of the court these days.'

'It will do you good to leave this place and seek company,' Harald replied with a frown. His cousin had been
in mourning too long for the wife he had married at nine-
teen and lost barely more than a year later. Berenice had
died of a fever after giving her husband a son, Stefan,
and the boy was now a sturdy lad of five years. 'Besides,
it is time that you gave me Stefan for his training as a
squire. Most lads would have entered school a year since.
You do him no favours by leaving him to the women,
Ralph.'

Ralph was silent for a moment, his expression harsher
than he realised. He was a man that others respected and
feared, a strong, powerful man with stern principles and
standards few could follow. Yet when he relaxed and
smiled he was pleasant to look upon and had an unconscious charm. Women admired him, but he was often
thought unapproachable, and it was said that his heart
had died with his young wife. When he spoke at last, his
words were just and considered.

'You are right, Harald, and I know it. I have been
remiss with Stefan. He grows too independent for his
nurse. He must be schooled, for how else will he gain
his knighthood? You shall take him with you this afternoon, my friend. I beg only that you will have a care for
him for his mother's sake.'

'You had no need to ask. I loved Berenice dearly,
though she was but a distant cousin of my mother's.'

Harald hesitated. 'You will not wish me to say this, Ralph—but you should think of marrying again. A man needs a wife to give him sons.'

'Pray do not!' Ralph held up his hand, a look of grief sweeping over his hard features. 'My demesne is large enough for my ambitions and I have a son to inherit all my lands. Why should I need more?'

Harald refrained from giving him the answer he knew would be unwelcome. Children died all too often of virulent fevers or accidents. He himself had five sons and two daughters, having married for a second time within six months of his first wife's death. It was the way of the world, for women were lost in childbed and there was no sense in repining. Life must go on and one woman was much the same as another in his experience.

'I know you loved Berenice, but—'

'Please!' Ralph's plea was a command, and a nerve twitched in his cheek. 'Let us speak of other matters. What think you of this quarrel that rumbles on between the King and Sir Thomas à Becket?'

As Harald launched into a tirade against the King's quarrel with the Archbishop, Ralph drew a breath of relief. He did not wish to discuss the fragile young wife, who had not been strong enough for childbearing. His hands clenched at his sides as he felt the familiar ache in his breast. He had grieved for a life needlessly lost. How could he ever think of marrying again when his unkindness, his thoughtless desires, had killed Berenice?

And there was the secret guilt that haunted him, because, though he had desired her, as a young man would for her beauty and sweetness, he had never truly loved her. She had proved too young and too foolish to hold his affections, and he feared that his reserve, his coldness, had destroyed her. She had known that he did not love

her and because of that she was dead. It was a heavy sin
for which he had done penance these past years.

He had let the women fuss over Stefan as they would,
because his son was a permanent reminder of Berenice's
tragic death, but his weakness would reflect badly on the
boy. He must be schooled and trained in the arts that
would make him first a page, then a squire and then worthy to receive his knighthood. Harald of Wotten was a
good man and just; he would look after Stefan and over-
see his education and the boy would be sent home to
spend feast days with his father. It was the end of one
part of their lives and meant that Ralph had no ties to
hold him to this place and must begin to think of the
future.

The King's request that he journey to Aquitaine and
seek out Queen Eleanor at her court was one that he felt
bound to honour, for he had received his own knighthood
at Henry's hands.

King Henry II was in Ralph's estimation a worthy ruler
of England. Henry had rescued the country from the
chaos it had fallen into under King Stephen's reign and
instituted many reforms. He had subdued Wales and regained northern territories that had been lost to Scotland,
but he had also brought in a law pertaining to the trial
of churchmen who had transgressed, which had aroused
the fury of many influential men. The most important of
these was Sir Thomas à Becket, a stubborn man who had
refused to bend in this matter of a law he felt unjust.

For the moment Ralph was not prepared to take sides.
It was, he believed, a matter between the King and his
Archbishop. Ralph's loyalty was to the King and his mission to visit Queen Eleanor. The marriage between Henry
and Eleanor, at first passionate and fortuitous for both,
had deteriorated these past years, and Henry had heard

rumours of his wife that displeased him. Some said that Eleanor meddled in matters of state that did not concern her, that she planted treason and sedition in the minds of her sons, turning them against their father. She had left England because of a quarrel with her husband and Henry was not altogether happy with her behaviour since. It was Ralph's task to carry letters to the Queen at Poitiers and bring back her answer.

For the moment that was all that mattered; this personal unrest, this feeling of emptiness, must be put aside. Ralph had devoted his life to the welfare of his son and the people on his estate. In the future he must begin to look elsewhere for a purpose to his life. Once, when he was young and full of shining ideals, he had thought of taking up the cross and going to the crusades, but that was before his careless behaviour had killed Berenice… Now he knew that he was not worthy. He was, in fact, a most imperfect knight.

The court had spent the day hawking on the marshlands beyond the forest. Alayne's peregrine had flown well, its speed, strong flight and tenacity much admired. Indeed, she had received more than one offer to buy the bird, but refused to part with it.

'I love my sweet Perlita,' Alayne said to one gentleman who persisted with his offer. 'I shall never part with her for gold or jewels. She is far too precious.'

A party of ladies and gentlemen were riding close enough to hear her answer and one of the gentlemen asked what would buy the peregrine, if gold would not.

'Why, nothing, my lord,' Alayne replied, her azure blue eyes sparkling with mischief. 'She shall never leave me unless I choose to give her.'

'A wager! A wager!' cried several voices.

'I'll wager the Lady Alayne would more willingly give her love than that bird,' one of the ladies cried and trilled with laughter.

'For shame!' another voice said. 'She cannot be won, for many have tried to win her smiles and received naught for their pains.'

'You are too unkind, my Lord Malmont,' Alayne said and laughed at the man who had spoken. 'You may have a smile for the asking, but the man who would win both me and Perlita must first win my heart.'

'Set me any task and I shall perform it,' he quipped, hand clenched dramatically against his breast while his eyes danced with merriment. 'For to win both you and that hawk would be a prize indeed.'

'You mock me, sir. I think you prize the bird more than the lady,' she replied and made a face at him, for she knew him to be another lady's admirer. 'I do not believe that I shall ever love. My heart is made of stone. I cannot love any man.'

'A challenge!' cried Baron de Froissart. 'The lady's denial cannot be allowed to go unchallenged. We must have a contest for the heart of this lady.'

Several gentlemen murmured agreement and there was much laughter and jesting as the party rode back through the forest to the palace.

Alayne found there was good-natured but fierce competition as to who should have the honour of helping her dismount from her palfrey. She laughed at their eager faces, then summoned a young page standing nearby, causing the knights to pull faces of dismay and complain that they had been overlooked for a mere stripling.

'I am not to be so easily won, gentle sirs,' she told them with a smile and gave her peregrine to the page, warning him to take good care of her before jumping down from her horse unaided. 'If I am to be won, it will be no simple task.'

She was immediately asked to set her challenge, but merely smiled and shook her head before walking into the palace. The coolness of the thick stone walls met her immediately, seeming dark and making her shiver after the heat of the sun. For some reason she felt uneasy, though she did not know why she should, nor what reason she had for feeling that way. The light-hearted exchange between the courtiers was no more than happened any day, though she was not usually singled out. Other ladies were more inclined to respond to such teasing and enjoyed setting tasks of heroism or skill for their admirers to perform.

She was foolish to be anxious. Yet the prickling sensation at the nape of her neck was intense. Turning, Alayne saw that a man was standing a little way off. He was partially hidden by one of the huge stone pillars that supported the arched ceiling above the great hall. She could, however, see that he was tall, powerfully built, with broad shoulders: an impressive man dressed in the English fashion in cloth of black and silver, his dark, almost black hair straight and just long enough to brush the neckband of his tunic. His features were strong, harsh, his mouth set hard as if he disapproved of all he saw about him.

Alayne knew that she had never seen him at court before and, for one moment, as their eyes met, she felt something stir within her. He had such intent eyes, the irises a deep grey that seemed flecked with silver—or was that a trick of the sunlight that came slanting in at the high window?

Alayne felt her spine tingle as she looked deep into those mesmerising eyes and felt the pull of his personality. Who was the newcomer and why was the tingling at the nape of her neck even stronger now than it had been? Was she being warned of something? Why was he staring at her in that particular way? And yet there was something about his expression that made her think he hardly saw her, that he was lost in some lonely place in his thoughts. He seemed brooding, distant, as if nursing some secret sadness.

Hearing the others enter the hall, the noise of their chatter and laughter filling the echoing space, the strange feeling of being threatened left her all at once and she laughed at herself. She had nothing to fear. The Queen had promised she would not be forced to marry and there was no reason why she should. For as long as she had Queen Eleanor's protection she was perfectly safe.

'Ah, there you are, Lady Alayne,' de Froissart cried as he saw her. 'We thought we had driven you to flight with our teasing.'

'No, indeed, sir,' Alayne replied.'

'Since you will set no challenge, we have decided to be judged by the court. The best amongst us shall compete for your favour at a tournament,' he said, eyes alight with wicked mirth. 'The winner earns the right to court you.'

'I am not to be won by such a contest,' Alayne said, but could not keep from laughing. The teasing look in the Baron de Froissart's eyes made her heart beat wildly despite herself. He was a charming man and of all the courtiers she liked him the most, though she did not believe that he, or any man, had touched the inner citadel within her. Sometimes she believed that her heart was dead, killed by the brutality of the man she had been forced to wed when she was little more than a child. 'I promise only a token to the winner, but my heart is not so easily captured.'

'Then what will win you?'

'I do not know,' Alayne admitted. 'My love, if it is ever given, will be for a gentle knight; a strong, true, loyal knight who lives by his ideals.' Her eyes were for some reason drawn to where the stranger stood, but he was no longer there. She felt disappointed though she knew not why, recovering herself almost at once. 'This is but foolish nonsense, sir! Who can say where love comes from? We find it where we least expect it and cannot love to please others. Do the poets not say that the greatest pleasure of all is to languish for a love that is not returned?'

'Cruel! Cruel lady,' de Froissart cried and smote his fist against his breast. 'So be it, we shall labour for the prize of being the knight who languishes at your feet without hope for love of you.'

She turned from him at once, hiding her amusement. The Baron was indeed a charming companion and she took little notice of his teasing, for she had decided that he was not the one who had been sending her poems and flowers. She rather thought it might be one of the young pages, because she had seen him watching her with a yearning expression that had touched her heart. Life at court was sometimes difficult for the pages, who were at the beck and call of all, and she had seen more than one young boy in tears when he thought himself unnoticed.

'You must fight for whatever pleases you,' she replied and left him staring after her.

'Cruel enchantress,' de Froissart called after her. 'You break my heart, lady.' He waited for some response but, lost in her thoughts, she hardly heard him as she made her way towards the twisting stair that led to the turret room she shared.

Alayne's habit of taking solitary walks about the gardens had made her aware of such things. She sometimes saw a snatched kiss or a clandestine meeting between a lady and her knight, but she kept such glimpses to herself; these things were secret and must be respected, and the tears of a page were every bit as sacrosanct to Alayne. She had once given a scarf to a boy in tears, doing her best to comfort him after his master had beaten him. She rather suspected it might be this boy who had been leaving tributes for her.

Walking up the curving flight of stone steps that led to her solar in the west tower, she was thoughtful. It might not be Baron de Froissart who had been leaving her tributes, but she had a feeling that he was taking an interest in her. She was not sure how she would react if he made a direct appeal to her as a potential lover. She did not think she would mind being kissed and treated as an object of reverence and desire—but what if he demanded more?

Alayne's marriage had taught her what brutes men could be at certain times, especially if their desires were frustrated. Some of the ladies talked of the joys of *fine* love, but could it ever be as sweet as the troubadours claimed in their songs? Alayne's own experience had been very different, and she recalled her marriage, which had in truth been no marriage, with only horror and revulsion.

Alayne shared her chamber with Marguerite de Valois and was not surprised that the lady was already there, changing from her outer garments of surcote and heavy wool tunic into a softer, lighter robe of cloth of silver, which she covered by an over-gown of deep blue. She smiled as Alayne entered and began to disrobe, taking off her plain white wimple. The wimple covered her head entirely and was more modest when out riding than the fantastic headdresses that the ladies adopted for court wear.

'Did you chance to see Sir Ralph de Banewulf in the hall?' Marguerite asked as Alayne shook her head, letting the shining mass of dark hair tumble down her back. 'My father told me he was expecting to see him here by today at the latest. He brings letters from the English King to her Majesty.'

'I saw someone new,' Alayne said. 'A tall, dark man, rather stern looking—' She broke off as she remembered his eyes and the way he had seemed to stare at her.

'Yes, I dare say that was he. His mother was cousin to my father. Sir Ralph is widowed these five years. His wife died some weeks after giving birth to their son. She was very beautiful and they say he still grieves for her.'

'That is sad,' Alayne said, remembering the brooding, almost haunted expression she had seen in the stranger's eyes. 'Such faithful devotion to a wife's memory is not often found.'

'No, that is true. Most men marry again as soon as possible for the sake of getting more heirs. I think he must have loved her very much. It is romantic—like the songs the troubadours sing for us.'

'Yes, it would seem so,' Alayne agreed, remembering the expression in the newcomer's eyes. Perhaps that explained his stern manner. He was hiding his grief. 'I did not think men married for love. It was not so in my case. My husband's lands joined my father's on one side. They arranged the match between them for their mutual benefit. My father said they were both stronger for the alliance, more able to defend their own demesne from any attack. My son was to have inherited all their lands in time and my father was disappointed that I did not give him the grandson he craved.'

'But you were married only a few weeks.'

'My husband had an accident the day after our wedding. He—he was drunk and fell down the stairs.' Alayne's eyes held the sparkle of tears, but she blinked them away, refusing to weep. 'He broke his back, but did not die at once. I nursed him for some weeks, but he did not recover.'

She turned away as the bitter memories crowded into her mind and would not be denied. Baron Humbolt had cursed her with his every breath, blaming her for his inability to be a true husband to her. His hatred had been hard for a young girl to bear, as had the cruel, crude language he used to her—the language of the stews. Almost as humiliating as the way he had tried to use her on the wedding night.

But she would not think of that! She had promised herself that she would never allow another man to humiliate her in that way.

'I am so sorry,' Marguerite said. 'It is little wonder that you have no wish to marry again. My father says it is almost time to arrange my marriage…' She broke off and sighed deeply. 'I hope he chooses someone kind, someone I can like.'

'He has not spoken of his choice for you?'

'Not yet, though…I think he may have someone in his thoughts, but I cannot be sure.'

Alayne guessed what was in her mind. 'You think he may approach his kinsman? Sir Ralph de Banewulf?'

Marguerite blushed. 'Perhaps, but I must not presume. These things are a matter for discussion and contract. Sir Ralph may not wish for such a match.'

'Is there no one you like? Someone you would choose to marry if you could?'

Marguerite's blush deepened. She hesitated for a moment, conscious of Alayne's eyes on her, then said, 'There might be, but he has not yet won his knighthood. My father would never permit me to wed a lowly squire.'

'Does he love you?' Alayne was intrigued. She was not sure why, but she had the feeling that her friend was not telling her the whole truth. There was someone—but was it really a squire who had yet to win his spurs? 'Do you love him?'

'It would be foolish of me to love him,' Marguerite said and for a moment sadness flickered in her lovely eyes. 'I know I must marry as my father dictates.'

'Yes, I suppose you must.'

Alayne knew that her friend had no choice but to obey her father. Having been married and left in possession of a small but adequate fortune in her own right, Alayne had been able to seek protection from her Majesty. It was not the same for Marguerite.

'Perhaps you will be lucky,' she said, more to comfort her friend than in belief. 'Come, if you are ready, perhaps we should go down. The Queen may need us.'

Marguerite nodded, smiling as if determined to banish her fears. 'I hope Sir Ralph has arrived,' she told Alayne. 'I am looking forward to meeting him.'

Alayne's thoughts returned to the man she had noticed earlier. He had seemed so cold, almost angry. Why was that? Had his expression when he looked at her been disapproval as she had at first thought or merely the sadness habitual to a man who was still grieving for the wife he had lost?

Chapter Two

The company was very merry that night, the courtiers still teasing Alayne, the knights devising tests of skill and courage that they seemed determined to carry out in her name. She could not refrain from laughing at their foolish banter, though she continued to be firm that she would give only a trinket to the winner of the tournament and that her heart was not to be so easily won.

'You must forgive them their foolishness,' the Queen told her as she bid her sit on a stool at her side and tell her how this talk of a tourney had begun. It was a rare privilege to sit in the Queen's presence and not given to many. 'They grow restless at court and need this contest to rid themselves of too much energy. It would behove most of them to take themselves off to a war somewhere.'

'Why do men like to fight, your Grace?' Alayne asked, genuinely puzzled. 'My father quarrels with his neighbours and his men fight amongst each other.'

'It is in their nature,' replied Queen Eleanor. 'And a true knight is brave in battle. I have always admired Saladin, despite his infidel beliefs. He is a true man and a clever soldier—but most men are faithless and we do well to remember it, Lady Alayne. Happiness lies not in the personal life, but in power, especially if you are a queen.'

Alayne sensed that the Queen was angry, but before she could ask her what had occurred to arouse her ire, she saw that a man was approaching them. It was the man she had seen standing in the shadows of the great hall when she returned from hawking. He bowed low before the Queen, his eyes dwelling on her for a moment and seeming to register both approval and admiration.

Eleanor of Aquitaine was a handsome woman with nut-brown hair and dark eyes, but there was much more than beauty to this woman. She was clever, proud and spirited, more fitted perhaps to kingship than some men. Alayne had heard it said that she took a keen interest in matters of state, not only in her own province but in England, encouraging her sons in defiance of their father. At the moment, her eyes were flashing with annoyance and something in the way she looked at the stranger told Alayne that her anger had something to do with him.

'So, Sir Ralph,' she said, 'I trust my servants have made you comfortable? You have your own chamber?'

'Why yes, your Grace,' he replied. 'I did not need so much. A place to sleep by the fire in your hall would have been sufficient. I do not expect to remain more than a few days.'

'My husband has asked weighty questions in his letters,' Eleanor returned a little harshly. 'It may be some weeks before I am able to find the time to answer them as I would wish. In the meantime I would not have his messenger given less than a warm welcome to my court. You must make yourself at home here, sir. We live comfortably, as you will find; there is food in plenty and entertainment. Indeed, my knights have planned a tournament in this lady's honour. Lady Alayne will be Queen

for a day and receive all the honours due her. Perhaps
you might care to join in the tourney? It will help to pass
the time while you wait for my answer.'

Sir Ralph bowed, his dark eyes narrowed as they cen-
tred on Alayne's face. For a moment he was silent and
she felt her cheeks grow warm under his scrutiny as he
seemed to measure her. Had he found her wanting? His
cold manner seemed to indicate that he had and she lifted
her head proudly in response, stung by his seeming con-
tempt. He had no right to look at her that way!

'I have heard much of the lady,' he said and his voice
was deep and soft, sending a little shiver down her spine.
'It is said that she has a heart of stone and cannot be won
in such a contest.'

Alayne met his look without flinching, knowing that
he had heard her laughing challenge to Baron de Froissart. It *was* disapproval she had seen in his eyes more
than once, she was certain of it now! Did he think her
vain, a heartless flirt who enjoyed having the knights risk
life and limb in a vain effort to win her favours? For
even though the contest would not be to the death, as
was sometimes the case when knights sought revenge or
a redress of honour, there was always a chance that they
might be badly hurt or wounded.

'I have promised no more than a token to the winner,'
she said, a look of pride on her face. She little knew how
her eyes sparkled or that anger enhanced her beauty. It
was a part of her witchery that she was truly unaware of
the power she held over men's hearts and bodies, the
power to make them burn for desire of her. 'It is a foolish
idea, but their own. I would have no one fight for me,
Sir Knight. I would advise you to ignore the challenge,
for it is mere nonsense.'

'I thank you for your advice, lady,' he said and made

her what she thought a mocking bow. She little knew that the stranger had felt the sensuality of her beauty despite himself, his body responding to her in a way that he had not felt for many years. His frown of displeasure was for himself, his own weakness, rather than for her. 'It is many years since I took part in such a tourney and I fear I would not be a worthy challenger. You must, I pray you, excuse me.'

He bowed to the Queen once more and walked on, leaving Alayne smarting. Who was he to dismiss her in such a way? She felt as if he had thrown water in her face. She was insulted by his manner and resolved to have nothing more to do with him.

'English manners,' the Queen remarked wryly as he moved away. 'You must not mind him, Alayne. The English are often arrogant and too sure of themselves. I met many such as de Bane-wulf when I resided in that land; they are as cold as their climate—though some are good men. Loyal if they give their heart to a cause, though not always with their ladies.'

It was King Henry's infidelity that had caused her to quarrel with her husband and leave England.

Alayne was thoughtful. 'I have heard that Sir Ralph mourns the wife he lost five years since.'

'Yes, I have heard that too,' the Queen said. 'I believe I remember Berenice. Her father brought her to my court once. She was a gentle, shy girl, and fragile. She might have been better in a convent than married to a man like that.'

'What do you mean?' Alayne asked. 'Is he cruel and unkind?'

'No, I think not,' Eleanor replied. 'But there is passion there beneath the ice. Do not be fooled by that cold manner, Alayne. Sir Ralph is a lusty man and his wife would need to match him. I think Berenice would be too gentle, too easily crushed—poor child. She was but fourteen or so when they married, fifteen when her son was born, and delicate. She could not survive the strain of giving birth to a child and never recovered. She was struck down with some kind of wasting fever, I have heard, and died in terrible pain.'

Alayne crossed herself. 'Poor lady. I fear there are many who die in such case, your Grace. The birthing of a babe can be a dangerous thing for women and too many are taken by a fever.'

'It happens, particularly when the woman is too slight and fragile, but for a strong woman it is not such a terrible thing. I bore sons and lived, Alayne—and I believe you would too. If that is your reason for fearing marriage?'

Alayne shook her head, her cheeks crimson. 'No, your Grace. I told you my story. I would have gladly given my husband a son if—if he had been other than he was.'

'Well, well, I shall not embarrass you,' Eleanor said and patted her cheek. 'You know that I shall not allow you to be forced into an unhappy match, but one day you may change your mind, and then I shall be happy to give you to the man you choose to wed.'

'I do not think that day will come.'

'Is there no one here to stir your heart, Alayne?'

'None that I would take to husband.'

'Ah, then perhaps there is someone you would choose as your lover?' Eleanor laughed as she saw her flush. 'No, I shall not tease you. There, I release you now. Mingle with the company and send Marguerite to me. I have something I wish to say to her.'

Alayne made her curtsy and went to find Marguerite. She passed on the Queen's message, then glanced around the large chamber, which was full of ladies and their knights, intent on making merry. A troubadour was singing a love song to a small group of ladies, who seemed entranced by his words. Several other ladies were taking their ease on banks of cushions; others sat more primly on hard wooden benches or stools, listening to conversation. The art of witty conversation was greatly prized at Queen Eleanor's court. Alayne debated whether to join one of these groups, but decided to take one of her solitary walks instead.

She liked to walk alone in the evening air. At this time of year it did not grow dark for some hours yet and the air was warm.

As she went out into one of the many sheltered courtyards, she caught the perfume of night-scented blooms and inhaled with pleasure. A little stream tumbled over an artificial fall of rocks into a pool where tiny fish swam and Alayne stood for a while, watching them, before a slight sound behind her made her turn. A man was standing there, watching her, and the sight of him made her heart jump, though somehow she was not afraid of him, as she sometimes was of others.

'It is late for you to be here alone, Lady Alayne.'

'I often walk alone, sometimes in the evenings. I do not fear it while I am under the Queen's protection, sir.'

'There are some men for whom that would mean nothing,' Sir Ralph said. 'No matter how innocent the lady, some would violate her given the chance—I have seen men of that ilk here this evening. Even if you think no harm to make mockery as you do, lady, you would do well not to give them the chance to take cruel advantage of you.'

'What do you mean?' Her heart had quickened and now she was afraid of the intensity she saw in his eyes.

He seemed to be accusing her of deliberately inciting the men who courted her. What could he mean? 'Are you…?' Her breath caught and she could not go on as she saw his hands clench at his sides.

'Nay, Lady Alayne,' he replied. 'You have no need to fear me, for I would not violate any lady, whether she be innocent or the wickedest wench alive.'

Something in the way he was looking at her made Alayne think that he disapproved of her and she raised her head proudly. 'You seem to criticise me, my lord. Do you think me a wicked wench because I laugh when the courtiers try to court me?'

Again, she didn't know how tempting she was as she stood there, her head tipped back, challenging him. Had he been young and carefree, he would have been tempted to crush her in his arms and tell her that she was the most desirable woman he had ever seen—but that way lay only pain and grief and he had been burned before.

'How can I think you anything when I do not know you?'

'I know you heard Baron de Froissart asking me what would win my heart earlier this afternoon. I gave him no reason to hope, nor have I encouraged others. It is the way of the court to jest over such things.'

Sir Ralph bowed his head. Was it possible she was that innocent? It hardly seemed likely. She had been wed before and must surely know her own power? Once again he felt the overwhelming desire to take her in his arms and kiss her, but crushed it ruthlessly. It was madness! She was not for him.

His manner was stern, seeming to disapprove as he said, 'I beg your pardon if I have misjudged you in any part, Lady Alayne. I am a stranger here and your ways are not my ways.'

'No. Therefore you should not judge.'

Her eyes sparkled with defiance as she met his chilling gaze. She was not used to such brusque manners from the knights who courted her with sweet words and songs—and she did not care for it.

'You are very right,' he agreed and inclined his head, a faint, rueful smile about his mouth, softening it so that she was suddenly aware of a foolish desire to be kissed. But not by him. No, certainly not by him! 'I have clearly insulted you, which was not my intention. I would say only that my advice holds true. It is not wise for a woman as young and lovely as you to walk alone, either at night or during the day.'

Sir Ralph bowed to her once more, turned and walked away, leaving her to stare after him in frustration. She thought him cold and arrogant, though his assurance came from within and was not the posturing of a fool. He was a man who knew his own power and authority, and lived by it. Yet beneath the ice she had sensed heat, a passion that had seemed to burn her, touching a place within her that she had believed no man could reach.

No, no, that was nonsense! She had merely found him interesting, a complex character. It was not as easy for her to read his mind as some other knights, who showed their feelings openly. What was it that he wanted to hide? And why had he chosen to warn her that she might be in danger? Was it true? Was she in danger even here?

She shivered suddenly as a chill touched her spine. Surely he was making too much of the risks? No one at court dare disobey the Queen, for she would punish them heavily if they did, especially if they flouted the rules of chivalry that she had set for her courtiers.

Alayne had always believed herself perfectly safe wherever she went at court, but now the shadow in the corners became menacing and she retraced her steps swiftly towards the hall, the light of the smoky torches and the laughter of her friends.

'Ah, there you are,' Baron de Froissart called to her as she made her way towards a group of ladies. 'We wondered where you were, lady. Sir Jonquil has prepared a poem for you—will you hear him?'

'Yes, yes, you must hear him!' clamoured a dozen voices. 'We want to hear his poem!'

Alayne smiled, her confidence restored in the familiar atmosphere of laughter and teasing. She was foolish to let the brooding of that strange English knight upset her!

Sir Ralph did not immediately return to the hall after leaving Lady Alayne, though he was relieved to see that she did so almost at once. He frowned as he wondered what had made him speak to her as he had. It was not his business if she chose to walk alone, nor if she flirted carelessly with men he considered unworthy. She had been married and must understand the danger she courted.

No woman could look and act as she did and be as innocent as she would have it! There was something about her that had drawn him despite himself, a witchery or enchantment that made his blood pulse in his veins. She claimed to be innocent of guile and for a moment he had almost been swayed by those proud eyes, but he had learned not be moved by a woman's tears and looks of reproach. Berenice had been young and foolish, but the Lady Alayne was very different. Any man foolish enough to let himself be caught in her toils would surely rue the day he had met her!

Ralph had heard much of the fabled Court of Love and of the rules of chivalry surrounding it. Such nonsense would no doubt appeal to vulnerable young women, who thought it amusing to tease and arouse the men who courted them, but Ralph knew too well that all men were base. It was dangerous to walk too near the edge with men in whom the beast lived near the surface—even he had been tempted to taste the honey Lady Alayne's lips seemed to promise and it was unkind memory, not chivalry, that had held him from the brink. If it were not for the memory of another woman's tears... His thoughts were diverted as he heard voices, close by but in the shadows.

'De Froissart wants her. If he has his way, she will be his lover and perhaps more ere too long has passed.'

'He plays games. She is not to be won so easily. She ignores my tributes as she ignores me. She has set her face against marriage and cannot be reached.'

Two men were arguing, their voices sour and heated, and Ralph sensed instinctively that they were discussing the Lady Alayne.

'But if she were to change her mind?' the first man said. 'This tourney in her honour may win her. You know how the ladies love to watch good sport, and she will be the Queen of the day. Her head may be turned by all the excitement. De Froissart is a past champion. There are few that could succeed against him. He will win the right to court her and, if she yields to him as a lover...'

'You think her father would demand marriage as the price of her honour if he knew?'

'The Baron de Robspierre seeks power and fortune. De Froissart is rich enough and popular at court. I have heard him speak of winning honour at England's court. The lady's father would welcome such a match.'

'I would see him dead first!'

'Then you must enter the lists against him. You must

receive her favour. Gain her confidence and make her like you. All the ladies love a brave warrior. Many a wench has fallen into my arms after watching me fight. Take her while she is hot for you! Once she is yours, you may find a way to tame her.'

'I have not the skill to defeat de Froissart in a tourney. Others, yes; I believe I might prevail with them, but de Froissart is a mighty warrior.'

'Play the coward's part and you will lose your chance.'

'I have a plan…'

The voices were growing fainter, as though the men had walked on. Ralph strained to listen, but he could no longer hear what they said and was unsure which direction they had taken. He did not know the voices, but recognised the greed and evil that drove them to their wicked plotting.

Ralph had made inquiries concerning the Lady Alayne earlier that evening, for she intrigued him and he knew that she was wealthy in her own right, but she was also her father's heiress for he had no other children and no brothers or close kin. It seemed that Alayne was even more vulnerable than Ralph had first thought. Her beauty and that way of smiling, that hint of pleasure that lay deep in her eyes, that warm, sensual allure she exuded without being aware of it, were all potent and enough to make her a prize for any man even had she not been wealthy.

His warning, delivered in a moment of anger, though more with himself than her, had been against violation of her person and her trust, but now it appeared that she was in danger of losing much more: her freedom and perhaps even her life one day. For such men as he had overheard were ruthless and she would be but a pawn in this plotter's game.

Something deep inside him rose up to deny such an eventuality. No, they should not harm her! Not while he lived. The next moment he gave a harsh laugh at his own reaction.

What was it to him? She had shown her feelings openly. She did not like him. She had been angered and insulted by his advice earlier. If he tried to warn her of this plot, she would probably not believe him. Besides, what did he really know?

He had heard two faceless voices speaking in the dark, discussing the tourney. No doubt many of the knights had spoken in similar terms of their chances of winning the lady's favour. One of those he had heard wished to gain the lady for himself, most likely because of the rich lands her father owned and the fortune her husband had left her. Her father and husband had clearly thought to unite their lands through the lady's sons, but she had none and was therefore the greater prize for unscrupulous men. Once married, her husband would own all that was hers, and if her father should die soon after a vast fortune would be the husband's for the taking. She would be her husband's possession, his chattel, to use as he would. That thought turned Ralph's stomach sour and made him scowl in the darkness.

Ralph scorned the greed that spurred such men, but he knew it to be a powerful vice. He had married for a far different reason, and yet he had brought Berenice nothing but pain and a cruel death. He was as base as any other of his sex, though he had strived to be better, to earn back his self-respect, and he had suffered for his carelessness.

He could not stand idly by if the Lady Alayne was in some danger, for he would be as guilty then as he was of Berenice's death. If he had acted differently that

day…if he had only taken the trouble to try and understand his wife…but that way lay only madness. He could
not give Berenice back her life, but he might help Alayne.

Should he speak to the Queen about what he had
heard? Ralph knew that Eleanor had been angered by the
tone of Henry's letters and what she had heard of her
husband's infidelity. It was unlikely that she would listen
to anything Henry's messenger had to say, especially as
he could offer no proof.

He would be foolish to try. Ralph wrestled with his
thoughts. He was not responsible for Lady Alayne's
safety! She was nothing to him, nor could she ever be.
Yet something about her had stirred feelings he'd believed long dead, buried beneath a mound of grief and
anguish.

He had been bidden to languish here at Poitiers until
the Queen was disposed to answer her husband's letters.
That might be a matter of days, weeks, or months. The
time would hang heavy on his hands, yet he would use
it to discover what he could about the men who plotted
to use Lady Alayne for their own ends. Perhaps if he had
proof, the Queen would listen if the lady would not?

Until he had overheard that whispered plotting, Ralph
had considered Baron de Froissart the lady's greatest risk
amongst the knights. He was clearly enamoured of her
and meant to seduce her if he could with sweet words
and brave deeds, but these other, secret plotters were a
more potent danger. They planned to take by stealth what
the lady would not give willingly, and that was something no true knight could ignore. He was bound by his
oaths of sacrifice and chivalry to protect the innocent and
punish evil.

Ralph decided that he must do what he could to save
the lady from the evil that threatened her, even if he

earned naught but her scorn for doing so. Perhaps if he could help an innocent lady—for in his heart he believed her thus, despite her flashing eyes and enticing smiles—he would in some small way repay his debt to Berenice.

Alayne and Marguerite helped each other undress. They both had serving wenches to care for their clothes and wait on them when they required service, but they often sent the girls to their pallets of straw early out of pity. It was a hard life at the palace for serving wenches. They spent their time fetching and carrying from dawn until dusk, snatching food in the kitchen from the remains of what was brought to the nobles' table, and avoiding the clutching hands of both the serving men and their masters. There were a brood of their children somewhere about the palace, born in corners and hidden by their mothers until they were old enough to become of use in the kitchens or stables.

'Sir Ralph spoke to me,' Marguerite said, a flicker of pleasure in her pretty face as she unfastened Alayne's intricate headdress and removed it for her, laying it on an oak coffer beneath the narrow arched window. It was dark outside now, for a cloud had passed across the moon. 'He seems a very perfect knight, chivalrous and kind. Did you chance to meet him, Alayne?'

'Her Majesty introduced us,' Alayne said, deciding to say nothing of her further meeting with the English knight. 'He did not say very much, except that he had no wish to fight in the tourney.'

'He was knighted by the English King,' Marguerite said. 'I believe he was a favourite at that court before his marriage. He served the King in his struggles with rebellious nobles, so I have heard. I do not think him a coward, Alayne, even if he does not wish to fight.'

'No, I think perhaps you are right,' Alayne said, remembering the hint of steel in his voice as he had warned her against the folly of walking alone in the evening. 'I dare say he thinks such pastimes foolish and a waste. If he fights, he does so in a good cause, I would judge.'

She had helped Marguerite to remove her headdress and now she pulled off her own tunic and ran barefoot to the bed in her shift, seeking the warmth to be found beneath the heavy coverlets. Even in summer the stone walls of the palace kept out the heat, and in winter it was so cold that they slept beneath piles of furs on top of their silken quilts.

They had undressed by the light of one rush tallow, which Mar-guerite extinguished before she joined Alayne beneath the covers.

'May God bless and keep us both this night,' she said and crossed herself. 'I think I like Sir Ralph,' she whispered softly as she settled down to sleep.

Alayne smiled to herself in the darkness. Marguerite clearly believed her father would do his best to arrange a match between her and the English knight, and seemed content that it should be so—despite her confession that she loved another.

Of course Marguerite had no choice but to obey her father, as Alayne had had none at the time of her marriage. She was not cold, but a little shiver ran down her spine as she remembered her horror on learning that she was to wed a man of her father's age, and the fear had begun as she saw the way he looked at her. Then, on her wedding night, when she had bolstered her courage to the limit to accept whatever he did to her, she had discovered that he was incapable of bedding her.

A tear trickled from the corner of her eye as she recalled his efforts and his abuse. When at last he had realised it was useless, he had struck her across the face, making her lip bleed. She had wept into her pillow as he left her bed, swearing and cursing her as though his inability was her fault. She had not known it then, but he had spent the night drinking strong wine, and in the morning he had greeted her with more drunken fumbling and abuse.

Leaving her to weep again, he had gone charging from her chamber and tumbled headlong down the stone steps of the tower. It would have been better if he had died instantly, for his back was broken and he was in terrible pain from that moment on until he finally died. Alayne had taken the brunt of his cruelty as she nursed him, ridden all the while with guilt—for it must surely have been something in her that had made him unable to be her husband. He had told her that she was a cold bitch and no proper woman.

His accusations and bitter curses had made her life miserable until he finally died, mercifully, in his sleep one night. Alayne had given thanks for her release and his, but then her father had told her that within six months she would be married again.

'You are too young to be a widow,' he had told her. 'Besides, if we are clever, we may find another suitor of more consequence than your fool of a husband, Alayne. Valmont's lands are not adjacent to ours, but they are near enough to make it a good choice. And there is always de Bracey...'

'Never!' Alayne cried, turning pale. 'I do not know how you could suggest it, Father. That man is—' She shivered and could not go on. 'He frightens me. Besides, you quarrelled with him over land that he stole from you.'

'All the more reason that you should wed him,' her

father said. 'Your sons will inherit it all, Alayne. Think of that—think of the power such a fortune will bring to your sons.'

Alayne pushed the thoughts from her mind. She had believed them almost banished, but the English knight had brought them back to her with his warnings. She ought to know that men had their baser side, for she had witnessed it at the hands of her husband and her father. Her father had struck her when she defied him, threatening to force her to obey him, but she had outwitted him and lived safe at court these many months. Yet her mind was never quite at ease, for she knew that her father was a stubborn man and would not easily relinquish his plans for her.

She closed her eyes, trying to empty her mind so that she could sleep, but all she could see was the face of the English knight. His eyes seemed to burn with a fire that seared deep into her soul, causing her to moan softly and bite her lip. No man before him, not even de Froissart, had managed to make her so restless. There was inside her a yearning, a need that she could not identify, but she knew it had begun when he'd looked at her so strangely in the walled garden.

'Why do you plague me so?' she asked him in her thoughts. She had been at peace with herself until he came, but something had changed and she was not sure why he troubled her so.

Chapter Three

It was a part of Alayne's duty to wait on the Queen in the morning, taking her the cup of sweet wine that she drank on breaking her fast and helping her to rise and dress for the day.

'I have given permission for the tourney,' she told Alayne as she drank deeply from the cup, the wine having first been tasted by the servant who brought it to her chamber. 'It will take place next week. Today is Saturday and tomorrow is the Lord's day, so we may not begin until the following day. The heralds shall announce it and ride into the villages about so that the people may come hither to enjoy the spectacle. We shall proclaim it a day of feasting and rejoicing.'

'I believe the knights are excited about the contest,' Alayne said. 'I must think of a suitable token to give the winner.'

'It need be no more than a scarf or a trinket,' the Queen said. 'Yet I think they hope for something more.'

'Then they hope in vain,' Alayne said with a frown. 'But I will not give so little as a scarf. They must fight for something of value. I shall give my gold bangle that was a wedding gift from my father.'

'Is that the one wrought with vine leaves in the style of the Romans?'

'Yes, the very one,' Alayne said, looking pleased because the Queen knew of it. 'Do you think it suitable?'

'It is very fine work and quite valuable,' Eleanor said. 'Are you sure you wish to give it, Alayne?'

'Oh, yes,' Alayne assured her. It was less personal than a scarf would be and, although she thought it pretty, it reminded her of things she would rather forget. 'I have others I prefer.'

'Then so be it—the bangle shall be the prize,' the Queen said and nodded. She gave a sigh and frowned as if something displeased her. 'It would be exciting if we had a new champion this time. De Froissart usually wins and it grows stale to see him vanquish them all. I think it a shame that he does not take himself off to join the Knights Templars and fight in a worthwhile cause.'

'I have heard that the Baron de Froissart fought in the crusade as a young lad, your Grace.'

'Indeed, he did,' she said and smiled. 'I was there and saw him win high favours, which he had from my first husband's hand. He was a page of no more than eleven then and fought as bravely as any squire. He was seventeen when he earned his spurs. None can call him a coward and, since he chooses to languish at our court, we must accept him—but I still think it a shame that he wastes his skills in play when he might fight in a more worthy cause.'

Alayne smiled and made no comment. The Queen liked strong brave men about her, and she would not really want de Froissart to leave her court. She was out of temper over something, and Alayne suspected it was to do with the letters from her husband, King Henry II of England. It was whispered that he had several times been unfaithful to her and that she had left him because of it.

Eleanor of Aquitaine was a powerful woman and a wealthy heiress. Her lands were coveted by many, but she guarded them fiercely and quarrelled with her husband instead of giving him the homage that she should as his wife.

When the Queen was ready, she asked several of her ladies to walk with her in the palace grounds. Alayne was of the party chosen, and as she strolled in the sunshine, chattering idly with her friends, she thought about de Froissart. He had won the last three tournaments, which was of course why he had suggested a tourney. She knew he hoped for a prize other than the bangle she had offered, but she was not sure of her feelings towards him.

It was true that he sometimes made her heart race when he teased her. Occasionally he would let his hand brush against hers, and he had recently twice helped her dismount from her palfrey. She had sensed that he wished to kiss her, and when he talked of *fine love* she knew that he meant he wanted to make love to her in the manner the troubadours sang of, with gentle wooing and languishing looks, the touch of a hand, and a stolen kiss— but for how long would he be satisfied with such privileges?

She could not allow the ultimate intimacy for which he longed. By the rules of courtly love it was for her to allow or to deny; this was her privilege as the lady in the *affaire*. To be kissed, touched with reverence, courted as an object to be admired and worshipped from afar—yes, she could accept and even welcome such a love. But in her heart she knew that that would not suffice for long.

Allowed such privileges, a lover would want more and she could not. She could not!

'What troubles you, sweet lady?'

Alayne jumped as the man who had been uppermost in her thoughts caught up with them, matching his steps to hers as she strolled in the gardens. She glanced round and saw that the Queen had turned back with her ladies. She had been dreaming and not realised that they were returning to the palace.

'I was thinking,' she said and smiled at him as he reached for her hand, raising it to his lips to kiss it lightly on the back. The look he gave her seemed to bathe her in warmth and a little tingle of pleasure ran down her spine as he released her hand. He was gentle and courteous, and it was pleasant to be courted in this way. If she had not experienced her husband's vile baseness, she might have welcomed de Froissart's courtship. 'So it seems you will have your way over the tourney, my lord. Are you pleased?'

'It is a matter of sport only,' he said and for a moment his eyes met hers and there was no laughter in them. 'Do not fear that I shall press for more than you wish to give, my lady. You are beautiful and you must have guessed that I languish for love of you—but I would not have you less than willing. I may win the tourney, but it gives me nothing I had not before.'

Alayne's heart beat faster. He was charming and she found him pleasing, but still there was a reserve in her. Besides, he did not arouse that restlessness in her that the English knight had done with just a look!

'I have given a bangle as your prize, Sir Knight, but you have not won it yet.' Her eyes teased him. It was pleasant to idle in the sun and talk this way with a friend. 'There may come a challenger to unhorse you.'

'I wish it might be so,' he said and sighed, and for the first time Alayne saw the truth of his heart, realising that there was more to this knight than she had previously imagined. 'I grow stale and bored at this court, Lady Alayne. It is only your presence that keeps me languishing here.'

'Then perhaps you should go,' she suggested. 'Where would you go, my lord?'

'To England,' he replied. 'I have heard that there are unruly barons there that plague the King and I would take service with him.'

'You do not think of taking the Cross again?'

'I have been to the Holy Land,' de Froissart replied. 'I paid my dues to the church. In truth, I have thought of other things…' He shook his head. 'No, the time is not right. Forgive me, lady. I know this kind of talk does not please you.'

Alayne stared at him in surprise. His words seemed to hint at something she had not suspected. She had thought he teased her merely in the hope of becoming her lover, but it seemed he thought of deeper matters. She turned away from him, walking back to join the Queen and her ladies as they went into the palace.

'Where have you been?' Marguerite asked her. 'Her Majesty says she will sit in the walled garden this afternoon with her tapestry. She wants you to sort her silks for her because you have the best eye for colour. I gave her the wrong blue last time and we had to unpick the stitches.'

Alayne nodded. She would be glad of something to occupy her mind. She had thought herself safe to indulge in a mild flirtation with de Froissart, but if he wanted her as his wife… She shook her head. No, she did not want to be his wife. She did not want to be any man's wife!

'I was dreaming,' she answered her friend. 'And de Froissart stopped me. I did not realise you had turned back.'

As they entered the palace, she turned round to glance back. There was no sign of Baron de Froissart, but she saw the English knight looking at her and he was frowning again. Why did he always seem to frown at her? What had she done that made him so disapproving?

Alayne's heart jerked and then raced wildly, her breathing becoming almost painful. His eyes seemed to penetrate her mind, to seek out her thoughts, to strip her naked to his gaze. And he did not appear to be pleased with what he saw. Oh, what did it matter?

And why could she not simply dismiss him from her thoughts?

Ralph set out to follow de Froissart a few moments after Alayne had disappeared inside the palace with the other ladies. He had not meant to listen to their conversation, but what he had chanced to hear had made him realise that the lady had little to fear from that knight. It seemed that he had misjudged de Froissart; he wished to marry her and that would be the best thing that could happen to her. Once she was safely wed, she would no longer be at the mercy of unscrupulous rogues who sought her for her fortune. De Froissart was in love with her and he had an adequate fortune of his own.

There was no doubt that it would be a good match for Alayne. She needed an iron hand in a velvet mitt to tame her, for there was fire in her though she pretended to modesty. The baron loved her and was therefore the best person to be on the watch for her safety. Besides, Ralph had been thinking about that whispered conversation and he suspected that whoever had been thinking of entering the lists against de Froissart plotted some mischief. It would be as well to warn the baron of his own danger and Alayne's.

He was out of sight of the palace and at the edge of the forest when he heard the shouts and sounds of fighting. Someone was being attacked! Ralph was wearing court dress and no armour, but he did have his sword at his side. He found it wiser to have his weapon to hand at all times when outside the palace.

Running towards the sounds of the struggle he saw what he had half-expected to find—the Baron de Froissart was surrounded by six ruffians. They were not knights but stout fellows armed with cudgels and were laying about de Froissart as if they meant to kill him. Giving a cry of outrage at such knavery, Ralph charged into the fray, his sword drawn. As they heard his battle cry the men turned, looked startled, and then fled as one into the forest.

Ralph did not bother to give chase. De Froissart was lying on the ground and, from the moans issuing from his lips, Ralph knew that he had not arrived in time to save him from injury. He knelt on the ground at his side, turning him over gently and frowning as he saw the blood on his head and more seeping through the sleeve of his tunic.

'Forgive me, I should have come sooner,' he said as he helped the baron to rise and heard his muffled cry of pain. 'What harm have those scurvy knaves done you, sir? I think you have suffered a wound to your arm, but what more?'

'A few blows to the head, but I think my right arm is worst. It may be broken.' A moan of pain broke from the baron, but he gritted his teeth and allowed his rescuer to tend him.

Ralph gently rolled back his sleeve and examined the arm with gentle fingers, then he nodded his head. 'Yes, I believe there may be some damage, but not, I think, a serious break. Let me help you back to the palace and summon a surgeon, my friend. I think you will mend in time for I have seen much worse wounds than this recover.'

'I thank you for your help,' de Froissart said, swaying slightly as Ralph helped him to his feet. 'Had you not arrived, I fear they would have killed me.'

'I had not realised you were in danger until this morning,' Ralph said. 'I knew someone meant to win that tournament and the Lady Alayne by fair means or foul— but I am at fault, for I did not realise this was his plan, to disable you first.'

'Pray tell me more!' de Froissart glared at him. 'Do you say this was a plot to stop me taking part in the tourney?'

'I believe it may have been,' Ralph replied. 'It was to warn you of a possible plot against you that I followed you when you left the Lady Alayne a few minutes ago. I believe someone is desperate to win her and her fortune and will do whatever he thinks necessary to stop any rival from carrying her off as his bride.'

'What knave has done this? I'll spit him like the swine he is!' de Froissart cried and then half-fell as the pain in his arm almost overcame him. 'At least, I shall when I am myself again.'

'I know not his name. I heard only a few whispers last night in the gardens.' Ralph smiled at his frustration. 'At first I did not realise what they meant and then it was too late to discover the identity of the plotters. I can promise you the time will come when you may repay this debt,' he said, 'but not soon enough for you to win the tourney.'

'But that was his purpose!' de Froissart said and winced as he tried to move his arm. 'If I do not take part, some other fool will win the chance to court her—possibly Baron de Bracey's son Renaldo. I know his father covets her lands and he covets her. Between them they are the veriest rogues, the son worse than the father. This is the kind of thing they would plot between them!'

'There were two of them,' Ralph agreed. 'One seemed to hesitate while the other ordered. It may be that you are right and it was de Bracey and his son. I do not think I know them, but you will have your squire point them out to me and I shall keep an eye on them.'

'But you must do more than that,' de Froissart said and halted his slow, painful walk to fix him with a fierce stare. 'You must enter the lists and defeat de Bracey. If he wins, Alayne must let him be her champion for at least a few hours and I do not trust that scurvy knave. He will find some way to take advantage of her.'

'I believe you care for the lady?'

'Damn your eyes! What business is it of yours?' de Froissart growled. 'If you must know, I would marry her if she would have me—but that father of hers soured her for marriage. She was forced to take a man near old enough to be her grandfather and I believe he treated her badly, though she will never speak of it to anyone. The Queen whispered to me that she was most unhappy in her marriage and would not easily trust another man, and so I have been gentle in my courtship of her. I cannot tell whether she loves me in return—but I would do whatever she asked of me.'

'You would protect her,' Ralph agreed, 'and she is in sore need of protection. We must do something to make certain that de Bracey's son cannot win the right to court her. Is there no one apart from me who would fight in your stead?'

De Froissart's eyes narrowed in reply. 'I have heard that you are a worthy fighter, de Banewulf. Fight as my champion and protect the lady from those rogues, for my arm will not be stout enough to do it myself.'

'It is a while since I entered the lists,' Ralph replied reluctantly. He had no love of the tourney—too many men were injured in what was a vain cause and he fought only in a just one. 'I train as always, for I believe it keeps the body well and the mind alert—but I have no heart for fighting. The last time I fought I killed a man who was my friend. I fought in anger and vowed I would not fight other than for my King and country again.'

'We have all done things we would rather forget,' de Froissart said, his interest caught by Ralph's unthinking confession. 'Did you intend to kill him?'

'No. He was trying to tell me something I did not wish to hear,' Ralph said. 'I grew angry and we fought. I knocked him to the ground and he struck his head against a metal anvil—we were in the stable-yard near the blacksmith's forge—and his skull cracked open. We did all we could to save him, but it was hopeless. Later, as he lay dying, he told me that he had lied to make me angry to bring me out of my grief, and then he smiled at me before he died.'

'What was the lie that made you so angry?'

'He told me that the child that led to my wife's death was not mine but his.' Ralph's face was dark with sorrow. 'But he lied and I knew that he lied. My anger was as much for myself as for him. I killed her by my unkindness and I killed him in my anger. For a time I considered taking up the Cross as my penance, but I knew that I was not worthy. God's knight must be worthy of the honour to bear his symbol.'

'I know what you mean,' de Froissart said, nodding. 'I too have killed in anger and that is why I will not take up the Cross again—but you wrong yourself, de Bane-wulf. You did only what other men have done before you and your sin is not so great as many.'

'Yet I cannot forgive myself.'

'Then make this tourney your penance.' de Froissart threw the challenge at him. 'If you feel you owe your friend and your wife a debt, take up the sword in their names as well as mine. For if you do not, I fear for the Lady Alayne's safety.'

Ralph stared at him in silence for a long moment, and then inclined his head. It meant that he must break a sacred vow, but he would speak to the priest and ask for a penance to set him free.

'I shall do as you ask, but I cannot promise that I shall be victorious. I have trained with my men as I told you, but I have not fought to win since the day I killed Christian Payton.'

'Have the surgeon patch me up and I shall watch you train,' de Froissart told him. 'Then we shall see what we shall see…'

'You should be in your bed, my friend.'

'I am no weakling,' de Froissart growled and stifled a moan of pain. 'Let me only have my arm bound and give me a glass of good strong wine and I will watch you fight. Aye, and cheer the loudest of them all when you beat those knaves!'

Ralph smiled, realising that he had begun to like the man despite himself. 'I bow to your judgement and pray that I may do your faith in me justice.'

* * *

Alayne listened to the gossip circulating that evening. The courtiers could talk of nothing but the attack on Baron de Froissart. Most cried shame that such a thing could have happened, for it was whispered by all that whoever was behind the attack had hoped to take unfair advantage by making it impossible for de Froissart to participate in the tourney.

'It was wicked knavery,' Marguerite said to Alayne. 'Who would do such a terrible thing?'

'I do not know.' Alayne frowned. She was feeling chilled as she had on the day of the hunt, when the tourney was first suggested.

The Queen frowned over what had happened and spoke of cancelling the tournament, but the courtiers begged her not to spoil their fun, and when de Froissart put in a belated appearance at supper that evening he added his pleas to the others.

'I beg your Grace will not cancel the tourney,' he said in a loud voice so that all might hear him. 'For whoever has done this thing will be thwarted by my champion if he thinks to win by foul means.'

'Your champion?' Everyone was agog to know who he meant and whispered one to the other as they tried to name the knight who would fight in de Froissart's name. 'But who will you choose? Is he a stranger to court?'

'He has been here but a few days,' de Froissart said and smiled at Ralph, who stood just behind him. He was in great pain, for he had drunk only wine and refused the healing potion the surgeon had given him, saying that he would not sleep until he was certain that honour had been satisfied. 'I speak of Sir Ralph de Banewulf...' Hearing the murmurs of surprise, he held up his uninjured arm for silence. 'Sir Ralph saved my life, for I foolishly went unarmed too near the forest and was attacked by those foul brigands. Had he not arrived in time, I fear I might be dead—but as you see, I am not.'

Alayne's heart caught as she heard his words. The English knight had not wanted to fight in the tourney—why had he changed his mind?

Queen Eleanor was looking at him. 'Is this true, Sir Ralph? Do you fight as de Froissart's champion?'

'Yes, for he has asked it of me and I am in honour bound to do as he asks.'

She inclined her head, a little gleam in her eye. 'I believe this tourney may be interesting after all. Since you make it a matter of honour, sir, I shall let the contest continue—with but one small change. You fight for a gold bangle and for the honour of sitting with the Lady Alayne at the high table as we feast afterwards. I know there was some foolish talk of fighting for the honour of courting the lady, but this I forbid. Whoever wins has only the bangle and her companionship for the evening, nothing more.' Her eyes swept over the assembled company. 'Do you all agree, good knights?'

There were murmurs of agreement all round, but Ralph noticed the scowling faces of a few knights, and he whispered to de Froissart who looked in the direction of two men standing together. It was clear by their harsh dark looks that they were father and son, though the father had run to fat, his face and hands podgy and white. If he was not mistaken, the knave was riddled with the pox, thought Sir Ralph—and that was the man who had thought to seize the Lady Alayne for himself! Or was it for his son? The younger man looked healthier, but his mouth was vicious.

No, by heaven, they should not have her! Ralph made the silent vow to himself, angered that they should have dared to think themselves worthy to approach her. Yet they had thought to steal her from de Froissart by secretly disabling him—perhaps they had thought to murder him, and might have had he not overheard their plotting.

'I am so sorry you are wounded, sir.'

Hearing a gentle voice behind them, Ralph saw that the Lady Marguerite had approached them and was talking to de Froissart.

'It was a mere scratch,' de Froissart replied nobly, if not entirely truthfully.

'You should be resting. It was a mercy that Sir Ralph was close by to help you, my lord.'

'I have much to thank him for,' de Froissart replied.

Ralph's attention wandered, his eyes searching the company, looking for Alayne. She was standing a little apart from the other ladies, a pensive expression on her face that touched him. Why was she so sad? He had thought her light-hearted and teasing, a temptress who enjoyed her power over the knights, but now, seeing her when she thought herself unobserved, he realised that there was more to the lady than he had first thought.

'Excuse me, I shall leave you for a moment,' he said to de Froissart, but was cut off as the Queen stood up to address her company.

'I do not know whether the attack on Baron de Froissart was by brigands or not,' she said and her expression was stern. 'But if I discover that this was an attempt to stop him fighting in the tourney—or if anything similar should happen to his champion—I shall banish the perpetrators for life, and their estates shall be forfeit.'

There was a gasp of surprise from the courtiers, for this was a harsh punishment and they had seldom heard their Queen speak so coldly to them. It was clear that she was very angry, and that she would not hesitate to carry out her threat if she were disobeyed. Banishment from the court and the confiscation of lands was something that most knights would not risk. Defeat in the tourney meant the loss of armour, but that was a mere trifle compared with this threat.

'Did someone try to harm you because of the tourney?' Marguerite asked and looked at de Froissart in distress. 'That was a terrible thing to do, sir.'

'We may never know their reason,' was all that de Froissart would say. 'I thank you for your concern, but I think that if you will excuse me, lady, I must follow your advice and seek my bed.'

Marguerite looked concerned. 'Yes, of course. Do you wish for help?'

'My friend here will help me. I fear I should be too heavy a burden for you, fair lady.' He made her a shaky bow and then hissed at Ralph. 'Get me out of here!'

'Foolish,' Ralph scolded as he put his arm about the baron, who was almost fainting on his feet, but had insisted on accompanying him to the hall. He forgot his intention to seek out Alayne as he hastened to assist de Froissart. 'Come, I shall see you to your bed—and you shall take the surgeon's potion to make you sleep or I shall know the reason why. I need your help to hone my skills in the morning or this tourney will be lost—and, despite the Queen's decree, I dare swear the victor will claim his rights as he sees fit.'

'And you must be the victor,' de Froissart said and scowled at him. The pain in his arm was fierce, but it receded a little as they argued, which was of course the other's intent. 'You fight well enough, but must put your heart into it, de Banewulf. As my champion you shall not shame me—or you shall answer for it when I am well again.'

Ralph laughed, though he believed the threat real

enough. They understood each other and had formed a
bond of friendship. De Froissart was a true knight and
would make the Lady Alayne a good husband. Something
deep inside Ralph protested at the thought of her wed to
any knight other than himself, but he quashed it ruthlessly. She was not for him. He would not take another
bride.

Alayne watched as they left the hall together. She had
been shocked and distressed to hear the news of such a
wicked assault on the baron, the more so because she
was afraid that de Froissart might have been attacked
because of her. But who would do such a thing? Surely
none of the courtiers was so base as to take unfair advantage? Yet there were some that she distrusted, some
she took good care to avoid.

Glancing across the room, she saw that both Baron de
Bracey and his son Renaldo were present this evening.
A little quiver went over her and she felt afraid. She
would need no warning from Sir Ralph to stay close to
her friends this night.

She was not sure which of the de Bracey men she
disliked the most. The baron was revolting and diseased,
if rumour be true, but the son was evil. He had come to
her home with his father once as a boy and she had seen
him tormenting her kittens. When she had remonstrated
with him, he had laughed in her face and told her she
would wake up and find them missing one day. She never
had, but she had lived in fear of it for months.

And this was the family into which her father would
have her marry! She knew her father did not hold her in
affection, but how could he contemplate such a match?
She had only seen the de Bracey men at court a few
times; they were not popular and did not come as often
as some. Why were they here now? Was it possible that

Baron de Bracey had made up his differences with her father? Her father would force her into any marriage that showed him some advantage, she knew—but she would rather die than be married to either of the de Bracey men!

She looked away, controlling her feeling of revulsion towards the men as she saw the Queen beckoning to her. Crossing the room to Eleanor's side, she made her curtsy and, taking up a lyre, began to sing for the company. She ought to have gone to de Froissart as Marguerite had, she thought regretfully. It would have been polite and kind after his courtesy to her, but his declaration that morning had made her a little afraid of him. As a courtly lover she found him acceptable, but as a husband…no, that was impossible. Alayne sighed. She was not sure that she would ever find any man acceptable to her in that way.

Yet even as she denied it, the features of the English knight came to her mind. She recalled the way his eyes had seemed to devour her in the garden the previous night, his expression in part angry, in part—what? Perhaps hungry was the best way to describe the look he had given her. She could not be sure. She knew only that she had not felt the fear or revulsion that came to her when other men looked at her that way.

There was something that drew her to Ralph de Banewulf, though she was afraid to admit it, even to herself. It could not be that she had begun to fall in love with him—could it?

No, no, she was sure that she could never love, so what was it that caused such restlessness in her, making it almost impossible for her to sleep? Why was it that she had such fevered dreams, dreams in which the English knight took her in his arms and kissed her so sweetly that it made her whole body sing?

* * *

Sunday was for devotion and Alayne attended mass four times in the royal chapel. At all other times there was feasting, music and dancing in the halls of the palace, but on the Lord's day the courtiers were expected to be sober and respectful.

The ladies spent most of the day at their devotions and their needlework, while the men often went out riding. Alayne suspected that they sometimes found taverns in the villages where they could drink and sport with the wenches, though, of course, some of the knights were genuinely devout and refrained from sport of any kind.

It was after supper, which the Queen had taken privately rather than in the hall, that she first heard the whisper from Marguerite.

'They say that Sir Ralph asked her Majesty's permission to keep a vigil in the chapel last night,' she told Alayne as they were going up to their chamber. An early night had been decreed so that all might be ready to gather on the common at first light for the tourney to begin. 'It seems he had vowed never to fight in such a tourney again, and the priest granted him absolution of his vow, his penance to lie prostrate before the cross all night.'

'I wonder why he took such a vow,' Alayne said, her brow wrinkling in thought. 'Do you think he had committed some great sin?'

'My father thinks him a good man,' Marguerite told her. 'There are bound to be rumours, of course, but I cannot think him capable of evil. And he is devoted to his wife's memory. She died suddenly, they say, of a fever.'

'I thought she died after giving birth to her child?'

'My father told me she had recovered, but then her illness returned suddenly. Sir Ralph thought she was well again and they say he blamed himself for neglecting her—but it cannot have been his fault. He is a good man, do you not think so, Alayne?'

'Perhaps. I do not know him, but I do not think him evil,' Alayne replied, avoiding Marguerite's gaze. The English knight confused her and she did not wish to continue speaking of him. 'Have you heard aught of the Baron de Froissart? I have seen nothing of him since the other night and I asked the Lady Angelica for news, but she said she had heard he was prostrate on his bed this afternoon.'

'Well, I do not know how that may be,' Marguerite said. 'My father told me the baron was watching Sir Ralph practise with the sword this morning for three hours.'

Alayne nodded, looking at her curiously. 'Has your father said anything more of your marriage?'

'No…but he says that he may take me to the English court soon. My Uncle Godolphin is much favoured by the King and it seems that my Aunt Isabelle wishes to see me. I have cousins of marriageable age.'

'Then mayhap your father has not made up his mind about your marriage yet,' Alayne said. 'Perhaps your squire may yet be knighted in time.'

'Oh, no,' Marguerite denied and glanced away, her cheeks pink. Alayne sensed that she was embarrassed, perhaps wished that she had not mentioned her feelings for the young squire. 'That was but a foolish fancy. He is too young to be married and I—I believe an older man might make a better husband.'

'Yes, perhaps,' Alayne agreed, 'though not too old. You would not like that, Marguerite, believe me. I think Sir Ralph and de Froissart are perhaps of a similar age…'

'The Baron de Froissart is the elder of the two by some

three years,' Marguerite said and blushed again as Alayne gave her an inquiring look. 'My father told me that Sir Ralph is the same age as my brother Eduardo and I—I know that de Froissart is older than my brother, for they were once good friends.'

'You did not tell me that,' Alayne said. Perhaps it was because Sir Ralph was so stern in his manner that she had thought him older. 'I thought you did not like de Froissart?'

'Well, it is not exactly that I do not like him…' The lady blushed. 'I should not have said what I did to you, Alayne. There was some quarrel between Eduardo and Pierre de Froissart when they were training together as squires. I thought it more serious than it was. My brother told me the truth of it recently and it was merely a squabble, because Eduardo was disciplined by his master—for some minor transgression that Pierre had reported. He was but thirteen at the time Pierre went off to the crusades and resented that he was too young to go with him.'

'Oh, I see,' Alayne replied, noticing that her friend was overcome with her embarrassment and that she had used the baron's familiar name several times. 'So you think that de Froissart is trustworthy after all?'

'As much as any man,' Marguerite said and turned away as they entered their chamber. She yawned as she disrobed, clearly wanting to change the subject. 'I am tired and we must be up early if we are to be ready in time.'

'Yes, of course,' Alayne replied. She was beginning to suspect that her friend was more interested in de Froissart than she would admit, and that her story of being in love with a young squire might not be true. Why should Marguerite have lied about her feelings? Unless she had believed that Alayne was interested in Baron de Froissart herself? Could she have been a little jealous and spoken hastily? 'Goodnight, and may the Lord bless and keep us.'

Marguerite was already snuggling down beneath the covers, her eyes closed. Alayne slipped in beside her, closing her eyes and trying to sleep, but her thoughts were crowding in on her, making her restless. It seemed that Marguerite was as uncertain of her feelings as Alayne was herself—and that the girl knew the Baron de Froissart much better than she had imagined. If Marguerite's brother had been de Froissart's friend, it was likely that the families had met often…

Something was still puzzling Alayne as she finally fell asleep, but she could not quite grasp it. Besides, it did not matter now—far more important was the contest the next day, and the identity of the eventual winner.

As her eyes closed and she drifted into a pleasant dream, Alayne saw the face of the victor as she handed him his prize.

People were crowding on to the common land where the tourney was to be held that morning. Men, women and children of all ages, talking excitedly, the young ones running around like playful puppies, pulling at their mother's skirt and begging for treats from the hot pie seller. When the Queen and her ladies arrived there was already a sea of faces assembled. Merchants and their wives, dressed in their best, labourers taking an unexpected holiday from their constant round of toil, beggars looking to steal or beg a few coins, peddlers carrying their wares on trays and entertainers of all kinds, the atmosphere one of excitement and anticipation.

'Isn't it thrilling?' Marguerite whispered to her. 'Oh,

do look at that man eating fire! It must cause him pain, wouldn't you think?'

'I expect it is a trick,' Alayne said. 'My nurse told me that all such entertainers trick us in some way.' She smiled as she saw the doubts in Marguerite's eyes. 'But it is exciting to watch, I do agree with that.'

However, she could not help feeling excited herself as, with a fanfare from the heralds, she was led to the place of honour on the dais, which had been erected beneath a canopy of billowing silk. The ladies of the court were chattering, watching as she was announced the Queen of the tourney, some a little jealously, some merely pleased to be a part of all the excitement of the day.

Her heart was beating nervously as she took her seat to the cheers of the people. For one day her rule was law, at least in matters of the tourney and the knights who competed for the honour of sitting with her that night at feast. As was her due, she was being enthusiastically hailed as the Queen of Youth and Beauty, taking precedence over the true Queen for the moment.

It felt strange to be seated higher than the Queen, but, when Alayne hesitated, her friend and protector smiled at her and nodded approvingly.

'It is your right,' she said. 'Be wise, my lady, for remember, today your word must be obeyed.'

'I pray that I shall be worthy of the honour, your Majesty.'

Alayne looked about her. To one side were the tents and banners of the knights taking part in the contest. Their squires had worked through the night to have everything ready for their masters, and it was a matter of honour with them that *their* lord should wear the best armour and ride the best prepared charger.

'Listen, Alayne,' the Queen said. 'They are ready to begin.'

The heralds had begun to blow a fanfare before announcing the names of the knights who had entered the lists. Then a great cheer went up as the people shouted for their favourites. Mounted on great chargers, the heavy horses snorting, their breath making clouds on the morning air, the knights began to parade before the courtiers. Each rode along the line of ladies and gentlemen, bringing his destrier to a halt before the ladies and bowing both to the Queen of the day and Queen Eleanor. Each knight tipped his lance in salute as he paraded and confirmed his willingness for the contest.

Some of the knights were wearing favours tied to their arms, which had been given by the ladies they admired. A few of the knights looked hopefully at Alayne, but she merely smiled. She would show favour to none, even though her heart did a strange flip when Sir Ralph de Banewulf tipped his lance to her. She noticed that he wore no favours, and that his colours of black and silver were more impressive than most. He was a proud knight, his stern features giving no sign of his own feelings about this contest.

'I shall pray for Sir Ralph to win,' Marguerite whispered as he rode away. 'But it is a real challenge this time, for they say that he is not battle hardened and will not last the course.'

'I pray that he may not be hurt,' Alayne said and discovered that the palms of her hands were warm and damp for some reason. Why should it matter to her what happened to this knight?

'I believe he may surprise us all,' the Queen said, her eyes bright with anticipation. The English knight had added some spice to the tourney.

'What will happen now?' Alayne asked, gripping her hands tightly together so that they would not tremble and reveal her inner tension.

Queen Eleanor explained that there were different forms that a tourney could take. Sometimes the knights rode into the mêlée, meeting opponents at random, unhorsing those they could, fighting on foot if they were unhorsed for as long as they could.

'Any who are still on their feet at the end retain their honour and their armour,' Eleanor said. 'However, the vanquished are obliged to give it up to the victors.'

'Let us pray that is all they lose,' Alayne said in a low voice that only those closest to her could hear.

She knew that sometimes those unhorsed fell, never to rise again, dying of their wounds, and carried off by faithful squires and pages. She thought that she would find it unbearable should the English knight lose not only his armour but also his life.

This day, however, the knights were to meet in single combat. To be unhorsed meant the loser must retire from the lists. Quite often a knight would be satisfied if he remained unhorsed and did not enter again, for it was often a way of settling personal quarrels, but the victors could all ride again if they wished until the last challenger was vanquished and the victor remained. The stewards of the day were responsible for matching the first pairs and they announced the names of the knights who would ride against each other in the first contest. Alayne strained to hear as the pairings were announced.

'Sir Renaldo de Bracey to meet Sir Jonquil de Fontainbleau,' announced the herald. 'Lord Malmont to meet Sir Henry…'

'Oh, poor Sir Jonquil,' Marguerite whispered, but Alayne was intent on the herald and hardly heard her.

She listened carefully as the names were read out, her heart missing a beat when it was announced that the English knight would ride for Baron de Froissart against Sir William Renard.

'Is Sir William skilled in the joust?' Alayne whispered to Marguerite. Her nails had curled into the palms of her hands and she felt quite sick with apprehension. She was relieved when her friend gave a little shake of her head. Until this moment Alayne had not thought it mattered who won the contest, but now quite suddenly it was very important that Sir Ralph should be the victor.

'I think it should be an easy contest for Sir Ralph,' Marguerite whispered and Alayne breathed again.

All the knights had retired to wait until their contest was called. The first pair rode at each other furiously, the thud of their chargers' heavy hooves and the noise of lances striking against shields making hearts beat faster. Then there was a gasp as one of the knights was unseated and only a ragged cheer for the victor.

'Oh, poor Sir Jonquil,' Marguerite cried as he went down from the first thrust of de Bracey's lance. 'I fear that he is better at singing his poems than jousting.'

'I do hope he is not badly wounded.' Alayne watched anxiously, for Sir Jonquil was a gentle knight and one of her favourites. 'No, he is on his feet.' She watched as the vanquished knight tottered off the field with the assistance of his squire and page to the cheers of the crowd: Sir Jonquil was popular, the man who had defeated him was not liked. 'I fear he will be feeling mighty sore by nightfall.'

'I dare say his vanity is as much bruised as his body,' Marguerite said and laughed. She was clearly enjoying the contest, as were the other ladies who watched and cheered their favourites. 'To be vanquished so soon is a humiliating experience for any knight.'

'He should not have entered the lists.'

'I believe he wanted to impress a lady.'

'Poor Sir Jonquil,' Alayne said. 'I hope she will not scorn him for his failure.'

'Do you not know?' Marguerite's brows arched. 'Sir Jonquil is one of your most devoted admirers. His poems and songs are all for you, and the looks he sends in your direction can leave no doubt in anyone's mind that he is devoted to you.'

'No, no,' Alayne denied, her cheeks heated, but she was prevented from saying more by the herald's fanfare.

The next contest was more strongly fought, the knights riding against each other twice before one was sent flying from the saddle. He did not rise himself immediately and was carried off the field by his squire and two young pages.

'Do you think he is badly hurt?' Alayne asked anxiously.

'I believe he suffered a glancing wound to his side,' Marguerite said, 'but he was probably winded by the fall. His armour would have protected him from the knight's lance.'

All the knights wore a suit of chain mail beneath their tunics and surcotes, and they had a small, round, metal heaume beneath a similar covering of mail that protected their head and necks.

Five more contests took place before the one that Alayne longed and yet feared to watch. Several knights were carried from the field, but the word was that none were seriously hurt, and Alayne relaxed a little, but then it was time for Sir Ralph to ride against his opponent.

Alayne took a deep breath, her palms wet and sticky

again. She wanted to close her eyes, to shut out the sight that she dreaded, yet found that she could not remove them from the English knight. She was drawn to him. His tunic was white with a black rampant lion emblazoned on the chest, his shield black and silver; it bore the same coat of arms, but with a small bear at the tip.

'Why is the emblem on his shield different to the arms on his pennant and tunic?' she whispered to Marguerite.

'The bear is his own personal emblem,' Marguerite replied and leaned forward to call encouragement to Sir Ralph. 'It is the mark of a man who has shown great bravery in battle and granted only to a few.'

Alayne knew that the English knight was about to commence his contest, but could not call out in the way that Marguerite had, for her throat was tight with fear.

'God be with you, sir,' she whispered, her heart catching as the two knights rode at one another. Both lances struck, but one knight remained seated while the other went flying to the ground. Alayne let out a sigh as she saw that de Banewulf was the victor of this contest. Fortunately, the other knight seemed merely winded and after a moment was helped away by his friends.

'It seems that Sir Ralph is more skilled than was thought,' Marguerite said a little smile of triumph on her lips. 'Oh, well done, sir. Bravely fought, sir knight!'

Several of the ladies were cheering, though the knights who had not chosen to take part looked glum. It seemed that de Froissart's champion would give a good accounting of himself, and thus earn more than his share of admiration from the ladies.

But what was happening? Sir Ralph was riding towards where Alayne and the ladies sat. He tipped his lance towards them, and then cried out in a loud voice, 'I challenge all those who would wish to ride against me. I will fight all comers in the name of Baron de Froissart, the Lady Alayne and my late wife, the Lady Berenice. If unhorsed, we will fight on in hand-to-hand combat should the unhorsed knight wish to continue.'

Alayne looked at the Queen, her heart beating wildly.

'Can he do that?' she asked, for she had never known such a challenge to be thrown down before. It was usual for the victors of the first round to ride perhaps twice or thrice more before the eventual victor was declared.

'That is a matter for you, your Majesty,' Queen Eleanor said and smiled at her. 'Such judgements are in your power. It means that some knights will be saved from riding again, because only those that wish to fight on under the new terms need do so, while the others retire with honour—and retain their armour.'

'I see,' Alayne said as she realised that this would save some knights from unnecessary pain and injury. Having proved their worth by surviving the first round, they could now retire with honour and make sure of keeping their costly armour. It was a brave and generous offer on the part of the English knight, and one that she approved. She got to her feet and smiled down at Sir Ralph, taking a scarf and holding it out to him. He lifted his lance so that she could tie it on. 'With this token I make you my champion. To win this tourney all must defeat the English knight, Ralph de Banewulf.'

'You do me honour, lady,' he said, saluted with his lance once more and rode away.

Alayne's heart hammered in her breast. By throwing down his challenge, Sir Ralph had saved others pain and humiliation, but what of him? He must meet each knight who chose to ride against him, and for how long could he remain undefeated? She almost wished that she had refused permission, yet somehow she knew that he had thrown down his challenge for a reason.

'How brave and bold he is,' Marguerite said. 'I do not think that many will take up the challenge.'

'I pray they will not.'

There was an excited buzz around the field, for the contest had taken a new direction. Before it had been no different from a dozen other contests held here previously, but now a new sense of purpose held the spectators in thrall. This English knight was clearly a bold warrior for all that he had not fought a tourney for some time, and only the bravest of the French knights would dare to take up the challenge he had thrown down.

Some few minutes passed before the heralds blew a fanfare and then announced that two men had taken up the challenge. One was Lord Malmont, the other Sir Renaldo de Bracey; Lord Malmont was to try his hand first.

The two knights rode fiercely at each other; Lord Malmont's lance snapped as it hit the shield of the English knight, but he was not thrown. He wheeled his horse about, riding back to take a new lance from his squire, and then rode hard at Sir Ralph once more. This time the blow he received lifted him in the saddle and he was thrown from his charger's back, landing on the ground and lying as if winded for some moments, before rising to his feet.

'Will you fight on, sir?' Sir Ralph asked, but Malmont lifted his hands and shook his head.

'Nay, I am well defeated, my friend. I yield to you…' he said and then, on a little sigh, he swooned and fell to the ground once more as his squire came running to assist him.

'Your champion does well,' Queen Eleanor said as she leaned towards Alayne, a gleam in her eyes. 'I think we have been misled. He is a worthier warrior than we had thought.'

'He said only that he did not wish to fight, your Grace,' Alayne said, feeling a strange urge to protect his honour. 'He never claimed that he was not well able to acquit himself if he so chose.'

'You do well to speak up for your champion,' the Queen replied, a little smile flickering on her mouth, but quickly hidden. This tourney was proving even more amusing than she had expected.

There was a few minutes' pause before the herald announced Renaldo de Bracey's arrival. The two knights faced each other across the space between them and the atmosphere became suddenly tense; if all the other contests had been fought in a spirit of comradeship, this would not be. There was something about de Bracey's manner that seemed to bode ill for the brave English knight. De Bracey was not much liked by his fellow knights, and yet he was respected for his skill with the lance and the broad sword. He would not yield so easily!

'Now it is de Bracey...' The Queen leaned forward. 'Now we shall see what the Englishman is made of.'

Alayne held her breath. She could not answer, for her throat ached with the tension that filled her. Please God, do not let her champion be vanquished! She did not know whether she prayed for his sake or for her own, since she would not like to have to be with de Bracey all that evening.

The knights rode at each other, their lances striking each other's shields with a resounding clash, but neither yielded. Both whirled about and then charged down upon each other with renewed ferocity; the air was filled with tension as their lances struck once more, and Sir Ralph's broke at the tip. He turned back and seized another from his squire's hand, riding back at his opponent for the third time. This time his lance caught the other's shield in the centre and de Bracey swayed in the saddle, but regained his balance.

For the moment there was silence as the watching crowd wondered what would happen next. It was scarcely ever that knights stayed seated for more than three jousts, but then, as they drew breath, de Bracey threw down his own challenge.

'We should continue this fight with swords, de Bane-wulf!'

'Willingly, sir,' replied Sir Ralph.

Alayne's palms were warm and damp as she watched. What was going on? Somehow this seemed more sinister than the jousting! She sensed the dislike between the two men, perhaps even hatred on de Bracey's part.

'What is happening?' she whispered to the Queen. 'I fear some mischief here.'

Eleanor was leaning forward in her excitement. 'At last we have a true contest, for the winner will be a knight worthy of his honour as your champion, lady.'

Alayne felt sick with apprehension. Suddenly, the atmosphere had changed and she was afraid—afraid that the English knight would be wounded unto death.

Sir Ralph rode back to where his squire waited and was helped to dismount, de Bracey assisted by his own squire to do the same. The crowd held their breath as the two men advanced to the centre of the arena, their excitement reaching fever pitch as they began to shout for their favourite. It was very noticeable that hardly any voices were raised for de Bracey.

For some seconds the knights circled each other warily as though taking stock of their opponent; then, suddenly, de Bracey lunged at Sir Ralph, managing to land a heavy blow on his shield. It sent him staggering back, but even as de Bracey advanced he recovered and struck back, sending the other man skittering off balance. They circled once more and then battle was joined in earnest, each man raining blows upon the other's shield fiercely.

'Well done, sir! Nobly done.'

The Queen's tribute did nothing to alleviate Alayne's fear. She was terrified. She had seen nothing like this contest and could scarcely bear to watch as she whispered a prayer: may God protect the English knight!

'Please don't let him die.' No one heard her whispered prayer, yet her expression betrayed all to one who watched and smiled.

Thrust and parry, thrust and strike; de Bracey seemed to gain the advantage for a while, his blows forcing Sir Ralph on to the defensive, making him retreat, but then he avoided a heavy blow by dodging aside and causing de Bracey to lunge at air. That took de Bracey by surprise and he roared his rage at the trick, striking wildly at his opponent. Now Sir Ralph seemed suddenly another knight, more vital and alert, and his skill was clearly superior to the other man's, who began to look clumsy and foolish as he lunged and missed time and time again, only to receive heavy blows that sent him staggering.

'Yes!' cried the Queen. 'Oh, worthy, worthy knight! Now you have him. Press your advantage, sir. Do not let him escape you.'

Alayne's face was deathly white and she felt close to fainting. For a moment she had thought Sir Ralph was going to lose—to be hurt! And that was more important than anything she might be forced to suffer in de Bracey's company.

'Damn you, sir!' de Bracey roared as the English knight whirled about, striking and retreating, always taking him off balance. Sir Ralph was like a stinging insect, inflicting his blows but never staying in one place for long enough to be bludgeoned in return. 'Stand and fight like a man.'

But de Bracey was on the defensive now; it could be seen in his blustering, his clumsy blows that slid off Sir Ralph's shield uselessly. He was the heavier of the two and growing tired as he tried to keep up with the faster man, who seemed to weave and duck, leap aside at every chance, whirl like a heathen dancer and come back at him again and again until his head spun.

And then the heaviest blow of all landed and de Bracey's sword went spinning from his hand, his shield cleaved in two by a massive second strike by Sir Ralph's sword, leaving him unprotected and clearly unable to continue the contest.

'You may stop the contest now,' the Queen whispered to Alayne. 'Declare Sir Ralph the winner.'

Alayne was on her feet immediately and the heralds blew a fanfare so that everyone turned to look at her as she declared in a loud voice that the tourney was over. 'By my authority as Queen of the Day I award the winner's prize to Sir Ralph de Banewulf. All the brave knights who took part this day have given us good entertainment, but now we would have feasting and dancing—there is to be no more fighting by my decree.'

Sir Ralph turned to face her, bowing to her and then the Queen. Alayne was smiling, preparing to hand him his prize when he should come to claim it, when a hissing sound from the crowd warned both her and Sir Ralph that all was not well. De Bracey had seized a broken lance from the side of the field and was rushing at Sir Ralph's back as if he meant to strike him. However, even as he raised his arm, Sir Ralph whirled about and struck at him with his sword, the blade cutting deep into the chain mail that protected his arm and causing him to scream out with pain. As he went staggering backwards, managing to stay on his feet but clutching at the wound that spurted crimson from beneath the slash in his mail, Queen Eleanor rose in her majesty.

'You are henceforth banned from this court, Renaldo de Bracey. The tourney was over and you tried to take foul advantage,' she cried, anger flashing from her brilliant eyes. 'You have flouted the laws of chivalry and must be punished. Go from here and never let me see your face again! For if I do, you shall face the headsman's axe.'

There was a roar of satisfaction from the crowd, who began to pelt the disgraced knight with anything that came to hand; half-eaten fruit, sticks and stones followed him as he staggered from the arena, still clutching at his bleeding arm and assisted by his squire.

'Forgive me for usurping your place,' Queen Eleanor said to Alayne as she sat down. 'But I have heard evil things of that man and it was not in your jurisdiction to ban him from court.'

'I am glad you did, your Grace,' Alayne replied. She was still trembling for what might have been had the English knight not been equal to the wicked attempt to stab him in the back. 'For if there is one man I dislike and distrust, it is Renaldo de Bracey.'

The Queen smiled and nodded at her. 'So, he will not trouble us again,' she said. 'And now you must award your champion his prize.'

'With the greatest of pleasure.' Alayne stood up and, as Sir Ralph came to bow to her, she ran down the steps of the dais and held the gold bangle out to him. 'You are truly the victor here today, good knight. The prize belongs to you.'

'I fought for the Baron de Froissart,' Ralph reminded her and his expression seemed stern and forbidding as he looked at her. 'I thank you and I accept on his behalf, Lady Alayne.'

She felt the pleasure drain out of her as she looked into his cold eyes. Why did he disapprove of her so? What could she have done to make him look at her that way? It was almost as if he had thrown cold water in her face. Did he dislike her so much?

'Yes, of a certainty, you were his champion,' she said, pride making her cool in turn as she lifted her head to meet his gaze. She held the bangle out and found that her hand was caught, and, with that same dexterity that he had shown when he fought, he somehow brought her close to him without seeming to exert force. For a moment she was so near to him that she thought he would hear the beating of her heart, which seemed so loud to her own ears. Their eyes met for a moment in a way that scared, yet excited, her. His touch made Alayne's body feel strangely light, and then he lifted her hand to his lips, touching them briefly to the merest tips of her fingers. 'My—my lord…?' The whisper could be heard by none but he.

'My own prize,' he murmured in a voice as low as hers. 'All I shall claim of you, sweet lady.'

Then, as her hand was her own again and Alayne's heart did a wild dance of excitement, he bowed and turned away to the renewed cheers of the crowd. What had that look meant? Her mind was whirling in confusion, for she had received no true message from him. He seemed at one moment to dislike her and then… Surely she was not mistaken? It had seemed for the merest second that she had seen desire in his eyes.

She watched as his squires and pages ran to congratulate him, adding their own praise to that of all who had watched the contest, and then some of the knights who had fought earlier came out of their tents to greet his triumphal return. They were pleased to have seen de Bracey so soundly beaten, it seemed. But now heralds were blowing a fanfare, announcing that food was being distributed free to the people, and the crowd turned their attention to the feast that was offered them.

Oxen had been roasting slowly over a fire all morning and the smell of the cooked meat made Alayne hungry. She like the rest of the courtiers would return to the palace for their own feast and the further entertainment that awaited them there.

But what then? she wondered. Sir Ralph had challenged all comers to become her champion. He had claimed a kiss as his own prize—but would he claim more of her one day?

Chapter Four

Alayne was carried in triumph on a litter as was her due, to be fêted and made much of by the knights who sought to ask her favours while they could. It was within her powers to grant small boons. She could, if she wished, command a lady to let a knight sit by her at supper—and even, if she was mischievous, to permit him to kiss the lady he desired. Some ladies took full advantage of their brief reign to work their malice on others or to mock, but Alayne waived her privileges and said only that all her courtiers were free to enjoy themselves in her presence.

The hall seemed dark after the brilliant glare of the sun, and cool despite the huge fire burning in the hearth. Wine was being drunk freely and by the time the feasting began some of the courtiers were already a little intoxicated.

Alayne took her place of honour at the top table. She was a little surprised when Baron de Froissart took his seat beside her and looked in vain for Sir Ralph. Somehow she had expected he would sit at her right hand. He had not come! Her disappointment was overwhelming, but then in another moment she saw that he had been

given a seat further down the table, the Queen on his
right hand and Marguerite on his left. She blushed as his
deep grey eyes rested on her thoughtfully for a moment
and then, discomforted, gave her attention to de Froissart.

'Are you well enough to join us so soon?' she asked
him, for she had not seen him at the tourney and had
thought him lying on his sick bed.

'I am much recovered, I thank you,' de Froissart replied. 'I had excellent care from my good friends and the
wound was but slight after all. My only regret was that
I was unable to take part in the tourney myself.'

'But your champion won nobly and well.'

'Yes, most nobly. I saw for myself how valiantly he
fought.'

'You were there? I did not see you.'

'I spent most of my time in Sir Ralph's tent and
watched only the contest between him and de Bracey.'

'Oh…' Why was he looking at her so oddly? There
was something in the gentle smile he gave her that made
her tremble. During that last contest her attention had not
wavered from Sir Ralph. She had been fearful for his
safety and believed her feelings must have shown in her
face. 'Then you know Renaldo de Bracey has been
banned from court?'

She blushed and looked down at her trencher as his
gentle smile of understanding brought a flush to her
cheeks, but he did not speak and, when she looked again,
she saw that he was frowning.

'The Queen's edict did not go far enough, for only the
son was banished and I believe Baron de Bracey may
still be here in Poitiers. You should be wary of Renaldo,
lady—for I do not think he will take his defeat kindly.'

'You have no need to warn me of that family,' Alayne
replied, but was distracted by the sweet strains of music.

'As Queen and champion of the day, we should lead the dance, sir.'

'Alas, I fear I am not fit for dancing this evening, lady. My champion shall take my place as he did on the field of battle.' Standing up, he looked down the table towards Sir Ralph, who was laughing at something Marguerite had just said to him, and beckoned. 'Come, Sir Ralph, will you not continue as my champion and lead the dance? For it is the custom and I fear I have not yet the strength for it.'

Sir Ralph seemed to hesitate, then got to his feet and walked towards them. Alayne's heart thumped as he stopped by her chair and bowed his head to her. He was such a powerful man, his tunic and hose needing no padding to accentuate the hard, strong muscles that rippled beneath. His features were not softly handsome as some of the other knights, but when he smiled at her Alayne's heart missed a beat. In repose that face with its determined chin looked stern and she knew too well that his eyes could be cold, but now the light of laughter was in them and it seemed to warm her. She had a tingling sensation that swept through her body, even to her toes.

'Will you allow me this honour since the baron gives up his claims, lady?' Ralph asked as he made his bow to her.

'You are a worthy champion,' Alayne replied, maintaining her dignity despite the powerful effect his presence had on her. 'I am honoured to lead the dance with you, Sir Ralph.'

As he took her hand to lead her on to the floor, Alayne could not quite prevent her fingers trembling within his. He looked at her inquiringly and then smiled in a way that was meant to reassure her.

'You have nothing to fear,' he said. 'If I have spoken

harshly to you in the past, I would ask your forgiveness. My warning the other evening was meant only to make you aware, not to censure.'

'There is nothing to forgive, sir. I believe you spoke truly. While Baron de Bracey is still here in Poitiers, it would be wiser to take care never to be alone.'

He nodded, not smiling now but serious as they began the courtly ritual of the dance. It was a slow formal performance, involving much bowing and curtsying and pointing of toes. Alayne thought how graceful Sir Ralph was for a powerful man, but he seemed agile at all things as if he kept himself at peak fitness.

'You dance as you fight, sir,' she told him as their dance finally ended and the rest of the company crowded on to the floor to join in the merriment of a much wilder dance, where everyone joined hands in circles. 'Tell me, do you excel in everything?'

She was not destined to receive her answer, for her hands were seized and she was drawn into one of the circles.

She saw that Sir Ralph had escaped and returned to the high table, where he had stopped to speak to de Froissart. Then, as she was caught up in the frolic of the country dance, she lost sight of him and, when she looked for him again, she could not find him.

He must have retired from the feasting, she thought, a little disappointed that she would not have a chance to talk to him again that evening. However, she was in great demand and all the young men wanted to dance with her. Some of them were a little drunk, and she received at least two offers of courtship from admirers she had never known she had, refusing them gently with a smile.

Baron de Froissart excused himself before the feasting was over, but Alayne was not allowed to leave. She was

Queen of the Day and her company was demanded until the hour of midnight was passed, when she was at last allowed to leave and seek the solace of her own chamber.

Alayne looked for Marguerite, but there was no sign of her friend and she realised that very few of the ladies remained. It seemed cool and dark in the narrow, draughty passages as she left the great hall and walked towards the tower in which she was housed. Shivering, Alayne quickened her step as she realised she was alone. Behind her she could still hear the laughter of men who continued their feasting, but there was no one near her. The torches cast but a dim smoky light over the passage ahead and her heart beat with fear as she felt some menace there in the darkness.

She paused to glance back, calling out, 'Who is it? Is someone there?'

No one answered and Alayne tried to conquer her fears. This was foolish. No one would try to harm her here! She was letting her imagination run away with her. She almost ran the last few steps to the winding stairs that would take her up to the chamber she shared with Marguerite and then a dark shape stepped out in front of her. She sensed danger, halted and turned, thinking to run back to the great hall for help, but another shadow had appeared out of the darkness and she knew that she was trapped.

'Help!' she screamed loudly. 'Help me!'

And then something struck her a blow on the back of the head and she fell into the arms of the man who moved to catch her.

'Pray God you didn't hit her too hard,' one of the men said gruffly, though Alayne did not hear his words. '*He* won't be pleased if you've killed her.'

'I had to stop her screaming,' the other replied. 'I don't mean to hang for *his* work.'

Sir Ralph paused to drink in the beauty of the still night, absorbing the scents of flowers that bloomed after dark, spilling their sweetness into the warmth of the sultry air. Their perfume was sweet, but not as intoxicating as that of the lady he had danced with earlier. For a while as he held her in his arms he had known a wild desire to make her his own, something he had recognised for the foolishness it was, but growing ever stronger and less easy to control.

He had left the hall when Alayne was drawn into the laughing throng of merrymakers, knowing that his task was done for the moment. It was his habit to walk alone at night, and he had much on his mind. What was it about the Lady Alayne that disturbed him, stirring forbidden feelings within him, arousing desires he had vowed to forgo?

She did not look in the least like his late wife and yet something about her had brought back memories—memories of a laughing girl he had wanted to protect and cherish, a girl who had died because she was not strong enough to bear his child...because he had not loved her.

'May God forgive me!' Ralph muttered to himself. He was a fool to torture himself this way; he could not even be sure that the child Berenice had borne was his and not his friend's and yet—

His thoughts were rudely shattered as he heard a woman cry out for help. It had come from behind him—the gallery that led to one of the towers, which housed several of the Queen's ladies. Yet perhaps it was merely some play between the lady and her admirer? Ralph hesitated, unsure whether to investigate or not, and then he

saw two men coming from a side door in the gallery
carrying a bundle covered in a dark blanket. It seemed
to be bulky and causing them some trouble. Their manner
was furtive, anxious, and, instinctively, he knew that
what they carried was a woman. They were clearly intending to abduct her!

Ralph raced towards them, his fury at such foul behaviour knowing no bounds. This courtyard was deserted,
seldom used even during the day. Had he not come out
here purposely to be alone, they would have escaped unseen into the park and thence to the forest, their wicked
deed undiscovered until the next day, when it would have
been too late.

'Stop! Stand where you are, knaves!' he roared at them
like some lion defending its jungle domain. He con-
fronted them as they stopped and stared in dismay, drawing his sword and brandishing it at them fiercely. 'Lay
down your precious burden, rogues, or I shall spit you
where you stand like the swine you are.'

They were startled by his sudden arrival and stood
looking at him stupidly for some seconds before one of
them, who had been in the crowd at the tourney earlier,
realised who Ralph was and gave a cry of alarm.

'It's him what won the contest today,' he ejaculated in
fear, eyes bulging. 'Come, Petre, let us go. Why should
we taste metal for *him*?' And, so saying, he dropped his
end of the bundle and ran off into the darkness. It was
now possible to see the tips of the lady's shoes from
beneath a silver tunic as they dragged on the ground.

The other man clung to his end, seeming uncertain
though clearly unable to manage the abduction alone. He
was not such a craven as his companion and lifted his
head, looking at Ralph nervously.

'It was not my idea,' he said. 'I didn't hit her—it was

Jean. He was the one who planned it with...*him*. I only
came to help Jean because he said he needed me and
would pay well. Let me go and I'll tell you all I know.'

'Lay her down gently,' Ralph said. 'Uncover her! Be
quick about it or I'll give you a taste of my blade.' His
expression turned to ice as he looked down and saw what
he had expected: Lady Alayne was lying with her eyes
closed, her face deathly pale in the faint light of the stars.
'If you've killed her, you will die for this.' His rage was
such that it took all his strength of character to hold back
from killing the man where he stood.

'I didn't hit her,' the rogue said. 'I swear it on my
mother's grave. It was Jean. I don't think she's dead, my
lord.' A faint moan from Alayne seemed to indicate that
he spoke truly. 'Let me go, my lord, and I'll tell you who
wanted the poor lady taken.'

'Do not seek to fool me with your fair words,' Ralph
growled. 'You had no sympathy for her when you laid
hands on her. Tell me the name of the man who paid you
and I may spare you.'

The man sunk to his knees as Ralph loomed over him;
he had begun to shake as he realised the cold fury he had
aroused in this implacable knight and feared for his life.

'I pray your pardon, sir. I never wanted to hurt the
lady. But I've a wife sick at home and need the money
Baron de Bracey was to have paid us for this night's
work. He swore to Jean that the lady would come to no
harm and that he intended to wed her in all honour—'

'Enough!' Ralph waved his sword in dismissal. He
could run the man through, but he was not given to senseless revenge and he knew who to blame for this wickedness. Besides, Alayne was beginning to stir and he
could not tend to her and detain the rogue who had tried
to abduct her. 'On your feet. Run for your life, knave. If

I ever see you near her—if anything like this is attempted again—I shall seek you out and kill you. Do not think to hide from me, for I shall seek you out no matter where you go and I shall have no mercy the next time.'

'God praise you for your mercy, my lord. I swear she shall take no harm from me.'

'Go, then!'

The man scrambled to his feet and ran off into the darkness as swiftly as he could. Ralph waited a moment to make sure the rogue's companion had not stayed to watch, then sheathed his sword and knelt beside Alayne, lifting her gently in his arms as she gave a little start of alarm and then opened her eyes.

'Don't touch me!' she muttered and shrank away as Ralph bent to help her, his fingers caressing her cold face. 'What happened? Where am I?'

'Fear not, sweet lady. You suffered a blow to the head, which may cause you pain, but I believe you were not severely wounded. The knaves intended to abduct you and would have had I not heard your cry. Fortunately, I was in time to save you from real harm.'

Alayne gazed up at him, recognising him as her sight cleared and she began to focus properly again. She had been at first alarmed, but now she was reassured as she saw him and allowed him to help her to rise to her feet, but then she swayed as the dizziness swept over her. He held her to him, steadying her until it passed, and his hands were gentle as they stroked the back of her head, seeking out the place where she had been struck. She knew an overwhelming desire to weep in his arms, but held back her tears. She must fight this foolish need to seek comfort from a man she hardly knew!

'You have a little bump,' he said and smiled down as she looked up wonderingly into his face. 'I think you will have a severe headache, my lady, but perhaps no lasting ill.'

'If I have not, I have you to thank for it,' she said and grimaced as her head span again. This foolish weakness! Once again, she felt as if she wanted to cling to him, to weep in his arms, but succeeded in holding back the shaming tears. Yet when she tried to take a step forward she almost fell, would have had his strong arm not supported her. 'You will think me foolish, but I do not believe that I can walk unaided.'

'You shall not walk at all,' he replied. 'Have I your permission to carry you, my lady?'

'I think I must accept your kindness,' she said, her eyes closing. 'I do feel rather strange.' She gave a little sigh as he swept her up into his arms, carrying her with great care into the gallery and turning towards the stone steps that led up to the solar. Around them the torches were flickering, their smoky flare almost gone. 'It was late before they would let me retire. I came from the hall alone and I felt someone followed me and then...' She gave a little moan and pressed her face against his shoulder as a sob escaped her despite all her efforts to hold it back. 'Who would do such a thing to me?'

Ralph held her to his breast, a wave of tenderness washing over him as he heard the distress and fear in her voice, and guessed that this was not the first time she had been subjected to violence of some kind. He had seen something in her eyes before this, something that told him she had known unhappiness and it was that that had made him see the resemblance to Berenice. In truth they were nothing alike, but both had suffered.

'I do not know for sure,' Ralph told her as he carried her up the stairs, 'but it might have been an attempt to force you into marriage.'

'With Baron de Bracey or his son,' she said and gasped again. He felt her tremble as she clung to him in her distress, and was stirred to anger that she should feel so threatened. 'If that had happened I…would rather die. I shall never marry a man I cannot love or admire. I have vowed to take my life rather than be forced to endure such humiliation again.'

He heard such grief in her voice that he could not be in any doubt of what she must have suffered at the hands of her first husband. His mouth thinned as he cursed the fool who had hurt her so. What base brutes men could be! He tried to think of some words to comfort her, but there were none to wipe away the pain she had suffered. But now they were at the door of her chamber and it opened as they arrived, to reveal an anxious-looking serving wench.

'My lady!' she cried. 'I was about to come in search of you, for we feared something had happened to delay you.'

'Your mistress has been attacked,' Ralph told her. 'Show me where she sleeps so that I may lay her down, but stay by me so that you may swear if necessary that nothing has occurred here to despoil her virtue.'

'Oh, my poor lady! Such wickedness!' the wench cried as she hovered round him. 'God be praised that you brought her to us, my lord.'

Ralph deposited his burden softly on to the bed and stayed a moment to smile down at Alayne.

'You are safe now, my lady,' he said, and turned to the wench. 'You will say nothing of this to anyone.'

'I swear it!'

'Sir Ralph!' Marguerite emerged from the garderobe wearing only her bedgown. It was fashioned of thick material, but showed much of her womanly curves and she blushed for shame. He turned his back on her at once.

'Forgive me, lady. I did not know you were here.'

Marguerite slipped on an overgown and felt more comfortable as she replied. 'I have my gown on now, Sir Ralph.' She walked towards the bed where Alayne lay, her eyes closed. 'My poor friend. What happened to her?'

'She was attacked by two ruffians attempting to abduct her,' he replied. 'She has been hit on the head. I do not think it serious, but she may feel unwell in the night. It would be a kindness if the serving wench were to sit up with her this night.'

'Bring water, Bethel,' Marguerite commanded. 'I shall bathe Alayne's head and take care of her myself, and we shall share the vigil through the night. I thank you for your care of her, Sir Ralph. You may safely leave her to us now.'

'It was good fortune that I was there,' he replied, his expression grave, eyes black as midnight and lit with a silver flame that glinted in the depths. His nostrils flared in a face set as a graven image, the anger simmering beneath the surface. 'Please say nothing of this, either of you, at least until I have spoken to the Queen. I believe I know who may be responsible for this wickedness but I have no proof. I must seek an audience with her Majesty on the morrow and see what may be done to protect Lady Alayne.' He spoke softly, calmly, his deep outrage betrayed only by a tiny pulse flicking at his temple—but, by God, someone should pay for this night's work!

'I do not know who could be so evil as to do this,' Marguerite replied. 'I thank you for the service you have given this night, sir.'

'It was my privilege to be of help to the lady,' he replied and bowed to Marguerite. 'And now I must leave

or your reputations will be besmirched. Be careful and
do not walk alone until the canker of evil has been torn
out of this place.'

'I never walk alone in the gardens,' Marguerite replied.
'I know it was Alayne's habit to do so, but I do not like
the gardens in the dark, for they say that evil spirits walk
at night.'

'This time she was within the palace.'

'Within the palace?' Marguerite turned pale. 'God
have mercy! How can any of us be safe in such a case?'

'Trust me,' he replied. 'I shall not rest until this monster has been dealt with, and now I bid you goodnight.'

Alayne moaned as he went out and closed the door
softly behind him. She had heard their whispered conversation, but felt too ill to take part. Now she opened
her eyes as Marguerite bent over her.

'Can you bear it if I bathe your wound, sweet friend?'

'If you are gentle,' Alayne said and a tear slid from
the corner of her eye. She had been brave while Sir Ralph
was near by, but felt bereft without him. 'It does feel so
very sore.'

'After I have bathed it for you I shall give you something to help you sleep,' Marguerite said and smiled at
her. 'How good Sir Ralph is, Alayne. I think you owe
much to him this night.' She shivered as she thought what
might have become of her friend if he had not chanced
to be there when the abduction was attempted.

'If he had not rescued me, I should have been dead by
my own hand,' Alayne said. 'Nothing would induce me
to marry the Baron de Bracey—or his son!'

'Do you think it was one of them who planned this
thing?' Marguerite crossed herself. 'Are they so evil? Indeed, I do not like them—yet to abduct you so brazenly!
It is beyond imagining. I do not blame you for fearing

such men. But as for taking your own life, you must not say such things. It would be a wicked sin.'

'I would rather die than be wed to a man I hate.'

'Yes, perhaps it might be preferable,' Marguerite agreed with a little shiver. 'And yet I do not think I should be brave enough.' She smiled as she finished bathing the back of Alayne's head. 'The blow they struck you hardly broke the skin and there was almost no blood. I think Sir Ralph was right, there is no lasting harm done. God be praised!'

Alayne agreed with her, but as she closed her eyes after swallowing the sleeping draught Marguerite brought her, she thought that it was due to Sir Ralph's prompt action that she was here safe in her own bed. She could not bear to think what might have happened to her if she had been carried off to de Bracey's stronghold. Indeed, she *would* have preferred death to life with a de Bracey.

Alayne had slept at last despite herself, lulled to peace by the tisane Marguerite had made for her. In the morning she felt tired and listless, shocked now by what had happened to her and the realisation that she would even now have been in the power of men she hated had it not been for Sir Ralph.

Would she ever feel safe again? She needed no persuasion to stay in her room, for her pride had taken a knock as well as her head.

The pain had almost gone by the time she finally ventured from her chamber and went down to the great hall.

'You should not have left your bed yet, Alayne,' Queen Eleanor scolded her gently. 'I have been told of your injury and did not expect you to resume your duties yet.'

'I shall not allow what happened to make me an invalid nor to keep me cowering in my chamber like a craven.'

Alayne's head went up proudly, for she would not show the fear she felt inside. That would be to let those who had tried to hurt her win, and she would not give them or any other the satisfaction of seeing how much the brutal attempt to abduct her had distressed her.

'Besides, I do not believe that I thanked Sir Ralph sufficiently for what he did for me, and I would put that right.'

'Sir Ralph is not here at the moment,' the Queen replied. 'He had some errand, I believe, but may return soon.'

Alayne's mouth trembled in her disappointment. She had not thought he would leave her at such a time—but she must not let his seeming desertion upset her. He had already done much for her and she had no claim on him. Yet she would have given much to see his tall, powerful figure about the court.

'Then I must hope that he will return so that I may make my gratitude known to him,' Alayne said.

'Yes, we must hope that it will be soon,' the Queen replied and smiled a little to herself. She had pondered long on the problem of one of her favourite ladies and believed that she might be close to finding a solution that pleased her.

'But the whims of men are something beyond our understanding, Alayne. One day kind and gentle, the next a roaring tiger fit to tear your heart to pieces. Who can tell if Sir Ralph will ever return?'

Alayne felt a sickness in her stomach, for she did not see the Queen's smile or guess that she was being gently teased. Was it possible that Sir Ralph had left the court and would never return? She was not sure how she would feel if she were never to see him again.

'You have done well in your investigations, sir,' the Queen said to Sir Ralph at the interview she had granted him on his return. 'Now we know that de Bracey planned the abduction after his son was disgraced at the tourney and having failed, both have fled to their stronghold. I could send my soldiers to besiege them, but I think it a waste of time. We shall let them stay there like rats in a trap, for if they dare to venture out they will be taken and brought to justice.'

'I believe their fortress would be difficult to breach unless a sufficient army was sent to destroy it,' Ralph agreed. 'That would be costly in both lives and gold, I fear. I dare say the rogues will stay there and hide for a few months. Yet there are others who may plan a similar deed.'

'You know of other plots to abduct the lady?'

'No, your Majesty,' Ralph admitted. 'I claim no knowledge—but the lady is vulnerable while she remains unwed. She is both beautiful and rich, a powerful combination to tempt most men—some beyond the bounds of bearing. Would it not be better for the lady if she were to marry?'

'Are you asking me to arrange a marriage with her for you, sir?' The Queen studied his face intently, but met a frowning response, though her intuition told her much that he believed well hidden.

'I do not deem myself worthy of her,' Ralph replied stiffly. 'But I believe the Baron de Froissart thinks highly of the lady and would wed her given a chance.'

'Indeed?' Queen Eleanor arched her brows. 'Does he

ask you to make his pleas for him? I had thought him
man enough to make his own.'

'I did not mean to speak for de Froissart,' Ralph replied, and again something in his eyes, a little flicker of
heat that he could not control, betrayed him. 'It is merely
that I believe him an honourable man and I would not
see the lady wed to a rogue.'

Amusement flickered in the Queen's eyes, though it
was swiftly hidden. In the matter of love her instincts
seldom lied and she was certain that she was right this
time. All that was needed was a little help from her and
the matter might be settled.

She rose to her feet, impressive, majestic and compel-
ling, a little smile upon her mouth. 'So be it. I have heard
you out, Sir Ralph, and now I shall tell you what I have
in mind…'

'Go to England with you and your father?' Alayne
stared at her friend in surprise. 'And the Queen has
granted permission without consulting me? How can this
be? She gave me her word that I might stay here for as
long as I wished.'

'Her Majesty is concerned for your safety here after
what happened the other night,' Marguerite explained.
'Sir Ralph has agreed to give us his escort on the journey,
which together with my father's men will make us strong
enough to withstand any attack. We are to stay with Sir
Ralph for some weeks, then visit the English court and
our cousins before returning home.'

'Oh…' Alayne's heart did a little flip, making her
breathless. They were to stay at the home of the English
knight! She stared at her friend uncertainly, her mind
whirling in confusion. What did this mean? Was there
some arrangement between Marguerite's father and the

Englishman? 'And afterwards—what shall I do when you marry?'

'It is not certain that I shall marry,' Marguerite told her with a blush. 'I believe my father has hopes in a certain direction but…I think Sir Ralph likes you more than he likes me. Besides, I have heard that he has no wish to marry again.'

'Because he still loves his wife, I suppose.' Alayne nodded. It had seemed romantic to her at first that the English knight should remain faithful to his wife's memory, but now she felt sad. 'But that would mean a lonely life for him, would it not?'

'They say that he seeks solitude, that he works harder than any of his men and lives the live of a monk.' Marguerite sighed. 'It must be wonderful to be loved so deeply, do you not think so, Alayne? To have a man love you for his life long…'

Alayne smiled as she saw the dreaming in her friend's eyes. 'I think that such love is to be found only in the songs of the troubadours,' she said. 'Oh, I admit that it is pleasant to be adored from afar, to be given tributes and poems and even to kiss a lover…'

'Have you kissed a lover?' Marguerite asked, looking at her with curious eyes. 'You seemed to take no interest in such things.'

'There was a young page who worked for my father when I was a child of twelve,' Alayne said and laughed. 'He kissed me once and I admit that it was sweet enough…' The shadows came to her eyes. 'My father sent him away. I missed him for a while—but then I learned the baseness of men's nature and forgot.' She shivered and closed her eyes for a moment.

'You have known great sadness,' Marguerite said. 'But I do not think all men are as your husband, Alayne. Sir

Ralph is a true and gentle knight and I think Baron de Froissart an honourable man.'

'Yes, I believe them both good men in their way,' Alayne admitted.

She turned away so that her friend should not see her expression or guess at the battle raging inside her. Something within her still shrank from the idea of being wife to any man, but there was a part of her that had begun to respond to Sir Ralph in a way she had not thought possible. She had not seen him for five days. He had sent his servant to inquire after her and a posy of flowers to wish her a speedy recovery, but she understood that he had only returned to court earlier that day. And now he was to escort her and Marguerite to England. They were to stay at his home. Alayne was not certain how she felt about that, but, if it was the Queen's wish that she should leave Poitiers for the time being, she had to obey.

When Marguerite and her father left for England, she would go with them. She had no choice and yet she feared the future. What would she find in the home of a man she hardly knew; a man whom she felt was destined to change her life?

Both Alayne and Marguerite rode their own palfreys, preferring to be in control rather than travel pillion behind one of the servants. They had learned to keep up with the hunt at Queen Eleanor's court and were excellent horsewomen, finding the journey tiring but bearable—though the sea crossing had not been pleasant.

'I feared we should all die,' Marguerite confessed when they landed at Dover. 'I am not sure I want to set foot on another ship as long as I live.'

Alayne smiled at her sympathetically. Marguerite had suffered more from the motion of the ship than she, for she had stayed on deck during much of the voyage, enjoying the fresh air and the experience. The sea was wild, untamed, its waters restless and terrifying when whipped to a frenzy by the wind. Yet she found it exciting. She would have stayed there longer had Sir Ralph not come to her.

'It looks as if we may have a squall heading our way, lady,' he had told her. 'I believe you would be safer below if we are to experience bad weather.'

'I would as lief stay on deck, sir. I do not fear the storm.'

'I fear it for you,' he said, giving her a stern look that told her he would brook no defiance. 'Please go below until the storm has passed.'

Alayne had gone silently, feeling chastened, and his harsh expression had stayed with her, making her wonder what she had done to make him so cold to her. When he held her after that terrifying attempt to abduct her she had felt safe and protected in his arms, but now he seemed to have placed a barrier between them. The feeling that he was angry with her had cast a cloud over Alayne. However, she raised herself from her own thoughts to offer reassurance to her friend.

'You will feel better now that we are on land again,' she told Marguerite. 'And who knows, perhaps you need never return to France.'

'Perhaps,' Marguerite said but looked doubtful.

Alayne looked about her for Sir Ralph's commanding figure. Apart from those few moments on board ship, when he had insisted that she go below deck, she had seen little of him since leaving the court. He was always busy, talking to his men, riding to the head and then the rear of their train, as if alert to the possibility of attack. Whenever they did happen to meet for a few moments, which was usually when they stopped at an inn to break their fast and rest, he seemed quiet, courteous but reserved. She believed that he was keeping his distance from her and was a little hurt. Had she done something to offend him? She could not think what it might be and asked Marguerite if she had noticed anything odd in his manner.

'He has much on his mind, I think. He carries important letters from the Queen,' Marguerite said. 'I know he means to leave us for a while when we reach England. Some of his men will escort us to his home, but he rides to meet the King at the White Tower in London. We shall wait for him and after a few weeks we shall all go to court together for the celebration of Christ's birth.'

'I see.' Alayne accepted but was not reassured by her friend's explanation. Sir Ralph had seemed so kind and understanding when he'd come to her rescue. Why had he withdrawn from her now? She was sure there was something more behind this odd reserve and yet could find no reason for it.

Before he left for his appointment with the King, Ralph took his leave of the ladies.

'I have sent a servant ahead to make sure that my steward knows of your coming,' he told them with a smile. 'Please treat my home as your own. I shall return as soon as possible and will hope to find you pleasantly settled.'

'You are very kind, sir,' Marguerite said. 'We wish you a safe journey.'

Alayne smiled but said nothing, turning away to follow her friend, but he caught her arm, his strong fingers pressing into the tender flesh as he held her. A little shiver went through her as she gazed up into his face, seeing the harshness of his features, the cool stare of those penetrating eyes and the uncompromising line of his mouth. There was such power in this man, such a firm will that sometimes she feared him despite his gentle ways.

'A moment, my lady, if you please.'

Was he angry? Alayne gazed up at him, feeling perplexed. He appeared angry, or at least battling with some strong emotion that seemed to wage a great war within him. 'You wished to speak with me, sir?'

'Yes.' He appeared to hesitate and the eyes that had seemed cold a second before were lit by a flame of silver that leaped up from within. She drew in her breath, afraid and yet fascinated by the pull of this man's power and strength. He took something from a tooled leather pouch that hung from a narrow belt at his waist. 'Queen Eleanor entrusted this to me, Lady Alayne. She bade me give it to you when we reached England. And I am honour bound to do her bidding.'

Alayne was surprised. Now indeed she sensed anger underlying the softness of his tone to her. She took the folded parchment from him, a quiver shooting through her as their fingers brushed in the transfer, making her heart jerk with something akin to both fear and excitement. Why was it that this man made her feel as no other had? She would have broken the seal of the letter at once if he had not forestalled her.

'No! I pray you keep it until you are alone. The matters contained within it require much thought.'

'You know what the letter contains?' She stared at him in surprise. What new mystery was this? Why should the Queen have told him what she had written to Alayne?

'Her Majesty shared her thoughts with me. But I would have you know that the decision is yours alone.'

'You frighten me, sir.' Alayne's hand trembled. His look and manner were severe, and again she thought he was angry, though she was no longer sure that his anger was directed against her.

Could he be angry with Queen Eleanor for some reason?

'You are wrong to fear me, my lady. My wish is always to protect you from harm.' He inclined his head to her stiffly and she felt that the reason for his reserve was contained in the letter he had given her. 'Forgive me, I have urgent business and must not stay. Go with your friends now and do not let anything distress you. You have my promise that you shall not be forced to anything against your will. Think carefully upon her Majesty's words and I shall return within ten days. We shall discuss the matter then.'

Alayne stood where she was, staring after his tall figure as he strode away. He was such a big man, strong and powerful, but there was gentleness beneath that stern exterior. She had glimpsed something once or twice when his guard was down and she thought that he would be kind to those he cared for.

She was aware of feelings he had stirred to life within her, feelings she had thought never to feel, and they puzzled her. She feared them and yet she welcomed them.

Her heart raced as she watched Sir Ralph mount his horse. What a complex man he was, so full of contradictions, but she believed that Berenice had been fortunate to be loved by such a man.

What could all this business of the secret letter mean? Surely not what had immediately sprung to her mind? She was trembling as she went to join her friends, who were waiting for her impatiently. No, no, she must be mistaken! Sir Ralph could not have been implying…

The Queen's letter seemed to burn through the soft

leather of her purse where she had tucked it. She was on fire to read it and yet terrified of what it might say.

The journey to Banewulf Manor was a matter of but two hours' easy riding though gentle green country that was pleasant to the eye, with rolling downs and the sea to one side, for they followed the coast road for some leagues rather than heading inland.

Alayne was pleased to find that the house was not merely a fortress as she had feared it might be, but had an attractive, solidly built manor house with four pointed turret towers, within the old castle compound. Although surrounded by thick stone walls and a moat, with a bridge and portcullis to protect against attack—an attack which had been all too likely during the reign of King Stephen—there was a thriving community in and around the castle. A small village of timber-and-wattle huts nestled at the foot of the rise upon which the castle was built, and there were extensive woods to the west, open downs that led in time to the edge of the cliffs to the east. However, the position of the house was sheltered and even on this autumn day the sunshine felt warm on Alayne's head. Not as warm as her beloved France, of course, but not as cold as she had feared it might be in England.

The horses clattered over the wooden bridge and under the stone arch that held the iron portcullis, which could be lowered swiftly in case of attack. In the cobbled courtyard servants had gathered to greet them and help them dismount. A white-haired man was addressing Marguerite's father with a little speech of welcome. After a moment Baron de Valois brought him to meet the ladies.

'My daughter, the Lady Marguerite—and the Lady Alayne, wife of the late Baron Humbolt.'

'You are very welcome, ladies. I am Master John Grey,

steward to Sir Ralph de Banewulf, and my master's letter bade me tell you his home is yours. You are to make yourselves comfortable and ask for anything you require that has not been provided.'

They thanked him and he summoned a smiling, pink-cheeked woman, possibly a few years older than Alayne, who told them that she was Mistress Morna Grey, the steward's daughter, and that it was her duty and her pleasure to serve them.

'I was nurse to my master's son until recently,' she told them as she led the way into the house, conducting them through the great hall to the wide staircase that led to an upper gallery. The house was built of stone, like the older keep that had been built nearly a hundred years earlier, but was of a more modern design, and there were shuttered windows on the upper floor rather than mere arrow slits as in the castle tower. 'But young Stefan has gone to be educated with his father's cousin and I have little enough to do of late. It will be a pleasant thing to hear ladies' voices in this house again, for there have been none but serving wenches since my lady's death. God rest her soul.' She crossed herself devoutly.

Alayne smiled and nodded as she listened, her eyes moving with interest over her surroundings. The walls were hung with thick tapestries, which gave warmth and colour to the house, and the upper floor had been well furnished with oak chests, coffers and stands of various kinds.

In the bedchamber to which she was shown, Alayne was surprised to find many items for a lady's comfort. Here, there was a tall counter on a stand with fine carving cut into its panels, also a handsome bed, several coffers, a board and trestle, laid with a beautiful cloth of embroidered silk and set with pieces of precious silver and gold. Near the hearth stood a handsome wooden stretcher for embroidery, and beside it a beautifully scripted and decorated bible lay opened on a carved wooden stand made specially to hold it.

Alayne ran her fingers over the bible reverently—such a work of art and devotion, which she knew must have taken one or several monks many years to complete. To find such a treasure here where she might avail herself of its beauty was something she had not expected. But the whole chamber seemed designed to please and comfort. Several stools and a wooden bench with a hard, straight back, but softened by cushions scattered against it, completed the feeling of comfort and peace that pervaded the room.

'I have seldom seen such luxury,' Alayne said to Mistress Grey. The whole of her father's house had contained but few of the items this one room held for her comfort. 'Are you sure you have given me the right chamber?'

'I have followed my master's orders, my lady. There are but two chambers prepared for a lady. The Lady Marguerite was to have that which was occupied by Sir Ralph's late wife—and this was his mother's chamber. Her name was Roxanna, and she was a lovely lady. Both her husband and son adored her.'

'I see—I thank you,' Alayne replied, feeling overwhelmed by such kindness. She had not been used to such consideration and for a moment her eyes pricked with tears. She blinked them away and smiled. 'I had thought this must belong to the mistress of the house.' For some reason she was relieved to know that it had belonged to Sir Ralph's mother and not his wife.

'A wench will bring you hot water to refresh you after the journey,' Mistress Grey went on. 'Perhaps you and the Lady Marguerite would prefer to sup together in her chamber this evening? It is larger than this one.'

'Yes, I thank you.' Alayne agreed. 'We are both tired and would fain rest.'

Mistress Grey smiled understandingly. 'My master has bid us take good care of you, my lady. You must ask for whatever you need.'

'I am sure I shall be comfortable here.'

Alayne waited until the servants had finished carrying in her baggage. She waved away her women when they would have begun the task of unpacking her trunks.

'Come back in a little,' she said. 'You must be tired, Louise and Bethel. Rest and relieve yourselves as I shall and then come to me.'

After the women had gone, Alayne took off her heavy mantle and let it fall on the bed, then removed her wimple. Her hair was thick and luxurious as it tumbled on to her shoulders. She shook it free and sighed as she felt the weariness of the day, then went over to the trestle and board. It was covered with a richly embroidered cloth of very fine, intricate work. Had Sir Ralph's mother made it herself? If so, she was an excellent needlewoman. Alayne believed it must be as beautiful as the Bayeux Tapestry itself, which the women of the time had sewn to depict the Battle of Hastings.

Laid out on the cloth were silver pots used for perfumes and unguents, also a comb and a mirror of burnished silver. A small gold vial held a few drops of perfume that still gave off a faint scent. The mirror gave Alayne a hazy picture of herself, but was not clear enough for her to truly see her own face.

Picking up a comb of silver worked with gold and precious jewels, Alayne drew it through her hair. She sighed as she laid it down again, knowing that she was

delaying the moment she dreaded. She sat down on the
bench, taking out Queen Eleanor's letter and began to
read.

Her cheeks became heated as she progressed and she
was glad that she had learned to read and was not forced
to ask a scribe to decipher it for her. The letter was very
personal and told Alayne that a marriage had been arranged for her by her Majesty herself.

> I believe that Sir Ralph speaks truly when he says
> that you are vulnerable, Alayne. A woman alone is
> at the mercy of any man who seeks to take advan-
> tage of her and your wealth makes you desirable to
> many. I know you have a fear of marriage, which is
> why I have persuaded Sir Ralph to offer you his
> protection. He himself has no wish to marry, but is
> prepared to offer you his name. It is out of my love
> for you that I urge you to consider his proposal.

Alayne stared at the signature in disbelief. How could
the Queen have written her such a letter—and why had
she been told nothing until this moment? She felt angry,
as if she had been led into some kind of trap, betrayed
by the woman she had most trusted. Had the letter not
carried the Queen's personal seal from the ring she wore
at all times, Alayne would have thought it false. She
would have suspected treachery of the worst kind. Even
now she felt that what she had just read must be a mistake. Surely she had misunderstood its meaning? And yet
she knew that she had not, for it was clear enough: the
Queen had given her consent to this match. Eleanor, her
friend and protector, had betrayed her trust. The Queen
surely had no right to do this without Alayne's consent
and knowledge. But it could not, must not, happen!

Oh, how could the woman she admired and loved as a true friend have done this thing? It was a cruel betrayal.

Alayne paced the floor of her chamber like a caged beast. This could not be happening to her. Sir Ralph could not have agreed to such an infamous proposal! Why should he? He did not love her. She knew that he was devoted to the memory of his dead wife. Besides, his demeanour on their journey to England had been distant. Perhaps, when she thought about it, his behaviour had not been cold, but equally it could not be called that of a suitor. Alayne had been admired by various knights in Poitiers and was used to smiles and compliments, not scowls and harsh looks from the men who sought her favours. Why should the Queen urge her to marry Sir Ralph? He was almost a stranger to her…though he *had* saved her from a fate that might have been worse than death.

For a moment she recalled the warmth and comfort she had felt in his arms and it cast her into turmoil. She had, despite herself, come to like the English knight— but not as a husband!

Alayne's head went up, pride coming to her rescue. She would refuse to marry him! Queen Eleanor's letter was a matter of advice, not a command. She would return to Poitiers at the end of the visit and then…ah, what then indeed? What was she to do with the rest of her life? She did not wish to marry and yet she had no desire to retire to a nunnery as most women did who refused to marry for a second time. What other course was open to her?

In truth she did not know. Her thoughts were too muddled, too confused to think of the future. In her heart she knew that she had begun to feel restless at court, vaguely dissatisfied with the shallow life there—but where else could she go? Not to her home, for her father would make her his prisoner and force her to a marriage of his choosing. What could she do? It seemed that there was no way out of her dilemma, unless she took the veil.

But she did not want to spend the rest of her days shut away from the world. She wanted…she knew not what? Alayne was distressed to discover that she no longer knew her own mind.

'Alayne…'

Marguerite's voice was a welcome invasion of her thoughts. She turned as the other girl asked if she might enter, hiding the letter in her purse and smiling.

'Is something the matter?' Marguerite asked, sensing a strangeness in her manner as she advanced into the room. 'Are you not pleased with your chamber? It is a little smaller than mine, but you have a fine view of the garden. Mine looks towards the forest and is darker despite its size. I thought I heard a wolf howling earlier, but we are well protected here within the castle walls.'

'Oh, no, how could I be less than pleased with such a room as this?' Alayne asked, recovering her composure. She was allowing herself to be upset for nothing. Sir Ralph would not force her to be his wife. He was a true knight, brave and honourable, and he had given her his word. She must trust him to keep it, for she had no other choice. 'Everything I could need for my comfort is here. I have not yet looked at the view.' She joined Marguerite at the tiny window and glanced out. It was possible to see only the outline of what would be a pretty walk in clement weather, for the sun had gone and there was but a shadowy moon. 'I believe the garden must be pleasant and there are fine rides to be had over the downs, I think.'

'I had not thought Sir Ralph's home would be as fine,' Marguerite said. 'I understand there have been many improvements since my father stayed here as a youth. I have never visited before this, but my father came to study here with Sir Ralph's father for a few years.'

'It is indeed a comfortable house,' Alayne agreed. 'There were not so many tapestries at my father's house and my husband would have scorned such luxury at his fortress.'

'The hangings are lovely, especially in this room,' Marguerite agreed. 'They give such warmth to one's surroundings. I think most women would find this house pleasant to live in at any time of year. It is certainly warmer than the palace at Poitiers.'

'Yes, indeed,' Alayne agreed. 'Though I believe it may be much colder in the depths of winter.'

'Oh, I dare say you are right,' Marguerite said. 'But—'

What she would have said was forgotten as a servant arrived to tell them that supper had been laid in Marguerite's room.

'It was to tell you that it had been brought that I came,' she cried and laughed. 'Come, Alayne. I want you to see my chamber. I have been told that it belonged to Sir Ralph's wife.'

Alayne followed her along the gallery, which overlooked the great hall below. Above them the vaulted ceiling towered, its arch spanned by great oak beams and decorated with gilded panels. Set at intervals were banners and shields carrying the de Banewulf arms, which were sometimes intertwined with those of the ladies they had married.

It was shadowy in the hall, a dim light creeping through the slits that served as windows in the lower chambers, but wax candles burned at intervals in darkly burnished pewter sconces giving off both light and warmth. Instead of the great chamber directly above the hall as was common to older castles, the gallery had been built in such a way that there were several smaller, private chambers, which was more comfortable but, Alayne imagined, vastly more expensive to build. Such expense seemed to indicate that the master of this house was both wealthy and generous.

Marguerite's chamber, situated at the other side of the house, was furnished much as Alayne's, except that a trestle and board had been set up before the fireplace and there were two magnificent carved chairs. It seemed clear that this room must have been often used by Sir Ralph and his wife for private dining, for such items were costly and seldom met with outside a royal palace. Alayne had never before used anything but a stool or a bench and found hers strange but comfortable.

The tapestries were richly embroidered, adding to the comfort of the chamber, but it did seem darker than the one she had been given, and Alayne felt an atmosphere. She thought it a little oppressive, almost brooding, which was foolish of her, but something she could not shake off. It was almost as if a sadness hung in the air and permeated the very fabric of the hangings. She gave a little shiver, feeling oddly cold. However, Marguerite seemed not to notice and Alayne kept her unwelcome thoughts to herself.

It must be her imagination, but she could almost believe the Lady Berenice's shadow haunted this room. No, that was foolish. She must shake off this mood and eat her meal.

'I have found an unfinished tapestry in one of the chests,' Marguerite told her when they had finished their supper. She went over to an oak hutch and lifted the heavy lid, taking out a piece of folded silk. 'Look, Alayne, is it not lovely?'

Alayne examined the material, exclaiming over the fine

work. A pattern of birds and flowers had been marked out with coloured threads, but only a small corner had been set with neat stitching of the costly silks. Yet it was possible to see how beautiful it might be when completed.

'Is it not a shame to leave such a thing unfinished?' Marguerite asked. 'It would make a beautiful hanging if it were completed.'

'Yes, I agree.' Alayne thought that someone who loved life and nature must have marked out the design and the work already done was lovely. 'Might it be a way of repaying Sir Ralph's hospitality if we worked on it together?'

'We could never finish it in the time we are here,' Marguerite said regretfully. 'But we might attempt it. Perhaps the work could be passed on to Mistress Grey when we leave.'

'Let us begin tomorrow,' Alayne suggested. She did not know why, but the tapestry intrigued her. 'But for this evening I am tired and must beg you to excuse me. I would seek my bed.'

'Of course,' Marguerite said and smiled. 'It will seem strange to sleep alone. We have been together for some months now—since you came to court, Alayne.'

'Yes, we have,' she agreed. 'But we shall be parted when you marry.'

'Yes…' Marguerite flushed. 'When I marry…or when you do.'

'I shall not marry.'

'You may change your mind one day.'

'I do not think so,' Alayne replied. 'Please, may we speak of something else?'

'I did not wish to distress you,' Marguerite said. 'But you cannot wish to remain at court forever?'

'No…' Alayne yawned. 'Excuse me, I am tired. I think I shall go to bed.'

'Yes, I am also tired. Forgive me if I upset you?'

'It was nothing.'

Alayne left her and walked back to her own chamber. It was strange not to share her room with her friend. At the palace there had been such a demand for space that the Queen's ladies always shared their rooms, but here there was a great deal of room and few ladies to share it. It was as Marguerite had said, a house that any woman would find comfortable.

After her serving women had helped her to undress, Alayne sat for some minutes, brushing her hair. She had her own personal things about her now, and they had added that final touch. She glanced about her, feeling a sense of content, as if the room welcomed her. Here the atmosphere was as inviting and happy as it had been sad in the other chamber, and she felt that Sir Ralph's mother must have been content here in this house. It must have been built for her as a bride, though it had been refurbished and improved recently, perhaps when Sir Ralph brought his own bride home.

Alayne's thoughts dwelt on the Lady Berenice for a while. Why was it that she had sensed unhappiness in that lady's chamber? Surely Berenice had been the happiest of women, to be so loved? The atmosphere she had seemed to sense must have been merely her imagination. Berenice had been loved and protected.

For a few moments Alayne's thoughts returned to the time of her marriage, her husband's brutality and his hatred of her when he lay imprisoned in his bed, unable to move the lower half of his body. It had not stopped him pinching and punching her when she tended him, and she had learned to dread being near him.

She could never suffer such humiliation again! Once married, a woman was her husband's property, owned even as he owned his animals and his house. Surely it was better to remain single, to retain that freedom she now enjoyed?

And yet she knew that a part of her was strangely attracted to the English knight. There were times when he had made her heart gladden and beat faster, and somehow she believed that he might treat a lady very differently from the coarse brute who had been her husband. She took out the Queen's letter again, reading it carefully and frowning over the part that said her Majesty had persuaded Sir Ralph to offer her his name. That must surely mean he did not care for her, would marry her only because the Queen had commanded him.

Alayne's pride was pricked. She would not marry a man who could not love her, why should she? If she decided to marry at all, it would be to a man of her own choosing.

The Queen had been anxious for her because of the attempted abduction, but she would never force her to marry—would she?

Alayne sighed as she crept beneath the bedcovers and blew out her candle. She must try to sleep and put this worrying problem from her mind. Sir Ralph would not return for some days; by then, perhaps she would have found a solution.

Chapter Five

For the next few days, Alayne and Marguerite worked on the tapestry discovered in Lady Berenice's chamber. By their combined efforts they completed two of the corners, working with the hanging held between them. It was a pleasant way of passing the time, for they liked to compare and choose the colours they used so that it would become a pleasing whole.

'That shade of blue is delightful,' Marguerite said, taking out a small skein of thread to hold it against the embroidery. 'But I fear there will not be enough to complete the hanging. We must blend in another paler shade or we shall not be able to finish it as we would wish.'

'I do not think we shall finish it,' Alayne said regretfully as she fastened her thread and cut it with the little knife that hung from the chatelaine at her waist. 'Sir Ralph said he would be home within ten days and it is eleven on the morrow. He will surely be here soon and then we shall be but a few days until we leave for the court.'

'Yes…' Marguerite sighed. 'I have become so comfortable here that I scarcely wish to leave.' She shivered and glanced at the fire. 'It grows colder of night now than it did. If the palace is as cold as it was at Poitiers, we shall feel bereft when we leave here, Alayne.'

'Yes, I believe we shall.' Alayne rose to her feet and went to look out of the window, which had not yet been shuttered for the night. There was a hazy moon and, as she watched, she saw a small party of riders coming towards the castle. A tingling sensation began at the nape of her neck and she continued to watch as they rode in under the portcullis, which had been raised for them at their approach. By their apparel two men were knights, the others their servants. She could not see clearly enough to identify the taller of the two men and yet she knew him. 'I think Sir Ralph has returned, Marguerite.'

Marguerite came hastily to the window. 'He is not alone,' she said with a slight frown. 'I wonder who he has brought with him.'

'We shall discover that on the morrow,' Alayne replied, her heart beating faster than before. She had longed for and yet dreaded Sir Ralph's return, for only then could she be sure of what was in his mind—only then could she be certain that he understood no marriage could take place. 'I am tired, Marguerite, and would seek my bed, if you will excuse me?'

'Yes, of course,' her friend said, though the hour was still early. 'I think I shall retire myself—we must be up early in the morning to welcome Sir Ralph home.'

Alayne kissed her cheek and went away to her own room, but just as she reached it someone came towards her from the shadows of the back staircase, which was normally used by the servants, and she caught her breath as she saw it was their host.

'Lady Alayne,' he said seeming almost as startled as she was at the unexpected meeting. 'I was told it was your habit to sit with the lady Marguerite at this hour.'

'It has been our custom to sit together in her chamber in the evenings,' Alayne replied a little stiffly. She was trembling inside, her heart beating so fast that she thought he must hear its wild thrumming. 'I have but now left her to retire.'

'It is early to retire, is it not?' Ralph asked, his gaze narrowing as he saw the discomfort in her face. Of course she had been hoping to avoid meeting him, must have been on edge these past days after reading that letter. He inwardly cursed Queen Eleanor for her well-meaning but clumsy interference. 'Forgive me, Alayne. I had hoped to return before this hour for I wished to speak to you at once on my arrival, but we were delayed and it was not possible.'

'You said you would be ten days, you have been no more.'

'I hoped to be sooner,' he said, his eyes dwelling on her lovely face. She looked proud and beautiful, but that hint of vulnerability, of fear, which had seemed to haunt her since the night of her abduction, was still there. He had hoped it might have faded over these past days. 'You read her Majesty's letter, of course?'

Alayne's cheeks were stained crimson. 'I was surprised by it,' she confessed. 'The Queen knows I have no wish to marry, and I think it unkind in her to spring this suggestion upon me in this way—and to use her powers of persuasion on you, sir. I believe you can have no wish for this marriage.'

'It was I who approached the Queen,' he replied, his expression stern, forbidding, giving her no hint of his true feelings. 'I felt that you were too exposed to unscrupulous knights who would use you for their own purposes, my lady. There was another knight I felt you might favour, but her Majesty did not agree. She knew that I had no wish to marry and thought that a union in name only might appeal to you more—that you might be able to accept my protection, while forbearing the more intimate duties of marriage.'

Alayne's cheeks flushed bright red. His gaze was intent, watchful, and she could not look at him as she said as calmly as she was able. 'And how would you feel about such a marriage, sir? I cannot think it fair to you— nor yet any man, for it is against the nature of marriage.'

Surely he could not mean what he had just said? To offer his protection while asking nothing of her in return was too generous, too noble for her to believe it sincere.

'It was that I wished you to understand,' Ralph said and took a letter from his pouch. 'I came here this evening to leave this in your room, my lady. I wanted you to understand my own feelings before we spoke.' He handed her the folded parchment with an air almost of embarrassment. 'If you read this, it may make you easier in your mind.'

Alayne accepted it, wondering why she did so. It would surely be better to refuse at once, to make an end to this awkward situation between them.

'I shall read it,' she promised. 'But I cannot say that my answer will be swayed by this. It is my intention to return to France after our visit here has ended.'

'That is your privilege and your decision,' Ralph replied. 'But I wish you will think carefully before giving your final answer. Indeed, I do not ask for your answer before our visit to court. I would have you grow used to the idea and to me, Alayne.' He smiled at her, revealing a tender side that made her spine tingle. How attractive he was when he was not scowling! 'I think both you and the Lady Marguerite will be pleased to see the visitor I have brought with me. The Baron de Froissart had presented himself at court and is now on a mission for King Henry. He but breaks his journey with us for a day and a night, and then will leave us—but I was sure that he would find a welcome with you, my lady.'

'The Baron de Froissart is a friend who must always be welcome to me,' Alayne agreed. 'I shall be pleased to see him, sir, and I thank you for bringing him to us.'

Ralph nodded, his eyes watchful. Her demeanour gave nothing away. Was he wrong to think that she might have a partiality for the French knight? He had known that he might lose her if he offered her the choice between them, but he would not have wished to take unfair advantage. De Froissart was aware of the situation, for Ralph had told him all. To his credit, the French knight had agreed that it must be for Alayne to decide her own fate. They both believed that Alayne must be married for her own safety, but Ralph had sworn he would not force the match the Queen had favoured upon her. She must make her own choice.

'I shall bid you goodnight, lady,' he said now and bowed to her. 'Sleep well and do not let ugly dreams disturb you. I know that you have suffered an unhappy union, but if you give yourself into my keeping, I would promise that nothing like that ever touched you again, Alayne. If your husband were not already dead, I should have killed him for you. Such beasts do not deserve to live!'

Alayne was startled by his fierceness. He was a man of such contrasts, capable of both kindness and great anger. She watched him walk away, her heart pounding. At times he frightened her terribly, but at others he made her feel safe and she wanted to take shelter within the circle of those strong arms.

Going into her chamber, she felt the sting of tears behind her eyes. If only she had never been forced into marriage! If she had never experienced the humiliation forced on her by her cruel husband, perhaps then she could have let herself love Sir Ralph with her whole self.

And there was a little voice in her head, an aching in her heart, that told her she loved him now, whether or not she wished it so.

Alayne's heart fluttered as she read Sir Ralph's letter to her. It was brief and told her that he had great respect and admiration for her and would be honoured if she would be his wife. He had never intended to marry again, for he had his heir and was content with his life, but he had lately come to believe that his home would be the better for a chatelaine and he would be happy to offer Alayne the safety of his protection.

> You have my promise that I would never seek to force upon you the kind of hurt you have suffered in your previous marriage, and whether our union continues in name only or becomes a true marriage would be your decision, Alayne. I ask only kindness and affection and offer you the same in return.

This letter had, she knew, been written by a man of culture. It was signed boldly and the sight of that signature made Alayne's heart race wildly. Sir Ralph was a passionate man, a resolute man—and how could she believe that such a man would ask no more of her than a smile and friendship?

She knew him to be a man of strong feelings and of pride—how then could she expect such a man to refrain from seeking her bed? He might promise it now, but for how long would he honour that promise once she was his wife?

Alayne closed her eyes as once again the cruel memories invaded her mind. She could still recall the malice and triumph in her late husband's voice as he had told her she belonged to him, that he owned her as he might a dog. He had made it clear that he could do with her as he would, that he considered her less than the meanest serving wench in his kitchens—and she shuddered at what her life might have been had he not tumbled down the twisting stone stairs of the tower.

A tiny voice in her head told Alayne that Sir Ralph would never be that cruel, that he was a very different man and might give her a kind of happiness she had never dreamed of, that she had in fact already begun to love him. And yet she could not accept what her heart dictated. A part of her might long for something she could not understand, her body responding to his lightest touch or even a smile, but her mind revolted against the idea of being a man's possession. It would be the wisest thing if she were to inform Sir Ralph of her decision at once, and yet, when she took up her quill, her hand would not form the words.

No, no, she decided as she laid the swan quill down again, not one word formed. She must not appear hasty or rude. Sir Ralph had spoken out of chivalry and kindness and she could never forget that he had saved her from abduction or the safe feeling she had discovered in his arms that night. She would not change her mind about marrying him, but she need not tell him just yet. She would choose her moment and speak softly so as not to offend him.

Sir Ralph's return home brought an immediate change to their lives. The house was more alive, the servants bustling about their work with a new energy. He commanded a banquet for the evening after his arrival, inviting some of his friends to dine with them in the hall. His kinsman Sir Harald of Wotten was there together with his wife and eldest son. He sat beside Alayne and told her that he had taken Sir Ralph's son into his own household to educate him.

'He will visit from time to time, but I would not bring him so soon for it might unsettle him. Christ's Mass will be time enough.'

'It seems hard that Stefan should have to leave his home so young,' she said, feeling sorry for the young boy who had been taken from his home and those who loved him. 'But I know it is the custom. I believe it was so for Marguerite's brother. She told me that he cried when he was sent away, but after a while he came back to visit and he was happy with his friends.'

'He has my two younger sons as his companions,' Sir Harald said. 'Stefan is a quiet boy, but he likes to study and will settle soon enough.' He looked at her inquiringly. 'You have no brothers yourself, my lady?'

'Unfortunately none lived beyond childhood. My father married twice, but both his wives died in childbed. I was the only one of his children to survive.'

'Then your father must treasure you the more,' Sir Harald said and smiled at her kindly.

Alayne did not reply. She knew that her father hated her because she was not the son he had wanted and he was angry with her for defying him over the matter of her second marriage. She sighed inwardly, but the minstrel had begun his sweet song of love and a juggler was performing marvellous feats of skill and balance. It was impossible to feel sad for long in such a house as this, where there were so many smiling faces and the spirit of true kindness seemed to prevail, everyone caring for each other.

Glancing round the hall, Alayne discovered that a man she did not recognise was watching her. His eyes seemed to study her in a way that she found disturbing, but she turned her gaze away. He was one of Sir Ralph's servants and of no real interest to her.

When the dancing began, the Baron de Froissart came to claim her. His smile was warm as he led her into the merry throng.

'I was distressed when I learned that you were to travel to England for some months,' he told her. 'But it spurred me to make a change to my own life and I must confess that I am well pleased. King Henry sends me north to deal with a band of outlaws that roam in the forest there. I am to take command of the garrison at Nottingham and make my home there for three years.'

'And this pleases you?' Alayne saw the satisfaction in his face and nodded. 'I see it does. You were bored at Poitiers, I believe?'

'The soft living at court is well enough for a time,' the baron replied. 'But I believe myself unsuited to the life. I grew restless there once my arm had healed, and needed more stimulation.'

'I am glad that your wound has healed, for it was wickedly done. And you are a soldier,' Alayne said. 'Indeed, I think you will be happier in your new position. I too found the life at Poitiers a little shallow at times. Even the best of pleasures grow stale in time if there is not a serious side to their purpose.'

'The life at court can be sweet for a time, but you were meant for a different purpose,' the baron said, his eyes intent on her face. Alayne trembled as she saw the warmth in their depths. 'You turn your face against marriage, my lady, but I think it would fill the empty yearning inside you. A woman needs the security of marriage and the love of her children.'

Alayne turned her head aside, her cheeks warm. It seemed that de Froissart saw too clearly. She could find no words to answer him for she did not know her own heart, and she would not offend a man who had been her friend.

'I would have stayed at Poitiers for your sake,' he went on, as she was silent. 'I would have done anything you asked of me. But I see it clearly now. You are not for me, sweet lady. You need a different kind of knight to heal your hurts and I would bruise you with my clumsiness. Therefore I have chosen another life.'

'I do not know what to say to you, sir. I mean not to offend, but I have no wish for marriage at this time.'

The music had ended. The baron took her hand to lead her to the side of the huge hall, where Marguerite stood in conversation with Sir Harald's wife. He smiled at her and pressed her hand as he sensed her awkwardness.

'Say nothing, for my words need no answer, Alayne. You do not yet know your own heart and it is not my place to speak of another's feelings, but I know that you do not love me. I would have taken you as my lover or my wife and served you faithfully, but I know my cause is vain. Yet I am ever your friend. Yours to command in need.'

'I thank you for your kindness,' Alayne said in a choked voice. The realisation that his courtship had been earnest and not merely a jest as she had thought had shaken her. She was sorry to part from a good friend, yet knew that she would have refused had he asked her to marry him.

After he had left Alayne's side, de Froissart asked Marguerite to dance with him. She accepted his hand, her cheeks touched with pink as he led her into the lively dance that followed. Watching them for a few minutes, Alayne understood something she had only half-suspected before—Marguerite was in love with the baron. Her warning against him had been given half in jealousy, half in misunderstanding, perhaps because at that time she had not understood her own heart. But she knew it now, for it was evident in her laughter, her eagerness.

Alayne felt sad, for she knew that he had taken a soldier's path because of his unrequited love for her. Why could he not have loved Marguerite? Must everyone be unhappy in this life?

'Why do you frown so?' Alayne turned her head as she heard Sir Ralph's voice close by, a sudden trembling seizing her as she gazed into his eyes. Such a large, powerful man and he looked at her so intently! Her eyes dwelt for a moment on his mouth. When he was not angry there was a soft sensuality about it that made her insides turn to water. What might it be like to be kissed by this man? 'Are you displeased, my lady?'

'No. Why should I be displeased, sir? You have provided us with a fine feast and entertainment.'

'I wanted you and Marguerite to enjoy yourselves. You have been used to the pleasures of court life and it must have seemed quiet while I was away.'

'Perhaps a little,' Alayne admitted. 'But it has been pleasant. We have not been idle or unhappy, I assure you.'

'We are commanded to attend the court in two weeks from now,' Sir Ralph said. 'I believe Marguerite and her father travel to their kinsman's home in the north for the

New Year, but I shall return to Banewulf after the celebrations for Christ's Mass.'

The look he gave her made Alayne's heart miss a beat and then race wildly, a slow heat beginning deep down inside her. It rose to flush her cheeks, making her uncertain and a little afraid of what he might say next. She knew that he was wondering if she would choose to return as his wife.

She could not meet his steady gaze, but looked down as she searched for something to turn the conversation, her nails turned inward to the palms of her hands.

'Marguerite found an unfinished hanging,' she said to cover her awkwardness. 'We have been working on it, but I fear it will not be finished before we leave Banewulf.'

'A pattern of flowers and birds...' Sir Ralph said, sounding odd. 'I remember that Berenice began it before she started to feel unwell, and then it was put away as she could not concentrate and did not wish to spoil it.'

Alayne was made curious by the tone of his voice, which was harsh and yet caught with emotion. She raised her eyes to look at him and saw that his expression had become bleak, his expression distant, as if he gazed into the past and found it cruel.

'I have heard that your wife died,' she said and then gasped as she saw the flash of pain pass across his face. How that hurt him! 'Forgive me. I should not have spoken.'

'She died of a fever after our son was born. She was too delicate for childbearing. Berenice should never have married—she was too good, too gentle.' The words seemed forced out of him, strangled by the intensity of his emotion.

'That is sad, my lord,' Alayne said, her throat tight

with emotion as she witnessed the grief that gripped him. 'Her death must have caused you much sorrow.'

'Yes, it did.' A nerve flicked in his cheek as he offered her his hand. 'Shall we dance, my lady? We stray to a melancholy subject and I meant this evening to pleasure you.'

Alayne nodded and gave him her hand. She was sorry that her careless words had brought him pain, for it was clear that it disturbed him to be reminded of his loss. He must have loved Berenice very much, she thought, and the thought brought a swift, slashing ache to her breast. When a man had loved this deeply, it was little wonder that he could not love again.

He had not offered her his name for the sake of the love he bore her, but from a desire to protect a woman whom he saw as in need of that protection. She thought he was a perfect knight, following the ideals of chivalry to its limit, and felt strangely humbled that he should offer her his name. Perhaps there was also a desire in him for companionship, a need for a little warmth and affection. He had spoken to her of these things and she could understand such a need, for she had often felt it herself. Indeed, there were times when she longed for more—much more.

Yet she knew that her husband had scarred her deeply. Could she ever hope to forget the humiliation he had poured on her, to find happiness in the love of a good man?

Alayne thought that it would be unfair to take everything Sir Ralph offered and give nothing in return. How could she trap him into a marriage that might never be more than pretence—he surely deserved more? In time he would want more, perhaps demand it as his right.

And yet he vowed that he had no wish for a true marriage. And she could understand that also—for he had loved too well and he could never replace Berenice in his heart with another.

Their dance was ending. Alayne smiled and thanked him as he handed her over to his kinsman, taking Sir Harald's wife into the next dance, which was a lively country affair.

'You are a little flushed, Lady Alayne,' Sir Harald said kindly as he gave her a look of concern. 'Perhaps you would prefer not to dance?'

'Could we seek a little air?' Alayne asked. 'May we go into the courtyard for a moment?'

'It would be my pleasure to escort you,' Sir Harald said. 'Though we must not stay long for you may take a chill—it is colder outside than you think. I believe we shall have snow before long.'

'I only need a moment to collect my thoughts,' Alayne said. She was silent as she tried to reconcile the confusion raging within her. She had been so certain that she could never marry any man, and yet something inside her was drawn to Sir Ralph. It seemed that an invisible cord had wound itself about her heartstrings, binding her whether she willed it or no.

'Has something upset you?' Sir Harald asked as they left the hall and ventured into the courtyard. The moon was bright, showing him the anxious look on her lovely young face. 'May I be of some service to you, lady?'

'Oh, no,' she assured him at once. 'Sir Ralph was speaking just now of his late wife and I think I was distressed by his grief.'

'Ah…' Sir Harald nodded, understanding. 'As I have been distressed by it myself many times. Ralph blamed himself for her death and would not be consoled, you see. We all thought he might die of his grief—especially after he fought with his friend Sir Christian Payton. We never knew why they quarrelled, but his friend hit his head as he fell and he died soon after in Ralph's arms—and in the following weeks and months Ralph seemed to withdraw into himself. I thought that he would become a hermit and it is good to see him much restored, Lady Alayne. I was very surprised to receive an invitation to this feast and to find two beautiful ladies here—but much relieved. I hope that my kinsman has taken my advice and will find himself a wife. It is not good for a man to live alone.'

'When did you give Sir Ralph this advice?'

'Just before he left for Poitiers,' Sir Harald said and looked concerned as she shivered and turned pale. 'You turn cold, my lady. We should return to the hall.'

'Yes, perhaps we should,' she said. It was clear that Sir Ralph had taken his kinsman's advice to heart, she thought, wondering why the knowledge hurt. She had always known he did not truly wish for a wife. Why should it cause her pain? 'I thank you for your kindness, sir.'

Alayne was asked to dance by another of Sir Ralph's friends when she returned to the hall and was happy to accept. He was a fresh-faced young man called Robert Greaves and squire to his master. Dressed in bright garb of blue tunic and yellow hose, he had eyes as clear as the summer sky and a sweet, soft mouth. She found him courteous and uncomplicated, his efforts to please her finding success as she laughed at his merry jests.

Watching her with the young squire, Ralph frowned, then pulled himself up for his unworthy thoughts and walked from the hall. As always his steward needed his attention on some matter of business that had come to hand.

After her dance with the young squire, Alayne decided that she would say goodnight to her host and retire. It had grown late, the fire burning low in the huge hearth, and she was beginning to feel tired, but when she looked for Sir Ralph she could not find him. He had disappeared, as had Marguerite and Sir Harald's wife.

Suddenly she was reminded of the night when she had been Queen of the Day for the tourney, and the terrifying abduction attempt afterwards. She was safe here, she knew, but still the memory haunted her.

Leaving the hall, Alayne hurried up the stairs to her chamber. Her maids were waiting for her and she allowed them to help her undress and prepare for bed before dismissing them. She was brushing her long hair, which fell in scented silken tresses to her shoulders, when someone knocked at her door and she went to open it, thinking it must be Marguerite. Opening it, she saw that Sir Ralph stood there.

'My cousin told me that you felt a little unwell earlier,' he said, his eyes moving over her anxiously. Alayne felt the power of that gaze, her heart jerking as she looked into his eyes and was drawn to him. Her mouth parted on a sigh and she felt that strange curl of heat deep within her. 'Do you wish for anything? Shall I send my physician to you?'

'I am quite well,' she said and smiled at him. 'It was merely that I was a little warm and wanted some air. You must not concern yourself, sir. I am not in the least ill.' For some reason she reached out to him and he took her hand, carrying it to his cheek for a moment, though in the next he had let it go. The gesture shook her, sending tremors running through her.

'My lord…' Her eyes were wide with surprise, her

parted lips unconsciously sensuous and soft with the desire she sensed but did not yet understand.

'Forgive me,' he said, a nerve flicking in his cheek as he felt the echo of her awakening desire reverberate within in him, arousing his need to a hot hardness that he had not felt in many a year. 'I should not have come— but I was anxious that you might have taken a chill.'

'I would have bid you goodnight, but could not find you,' Alayne said. 'It was kind of you to inquire after my health, sir.'

'I had some business to attend that took me from the hall and when I returned you had gone. I was anxious about you, but you have set my mind at rest,' he replied with a wry smile. 'I shall go and leave you to your rest, lady.'

His eyes seemed to draw her in and Alayne felt that she was being pulled towards him, her limbs weak with a longing she did not understand. She wanted to beg him stay, but knew that she must let him go. If any should see him here, she would lose her good name.

'I bid you sleep well,' she said and smiled.

'And I you,' he replied and then he reached out and touched her cheeks with his fingertips. 'You are as beautiful inside as out, Alayne. I pray that I may serve you in some way.'

Alayne trembled as she drew back, closing the door of her chamber in some confusion as he walked away. If any of the knights at Poitiers had spoken so to her she would have thought it a prelude to seduction, but there was something about Sir Ralph that told her he had been sincere in his concern and his wish to serve her.

She almost ran to her bed, pulling the covers up around her neck for the night had turned bitterly cold. Extinguishing the candle by her bed, she closed her eyes and tried to make sense of the sensations that the touch of Sir Ralph's hand had aroused in her.

No, she thought as she snuggled further beneath the fur rugs that covered her, she must not let herself love him. He did not love her and she would merely lay herself open to hurt if she admitted her love for him. Not the kind of hurt her husband had inflicted on her, but another kind—a kind that might be even more painful than that she had previously experienced.

Alayne's dreams were sweet, but when she woke they left her and she could not recall them. As she pulled on a warm robe and went to the window she saw that snow had fallen during the night, covering everything in a crisp white layer that had a touching beauty. As she watched she heard laughter and saw that some of the younger men were indulging in a snow fight, throwing handfuls of it at each other and chasing each other over the frozen ground.

She turned as the door of her chamber opened and Marguerite entered, already dressed for the day in a warm kirtle, overgown and fur-lined robe.

'What, still not dressed on such a morning?' she cried and laughed as Alayne drew back from her window. 'The baron left half an hour ago, and Sir Ralph went with him to see him on the right road. It is a bitter day for travelling, but the roads will be easier now that the frost has come.'

'Yes, it is easier to travel after a light fall of snow,' Alayne agreed. 'The roads had become wet after the rain and were almost impassable in places, I believe. It will be easier for the baron to travel while the frost lasts.'

'We are not to travel for a week or two,' Marguerite

said. 'But we go south and I am told that the roads are
a little better than those to the north.'

'Yes, I suppose so,' Alayne agreed. She saw the anxiety her friend was trying to hide. 'You are concerned for
the baron?'

'It is a lawless place he goes to,' Marguerite said. 'I
fear that I may never see him again—though he says that
we shall meet when I stay with our cousins in Nottingham.'

'You would like that, I think?' Alayne smiled as her
friend hesitated. 'You do not need to hide it from me,
Marguerite. I know you like the baron.'

'I love him,' Marguerite confessed and tears sprang to
her eyes. 'I spurned him once—before you came to
court—because I had heard ill of him. He was angry and
then you came to Poitiers and he had eyes for none but
you. When I told you of the squire I loved, it was a lie
to blind you to the truth of my folly. I know Pierre cares
nothing for me.'

'If he cared for me, it was only as a friend,' Alayne
said. 'Like others at the Court of Love, he played the
game of courtship most ardently because I did not show
favour to any man. He knows that I would never marry
him, Marguerite. I have made it plain and he accepts it.'

'Yes, he told me,' she said and wiped a tear from her
cheek. 'I thought there was no hope for me—but now
perhaps…'

Alayne went to her, kissing her cheek and smiling.
'Does your father know that you love Baron de Froissart?' Marguerite shook her head. 'Why do you not tell
him? He might arrange a match for you.'

'My father was set on a match for me with Sir Ralph,'
Marguerite said. 'But I do not think he is interested in
me. If he marries at all—' She broke off and looked at

Alayne. 'You might find happiness with him if you tried. I believe he is a truly good man, Alayne.'

'Perhaps,' Alayne said and turned away to hide her confusion. She felt as if she were torn in two by the conflicting emotions within her. 'He is truly a good man, but I am not sure that I could ever marry anyone.'

'Will you return to Poitiers?' Marguerite asked. 'Think what the future will be, Alayne—what it might already have been if Sir Ralph had not been there to protect you that night.'

'Yes, I know. I have thought of it often,' Alayne said. She heard a shout of male laughter from outside and glanced out of the window. 'Look, Marguerite. I believe Sir Ralph has joined in the game.'

Marguerite glanced out and smiled. 'They are like children,' she said. 'Get dressed quickly, Alayne. I have not often seen such a fall of snow and I want to touch it.'

Chapter Six

The snow lasted for three weeks but it did not keep them prisoners at Banewulf, for though it was cold and there were further falls they were not deep.

'In this part of the country we seldom get deep drifts until January or February,' Sir Ralph told his guests. 'This kind of snow is a blessing, for the ground freezes and makes the roads passable again.'

Alayne found that she liked the cold weather more than she had imagined she might. It was pleasant to go out walking on the downs that led to the cliffs and on one occasion she ventured right to the edge and stood looking down at the sea. It looked grey and angry, but she was too cold to stay there long and returned to the warmth of the house.

Robert Greaves was often her companion on her walks. He was a pleasant young man and, though admiring, treated her with the respect due to her position. She knew that Sir Ralph's servants believed she was to marry him, and these past days she had begun to think it might be the solution to her problems.

She had found a certain contentment in Sir Ralph's house that she had not known before, and enjoyed his company when he had leisure to spend time with them, although he was often busy with his steward. She had discovered that he had a pleasant singing voice, and that he was skilled in the art of dancing. Indeed, there seemed little he could not excel at and she found herself more and more inclined to think of him as a perfect knight.

He knew much of the scriptures by heart and he read Latin as well as any scribe. He was a raconteur and could tell fabulous tales, some of them true histories and some fables. Amongst his private collection of treasures, he had a beautiful book of hours inscribed by learned monks, also fabulous items of gold, silver and rare Venetian glass, and he took pride in showing his things to Alayne.

He also enjoyed the sports common to other knights and joined the training with his own men, practising in the courtyard for some hours most mornings. He enjoyed hunting for wild boar and occasionally the wolves that roamed in the forest nearby.

'Mostly we live at peace with them,' he told Alayne once when the men had been out hunting for wolves. 'But sometimes in winter when they are hungry they attack the villagers or their animals, and then we have to hunt down the rogues and kill them.'

Alayne accepted his words, for it was a part of life and her father had often done the same.

She had discovered a new way of living in his house and was sorry when the time came for them to leave for the court. Sir Ralph had not spoken of his offer of marriage again, and she believed that he was waiting for a sign from her. He had promised that he would not press her for an answer and his patience gave her the courage to consider his proposal.

Was it possible that they might be happy in this way for the rest of their lives? She had begun to lose her fear of him, to discover that his frowns often meant only that his mind was elsewhere. He was a busy man with many duties, for this was only one of the manors he held and messengers came often with matters requiring his attention.

'In the spring I visit my estates in the North,' he told her once. 'I would not live there in winter, for it is much colder than here—but it is pleasant enough once the roads are over the worst of the winter.'

It was clear that he was a wealthy man. Alayne knew that she would have a life of comfort and ease if she wed him, but she had wealth enough in her own right and that would not have swayed her if she had not liked the man himself.

And she had discovered that she did like him. The other feelings she had for him were shrouded in mystery. She might suspect they were love, but would not admit to such emotions—but her liking had come more slowly, out of a growing respect for him.

She could live with a man she liked and respected, Alayne decided, if only he would keep to his word and not expect too much of her.

It was very hard to know what to do. If she refused him, she must return to Poitiers in the spring—and what awaited her there? The Queen would probably arrange another match for her and, if she did not, Alayne's father might try again. He would not hesitate to wed her to that brute de Bracey if she ever came within his power again.

No, she thought, she was safer here in this house, happier than she had ever been. She had not yet decided, would not decide until they were at court, but she was beginning to think that she would not mind being married to Sir Ralph.

* * *

The weather was still frosty when they set out for the castle at which King Henry was holding court that Christmastide, the ground hard beneath the horses' hooves. It was a party of some thirty-five men and two ladies that set out from Banewulf that morning, a baggage train of packhorses and carts following behind with the servants. The custom was for men of wealth to transport the comforts of home with them, for there might be no lodging available in the castle and the company might be forced to seek shelter in the town.

However, after a journey of several days and nights spent in the guesthouses of a monastery or some great abbey, which were better furnished and more welcoming than most inns, they arrived at the castle. Set high upon a mound, it was an imposing edifice of square stone towers with thick walls enclosing the inner bailey. One of the early fortresses built soon after the conquest, it had few of the refinements of Sir Ralph's home and Alayne shivered at the sight. Castle Hardacre seemed a forbidding place and she was somehow uneasy as the party rode over the drawbridge and into the roughly cobbled courtyard.

'This is the home of Berenice's brother, Baron Foulton of Hardacre,' Sir Ralph told Alayne as he came himself to help her dismount, his hands lingering momentarily about her slender waist. Looking down into his face, Alayne felt that rising heat within her, but she was becoming accustomed to it now and fought her weakness. 'I have not seen William since his father died.'

He was frowning and Alayne sensed that he would have preferred to attend the King at some other place. However, the King often moved from castle to castle; it was difficult to maintain the court at one place for long and any noble could be called upon to offer his king hospitality.

'You are welcome, brother,' a voice said behind them and Alayne turned to see a tall, thin man. He was, she thought, a few years younger than Sir Ralph, pale and pinched of feature, his hair cut short about his head in the style of the monks, but without the tonsure.

'William,' Ralph clasped him by the shoulders and embraced him. 'You have become a man since we last met. I have not seen you since your father's funeral.'

'It has been too long, brother,' William Foulton said, his hard gaze seeming at odds with the smile on his lips. 'You have brought ladies to brighten our Christmastide.'

His pale blue eyes passed over Marguerite and came to rest on Alayne. She felt an odd chill at the nape of her neck, though she could not tell the reason for her discomfort. Baron Foulton was smiling, holding out his hands to her in welcome, but when she gave him her own she found his clasp moist and clammy. Her immediate reaction was a feeling of revulsion that made her want to wipe herself clean. She did nothing of the kind, of course, forcing a smile as she returned his greeting and thanked him for the hospitality he offered.

'You will find my home poor comfort after Sir Ralph's,' he told her. 'It is a fortress I hold for the King and has none of the luxury you will find at Banewulf.'

'You wrong yourself,' Ralph said frowning slightly. 'I found the accommodation well enough when I last stayed here.'

'When you wed my poor sister,' William Foulton said and sighed. 'God rest and keep her. She was a sweet child and I know you loved her—as I did.'

There was something about his manner at that moment

that set Alayne's nerves tingling. He was hiding something, she was certain of it—but what?

Sir Ralph's expression was grave as he replied, 'Berenice spoke of you often. Your letters were her greatest treasure, especially when she was unwell.'

There was a gleam deep within Foulton's pale eyes then that made Alayne wonder. Baron Foulton had welcomed his brother-in-law with every sign of warmth and pleasure, but she had the oddest feeling that it was false. If her senses did not lie, the baron hated Sir Ralph. Yet surely she must be mistaken?

Both men were smiling and talking in the friendliest of terms as they led the way into the great hall of the keep. Alayne felt the cold strike deep into her bones as she entered it, for there were few hangings to cover the roughly hewn walls and the chill penetrated the ancient stone. She could see that in places the damp stood upon the walls, and though a huge fire blazed in the hearth it scarcely took the chill from the air even when you stood close to the flames. She was glad of her fur-lined mantle and she saw that Marguerite was also shivering.

The ladies had been accommodated in the west tower, and a serving wench took them almost at once to their chamber. Because the coming of the court had strained the available space to the limit, they discovered that they were obliged to share with another lady. She welcomed them with a smile and told them her name was Ellen.

'I am cousin to Baron Foulton's mother,' she said. 'I came to nurse her in her last illness and have stayed on since she died. God rest her soul, poor lady. William is my betrothed husband and we are to be wed in the spring.'

Alayne congratulated her on her coming wedding, though she was not sure what kind of a life it would be for a young woman in this bleak place. The chamber they were to share was sparsely furnished with three truckle beds that could be pushed away during the day to allow for more space in the tiny room. There was but one coffer, one stool and a trestle and board. Alayne thought it one of the poorest chambers she had seen and was glad of her own things waiting to be brought up.

'I have given up my own chamber for his Majesty's companions,' Ellen told them as if she thought some explanation necessary. 'And my poor companion who usually sleeps here has but an alcove for her mattress. We are stretched to the limit by this visit. William can hardly bear the expense.'

'It must be very costly to house the court even for a short time,' Alayne agreed, thinking of the huge quantities of food that would be required by so many guests and their servants. 'But of course it is a high honour.'

'Oh, yes,' Ellen agreed, her pale face lighting with a smile of pride. 'William is conscious of the honour the King bestows on him, even though he fears he may be ruined. But you are tired and hungry. I shall have the servants bring food and wine.'

Marguerite pulled a face as the other girl went out. 'Mistress Ellen is no beauty, is she? I suppose she has no better prospects, but I should not care to be chatelaine of such a place. It is damp and cold and cheerless.'

'Hush,' Alayne said and frowned at her. 'She is not ill favoured, though perhaps a little plain. Not every woman is beautiful, Marguerite. Yet I must admit that I should not care to live here.' The castle was too like that which belonged to her late husband and brought back unpleasant memories.

'Nor to be married to William Foulton,' said Marguerite with a wry face. 'There was something unpleasant about our host—did you not think him a little strange? I dislike the way he looks at one.'

'He was a little odd,' Alayne agreed. 'I am not sure I would entirely trust him. But we are here until after Christ's Mass. We must make the best of things as we find them.'

Marguerite agreed, but she continued to grumble about their accommodation, and the wine brought with their food did not fare better with her for she thought it sour and thin.

Ellen had not returned with the servants. Alayne wondered if the other woman had left them to settle in out of kindness or whether she might have heard them discussing her and been offended.

However, when they met later that evening at the banquet given in the King's honour, she was perfectly civil, though perhaps a little cooler than she had been at first. Alayne thought it sad if they had carelessly offended her and went out of her way to be pleasant.

Both she and Marguerite were presented to the King, a sturdy man with strong features, who greeted them kindly. He seemed to take more interest in Alayne than Marguerite, and when he told her that he hoped to see more of her and Sir Ralph at court in future, she knew that he had been told of the marriage proposal. Indeed, he seemed to believe that it was already arranged. Perhaps that was not surprising, for it would be difficult to resist the Queen's suggestion.

Alayne felt a moment of panic. In her heart she had always known that the marriage was inevitable once Queen Eleanor had set her seal to it. Yet still she gave the King no answer other than a smile. Sir Ralph had told her that she would not be forced in any way and she clung to her belief that he was an honourable man.

That first evening at Hardacre Castle was very like those she had been accustomed to at Poitiers. A meal consisting of several courses of rich meats, fish from the carp pond, pigeons in wine, a roast boar and a swan swimming in a lake of succulent sauces was followed by festive entertainment. There was dancing, minstrels singing and a troupe of jugglers to make them laugh and marvel at their skills. In honour of Christ's birthday a religious play was performed by a band of mummers, reflecting the holiness of that special day.

On the eve of Christ's Mass boughs of greenery were brought in to deck the hall. With it came the smell of the forest, sharp and tangy, the scent mingling with the fresh sweet herbs caught underfoot and the smoky flame of the torches, which flamed from iron brackets overhead. Outside, the snow lay crisp and white after a fresh fall and the air was so cold that it seemed to freeze one's breath.

Alayne ate sparingly of the rich food brought to table that evening. She was seated at the far left of the high table, some distance from the King and with Baron Foulton at her right hand.

'You do not eat heartily, Lady Alayne?' her host questioned, his brows rising. 'Does the food not please you?'

'It is very rich, sir. I do not care to eat too much of this spicy sauce. I find it lays heavy on my stomach at night. I shall take a little of the quince tart, for that is light and sweet.'

He looked at her approvingly. 'You are a woman of moderate habits. I believe Sir Ralph will be fortunate in his marriage.'

'It is not yet confirmed, sir,' Alayne replied with a little flush.

'But understood, surely?' There was a gleam in his eyes that made Alayne wonder what was in his mind. 'His Majesty spoke of it to me. I do not think I misunderstood him.'

'I have not yet given my answer,' Alayne said, puzzled by something in his manner. It was as if he was trying to make her say something—but what? 'The Queen has urged me to accept Sir Ralph as my husband. However, we have not yet come to any agreement.'

'Perhaps you should think carefully, Lady Alayne. My brother-in-law is a difficult man to understand,' the baron said, and she was chilled by the look in his eyes. Now she was certain that he held malicious intent against Sir Ralph. 'Some would think him of a sullen disposition, yet my sister told me that he was kind to her. At least at the beginning he was kind. I believe she became very unhappy towards the last days of her life.'

Alayne felt a tingling at the base of her spine. What was he implying? Was he trying to tell her not to trust Sir Ralph?

'I understood the Lady Berenice was ill?' Alayne's eyes widened as she looked at him and saw clearly the hatred he bore his late sister's husband. He blamed Sir Ralph for her death! 'You cannot think her unhappiness was caused by some fault of her husband? Everyone says that he was devoted to her.'

'And she to him.' William Foulton's lashes veiled his thoughts from her as he looked down at his wine cup, toying with the stem. She waited for him to continue, but he had lapsed into a brooding silence.

Alayne was not sure what to think. She had sensed the falseness of the baron's welcome at the start, but now she believed she had seen a deeper hatred than she had imagined. Why should William Foulton hate his brother-in-law? She could find no reason, unless he blamed Sir Ralph for Berenice's death.

But surely that could not be true? Sir Ralph had been deeply affected by his wife's death; she had witnessed his grief herself, which was remarkable after so many years. Perhaps it was just the baron's nature to be resentful. He had the look of a mean-spirited man and Alayne found herself pitying the woman who was to be his wife.

It was some time later, when the feasting was over, that Alayne was told his Majesty wished to speak to her. She followed the servant who had come to summon her to where the King sat, at that moment in conversation with one of his nobles. However, it was no more than a few seconds before he waved the man away and beckoned to Alayne.

'Come forward, lady.'

Alayne made her curtsy and moved closer, waiting nervously for what he had to say.

'It is my habit to grant as many requests as possible from my loyal followers at this time,' the King told her with a smile. 'I have received a letter from your father. He requests that I return you to him so that you may be married to a man of his choice. Is this your wish also?'

Alayne had turned pale. The room seemed to spin around her and for a moment she was afraid that she might faint. She would never let them marry her to de Bracey! She would rather die.

'No, sire,' she said, taking hold of her senses and forcing herself to fight off the waves of nausea that had threatened to overwhelm her. 'I beg that you will refuse my father's request. He would marry me to a man I cannot like or respect.'

'That is what I have been told—a man, moreover, who was banished from court for breaking the laws of chivalry.' King Henry's gaze narrowed, his eyes thoughtful as they rested on her lovely face. She was a proud beauty, a prize for any man and worthy to be the bride of the knight he wished to reward for services done. 'Is it then your wish that you should be given in marriage to Sir Ralph de Banewulf?'

Alayne took a deep breath. She knew that she must speak now and what her answer must be. She had no choice but to marry—that was plain to her. It was certain her father would never rest while he saw advantage to be gained from her. And since she must wed, there was but one man she could bear to accept as her husband: the man who had shown her so much kindness these past weeks.

There was no help for it. The choice was made and in her heart she knew it for the best and accepted her fate. 'If Sir Ralph wishes me to be his wife, I should be honoured to wed him, sire.'

The King smiled in satisfaction. Sir Ralph had asked no boon for himself, but Queen Eleanor's letter concerning the matter had convinced Henry that it was the best for all concerned. The wench clearly needed a husband to keep her safe from her greedy father and his fellow conspirators, and Sir Ralph was attracted to her. It was plain in the way he watched her, his gaze following her as she moved about the room. He had given no other sign of wanting this marriage. Indeed, he had asked Henry not to interfere—but left to himself he would sink back into the seclusion he had sought since the death of Lady Berenice and that would not suit Henry's plans. He knew that there was considerable unrest in the country; it simmered beneath the surface, waiting to burst out, much of it the fault of that wretch he had risen to high honour who now sought to defy him. Thomas à Becket was a thorn in Henry's side and he needed all the nobles loyal to him at hand in case of trouble.

'That is well, lady,' he said. 'I shall inform Sir Ralph that the marriage will go ahead on the day following Christ's Mass. It shall be our pleasure to arrange it.' He waved a hand at her. 'Go and enjoy yourself. I see that there is to be no end to the petitioners this evening.'

Alayne glanced round and saw that several nobles were loitering nearby as if waiting for their chance to ask a boon of their sovereign lord on this most holy night.

Alayne walked away, her heart racing as she saw Sir Ralph coming towards her. She stood waiting for him to reach her, and saw that he was smiling in the way that caused her such confusion. But the die was cast now and she knew there was no escaping her fate. In two days she would become Sir Ralph's wife and then he would take her home to Banewulf. He had promised to accept a marriage in name only, but could she trust him to keep his word once she belonged to him?

'Alayne,' Sir Ralph said, and his expression made her suddenly breathless. 'I was looking for you. I wanted to give you a gift for the morrow.'

'I have embroidered something for you, my lord,' she said a little shyly, 'to thank you for all the kindness you have shown me—but it is in my chamber. I meant to give it to you tomorrow.' She had made him a belt of fine leather, embroidering it with his own emblems of the wolf and the bear in gold thread and beads.

'I shall be happy to receive it then,' Ralph said. 'But I wanted to give you this tonight—before we go to mass.'

He gave her a teasing look that sent her pulses wild, drawing her into the shadows of the huge stone pillars that supported the vaulting roof. Then he reached into the pouch at his belt and took out a small package wrapped in silk, handing it to her. 'This is a token of my faith, Alayne. I offer it to you and ask you formally to be my wife.'

Alayne's hand trembled as she accepted it, believing that he must have known of the King's intention that evening. A voice protested in her head that this was not what he had promised, but she thrust it away. There was no choice. She had given the King her word and there was no going back. As she unwrapped the package she saw that it was a heavy cross of gold set with cabochon rubies and pearls, a beautiful thing that she could wear upon a ribbon at her throat.

'Why, it is lovely,' she said, surprised and pleased by his choice. 'I shall always treasure it, sir.' Her hand reached out to him and he took it, holding it for a moment before turning it to drop a kiss upon the palm. A shiver ran through her but it was of pleasure, not revulsion, and she looked up at him, her mouth parting in wonder. He hesitated, then reached out to draw her nearer. For a moment he gazed down into her eyes and then he bent his head, brushing her lips with a soft kiss that made her pulses pound wildly. He stroked her cheek with his fingertips for a brief moment, then let her go. His touch had sent her senses spinning, her eyes wide with wonder as she gazed up at him. Why did her heart beat so frantically—and what was this strange need that possessed her? Her body seemed to be melting in the fire he had somehow raised in her.

'Well, Alayne—will you have me as your husband?'

'Yes,' she breathed, all doubt banished for the time being. 'Willingly…besides, the King commands it.'

'The King commands?' Ralph frowned, clearly startled. 'What is this? I know nothing of this, Alayne.'

She saw the coldness come into his eyes and caught her breath, wishing her words unspoken. For a moment she had glimpsed something in him that had made her feel that marriage to this man might hold happiness beyond her dreams, but now he seemed to be angry, to have withdrawn from her once more.

'His Majesty told me that my father wanted me returned to him so that he might arrange a marriage for me. When I begged him not to send me back, he asked if I would wed you instead…'

'And you agreed, of course,' Ralph said, a nerve flicking in his throat. 'What else could you do? The choice was not of your own making, but forced on you by this interference. Forgive me, Alayne. This was not of my asking, nor my intention.'

'Do not be angry,' she said and touched his arm tentatively. 'I had already begun to think that it was the only way—the best way for me to live. I did not want to go back to the empty life at Poitiers and I was happy at your home. I think I might like to live there forever.'

'Is that the truth?' he asked, his eyes seeming to bore into her as if they would bare her soul to him. She glimpsed some deep-felt emotion, though it was swiftly hidden, controlled. 'You had made up your mind to accept my offer before Henry spoke to you?'

'Yes…' Alayne's voice held a note of uncertainty that was not lost on him. He frowned down at her, but then his expression softened. 'Yes, I had decided what my answer would be when you asked me.'

'Then we shall take the opportunity to be wed before

we leave here, Alayne. I wish to return home as soon as possible after tomorrow—and it is best that we are wed before we leave.'

'Yes. It was his Majesty's wish that we should be married here.'

'Then we shall oblige him,' Ralph said and his mouth thinned to a hard line. 'However, my word holds true, Alayne. That kiss I gave you a moment ago changes nothing. Our marriage is in name only. My promise was that you should be forced to nothing you disliked, and though I would not have had it so, in part that has not held true. However, the rest remains.' He banished his frowns and held out his hand to her. 'I believe that the court is going to chapel now. It is time for the mass. Shall you allow me to escort you there?'

'Why, yes, my lord,' Alayne said. 'It would be most fitting.'

Her hand trembled as she held his arm. So they would be married, this perfect knight and she, and she would be his wife in every way except the one that terrified her—but for a moment as he'd kissed her so softly she had glimpsed something far sweeter: happiness beyond her imagining, a life so blessed that she thought it but a dream.

Ralph cursed as he went to his own chamber later that night. Damn Henry for his well-meaning interference! He had hoped that he was winning Alayne's confidence, that she would take him for his own sake because she wanted to be his wife—wanted all that marriage entailed.

He had made her a promise that he would not enter her bed by force and he meant to keep it, though he knew that he had set himself a hard task. She was so lovely, so appealing, and her smiles seemed to invite his kisses, her lips soft and tempting, and the slumbering passion in her eyes seeming to promise so much.

Alayne was unaware of her power to rouse men to a fierce desire to bed her. In Poitiers he had thought she could not be completely innocent of her own enchanting appeal, but in these past weeks he had come to know her. Her beauty went deeper than what the eye beheld, and her nature was as sweet and loving as a man might hope for in his wife—but she had been badly hurt. He knew that it would take great patience to overcome her fear of the marriage bed.

'God help me,' he muttered hoarsely. 'Let me die before I harm her.'

He had given his word and he must learn patience. Her lips were tempting, but only if she came to him, willing and eager to be kissed, as she had seemed to earlier, could they hope to find true happiness.

He had thought that she had truly come to trust and perhaps to care for him, but now he knew that she had been forced to take him as her husband and he could not be sure. Marriage to him must seem better than the life that awaited her as the wife of de Bracey.

Her willingness to accept this marriage did not mean that she loved him, Ralph de Banewulf.

Chapter Seven

'You look lovely,' Marguerite said as she helped her to dress in the gown she had chosen for her wedding. It was a simple white silk tunic covered by a blue surcote trimmed with silver and a dark blue mantle lined with creamy fur, which Sir Ralph had sent as a gift that morning. It was just one of many gifts that he had given her over the festivities, but one of the most welcome in this cold place. 'I am sure that you have made the right choice, Alayne. Sir Ralph is a good and gentle man.'

'He is a man of ideals,' Alayne agreed, a little smile on her lips. 'I like and respect him, Marguerite. If I must marry, he is the man I would have as my husband.'

'My father is disappointed for—he wanted the match for me,' Marguerite told her. 'But perhaps now he will be more inclined to listen—if Baron de Froissart should ask for me when we next see him.' There was a wistful note in her voice, dreaming in her eyes.

'I hope that he will,' Alayne said and kissed her warmly. 'I would see you happy, Marguerite, and I know that you love him. He must come to realise your value.'

'Unfortunately, I am not sure that he feels anything for me,' Marguerite said, her mouth drooping a little. 'But once he knows that you are married, he may take me as a substitute.'

'Oh, Marguerite,' Alayne said, 'pray do not hurt yourself in this manner. I am sure the baron cares for you in his own way. You said that he paid you attention once and you refused him. It may be because of that that he turned to me. If he sees that you have changed towards him, he may realise that he has always loved you.'

'Perhaps.' Marguerite's smile was wry. 'I would accept him even if he did not truly love me, Alayne. For me there is no pride where love is concerned—' She broke off as someone knocked at the door. Opening it, she found a young page standing there and asked what he wanted.

'I have a letter for Lady Alayne,' he said.

'Give it to me.'

'I was told to give it to no one but her.'

Alayne came to the door and took the letter from him. She thanked him and he blushed, then turned and ran down the stone steps that led away from the tower.

'It must be from Sir Ralph,' Marguerite said, and then, as she saw Alayne's face turn pale, 'What is it? He has not cancelled the wedding?'

'It is not from him,' Alayne said, her hand trembling. 'It is not signed.'

She held it out and Marguerite took it from her, reading the brief and ill-penned message swiftly and with growing dismay.

'This is wicked! To send such a message on your wedding day! How could anyone be so cruel?'

Alayne shook her head. She was beginning to recover from the shock of the hateful words that had accused Sir Ralph of being a murderer—of having killed his wife!—but the horror of it lingered like a cloud in her mind.

'Whoever wrote that must hate Sir Ralph,' she whispered, feeling the sickness rise in her throat. 'It is the work of a warped mind, do you not think so?'

'It is a terrible lie,' Marguerite said angrily. 'You must give it to Sir Ralph and let him deal with it, Alayne. This kind of accusation cannot remain unchallenged.'

'Yes, he shall know of it,' Alayne said and took the letter back from her, folding it and placing it in her coffer where she kept other papers she wished to retain. 'But not today. It would cast an atmosphere and I would have today a happy occasion.'

'Yes, you are right,' Marguerite agreed. 'You are sensible not to let it disturb you, Alayne. You know that what is written there is a wicked lie and that it was meant to hurt you. You should ignore it and show the world that you are happy to wed Sir Ralph—in this way you will show your indifference for the person who wrote this.'

Alayne agreed, lifting her head proudly. She would not let this attempt to distress her spoil her wedding. Such a scurrilous lie was not worth her attention. Marguerite was right; she must give the letter to Sir Ralph, for she believed she knew who had sent it. Sir Ralph must certainly be made aware of this wicked attempt to poison her mind against him, but she would tell him in a few days, when they were settled at Banewulf.

She was smiling as she went down the tower steps to the company awaiting her in the huge hall below. The wedding ceremony was to be performed by the King's own chaplain, and Henry had promised to give her to her husband himself.

Henry had been generous to them, giving Alayne a heavy gold chain set with emeralds, which were said to ward off the evil eye and the falling sickness; and for Sir Ralph there was a position in the King's household should he care to accept it with a pension of some one hundred gold marcs a year.

Alayne was trembling as she looked at the assembled faces. The King and his nobles richly dressed in fur-lined mantles and long tunics of good wool cloth, a scattering of ladies, far outnumbered by the men, and to the rear of the company one face that looked at her with what she could only think was spite. Had he expected her to draw back from the marriage because of his letter?

Alayne lifted her head higher and turned to greet Sir Ralph with a smile as he held his hand out to her. She took it and moved to her place at his side.

Listening to the priest intoning the solemn litany that committed her to this man, Alayne felt oddly detached, as if it were happening to someone else. She had not yet quite conquered her fear and her hand trembled a little as Sir Ralph slid the heavy gold ring on her finger, but when she looked up into his face and saw the expression in his eyes she was comforted.

This man was very different from the brutish husband who had taught her to fear him, and she felt a sense of peace steal over her, believing that now at last she was safe. This knight would protect her from those who had sought to use her for their own ends, and perhaps one day he would learn to love her.

The feasting would go on long after they had left. Sir Ralph had given the excuse that the weather was changing and he did not want to be trapped at Hardacre when the heavy snows came. Alayne believed he was anxious to leave the castle, perhaps as much for her sake as his own. She had been brought to the blush by the robust jesting of the nobles, and had been glad to be spared the embarrassment of the bedding ceremony, though, as she had been married before, she would not have been required to show blood on her sheets in the morning.

They travelled until dusk began to fall and then took shelter at an abbey for the night. As the guesthouses for men and women were strictly divided there was no possibility of their sharing a bed that night, and Alayne was happy enough to sleep with her serving women for companions, though they bemoaned her misfortune.

'We should have gone to an inn,' Bethel said to her. Bethel was dark and pretty, a plump comely girl who laughed a lot and lingered with the serving men when she could. 'Or stayed at the castle for a few nights longer, my lady. 'Tis a shame that you cannot be with your husband this night.'

'I am content to wait until we reach Banewulf,' Alayne replied. 'Sir Ralph is impatient to be home and it will be much more comfortable for us all there.'

'Indeed, you speak truly,' Louise said and smiled at her. Louise was tall and thin, quieter than Bethel and more thoughtful. 'Banewulf is much warmer than that draughty castle. 'Tis no wonder they all look such poor mewling creatures.'

'You have a wicked tongue and should curb it,' Alayne reproved, but with a smile that took the sting from her words. 'But I must admit that I did not much enjoy my stay there.'

Baron Foulton had given her a pewter wine cup as his wedding gift. She had wanted to refuse it, but had known that she must not. However, her thanks had been stiffly given and she saw something in his eyes that told her he was her enemy. He had warned her, but she had disregarded his warning and wed despite him. He would not forgive her lightly.

'I wish you good health,' he said. 'Too many gentle ladies die in childbirth. I hope that will not be your fate, Lady de Banewulf.'

How false he was! She believed that he meant the opposite of what he said. He wanted her to suffer the same fate as his poor sister—out of spite or revenge against the man he hated.

'I thank you for your good wishes,' Alayne replied. 'And accept them in all sincerity, as they are given.'

His sparse lashes flicked down to cover his eyes and she knew her message had gone home. He had done his best to make her withdraw from the marriage, and now he hated her—as he hated Sir Ralph. She must warn her husband of his falseness, but it could wait until they were at Banewulf.

On their journey to the castle Sir Ralph had spent much of his time talking with his men, leaving Alayne to the company of Marguerite and her serving women. However, he was attentive and courteous as they rode home, bringing his horse to a gentle walk beside hers and talking to her about the scenery and the various towns or villages they passed.

'We shall go to London in the late spring,' he told her. 'You will have the opportunity to visit the silk merchants and order new gowns then, my lady. In the meantime, if there is anything you require, you may give me your order and I shall have whatever you need sent to Banewulf.'

'I brought only some of my possessions to England with me,' Alayne said. 'But I would fain have my dear Perlita brought to me when it is possible, for though I

know she will be cared for in my absence, she will miss
me. We could perhaps send for the remainder of my possessions in the spring, when the tides and roads are easier,
my lord.'

'You will not want to return to Poitiers yourself?' he
asked.

'No, I have no wish to return to the court. And though
my late husband's lands belong to me by right, I have
never tried to claim them.'

'I shall do that for you,' Ralph said. 'If you have no
wish to visit them, it might be better to dispose of everything for a sum of gold, which will then be yours to
purchase a manor here if you so wish.'

His offer was generous for she knew that in law he
had the right to claim anything that was hers, but it
seemed that he did not intend to take that right.

'You are my husband,' she replied. 'You must do
whatever pleases you. I trust you, my lord, and when
we—' She had been about to speak of their return to
Banewulf, but the words died on her lips as movement
at the edge of the forest caught her eye. Someone was
there watching them—an archer, his bowstring drawn
tight! 'My lord, beware!' Even as she cried out the warning an arrow came winging towards them, narrowly missing them both. Had she not halted her horse and caused
Sir Ralph to turn sharply on his, it must have found its
mark.

'After him!' Sir Ralph's shouted order was hardly necessary, for his men had seen the incident and four of them
were already riding in pursuit of the assailant. 'Bring him
back alive if you can.' He looked at Alayne's pale face
and cursed. 'Damn the rogue! He shall be hanged if my
men capture him.'

'He might have killed you...' Alayne felt shaken.

'Why did he fire at you like that? I saw only one, but there may have been more. What was the purpose of this attack?'

'A robber hoping to take us by surprise,' Ralph said. 'There are many such in the forests I dare say. They feed on the King's venison and ambush the unwary. I do not imagine there was more than one, but, never fear, my men will find him.'

'I am not sure he meant to rob us,' Alayne said, looking at him anxiously. She felt that they had come close to death for the arrow might have hit either of them, though she had thought it meant for him. Speaking her thoughts aloud, she said, 'How could one man hope to rob such a well-armed party as ours? I think his purpose was to kill you.'

'No, no, you worry for nothing,' Ralph assured her, for she was clearly distressed by the incident, her lovely face pale and strained. 'Bands of robbers and beggars roam these forests and oftimes attack the unwary traveller. We were riding a little behind the others and mayhap he thought to overpower us and steal what we have before it was noticed by my men.'

Alayne thought it unlikely that any lone robber would dare to take the chance against so many. No, the assailant had taken the risk of firing one arrow and then made off into the woods, his purpose clearly murder.

'I think he was sent here to kill you,' she said again and the coldness spread through her as she remembered something else. 'I believe you have an enemy. There is a letter in my coffer that you should see, my lord. A page brought it to me on my wedding day. It accused you of a wicked crime and was written by someone who hates you. The intention was to prevent our marriage, but refused to believe such lies—and so out of his frustration he has resorted to this treachery.'

Ralph's gaze was serious as it dwelt on her lovely face. 'I thank you for your trust in me, Alayne. Why did you not tell me of this letter before?'

'I thought it did not matter and that I would show you when we were at home at Banewulf. I did not wish to spoil the happiness of our wedding day and feared it would cast a shadow.'

Ralph nodded, his steady gaze never leaving her face. She looked so pale and frightened and he was furious that he had been taken by surprise by whoever had fired on them—that *she* had been exposed to danger.

'You believe that you know who sent the letter, do you not?'

'I think it was Baron Foulton,' she admitted. 'He spoke ill of you on the eve of Christ's Mass. Besides, I thought him false from the start despite his smiles and apparent friendliness—and Marguerite was of the same opinion.'

'As I was myself,' Ralph said and sighed, that bleak expression on his face once more. 'I fear that William blames me for his sister's death.'

'But it was not your fault,' Alayne said. 'Many women die of fevers after being brought to bed of a child. No one could truly blame you for that.'

'No, perhaps not,' Ralph said and there was something about him then, a drawn, haunted expression, as if he wrestled with some strong emotion. 'But Berenice was unhappy, and I fear that was my fault.'

'Will you tell me why?'

Sir Ralph frowned and then gave a slight shake of his head. 'Perhaps one day,' he said. 'When we know each other a little better. For the moment I think we should make haste to find a lodging before night falls. If there are outlaws and brigands about, I do not want to be drawn into a trap.'

Sir Ralph's men had gathered about them protectively, and the opportunity for further conversation was lost. They rode swiftly to make sure of reaching the monastery before darkness fell.

It was almost two hours later that Alayne was settled in the sparsely furnished cell that served as her bedchamber for the night. Because of the danger and Sir Ralph's haste she had not had the chance to reflect on her husband's revelations about his first wife until now, but as she sat on the stool provided and allowed her servants to prepare her for bed, she was thoughtful.

She lay wakeful in her bed long after the serving wenches were snoring on their cots, her mind going over and over the events of the day.

Why should anyone want to kill Sir Ralph and why should Lady Berenice have been unhappy? She had a loving, generous husband and she was expecting his child—what had made her so downcast? Was it just that she had carried her child badly and felt ill or was there some other reason?

It seemed that Sir Ralph blamed himself for Berenice's unhappiness. Alayne worried at the problem as a dog will at a bone. Why should Sir Ralph blame himself for his wife's unhappiness? Despite herself, the doubts crept in. Surely there was no truth in the malicious letter she had received on her wedding morning? Could Berenice's husband have done something to make her fear him?

No, no, she told herself, quashing the insidious suspicion immediately. She would not let herself think such evil thoughts, for if she did then the writer of the letter had won.

* * *

Alayne felt a sense of peace when she saw the manor of Banewulf ahead of them. They had been several days upon the road, despite making all speed, and the weather had become colder. Overnight there had been a heavy fall of snow and the last few leagues had been treacherous as the horses struggled to keep their footing in the deep drifts. Now and then the mournful cry of a hungry wolf could be heard in the forest, sending shivers down Alayne's spine.

Ralph glanced at her as they cantered the last few strides into the courtyard. He gazed up into her face as he came to lift her down, setting her gently on her feet, his hands lingering momentarily about her slender waist. She looked tired and strained, less content than she had before the attack on them.

'It has been a difficult journey,' he said, restraining the anger he felt inside. That arrow might as easily have struck her as him! 'We shall venture no more abroad until it is spring, my lady. You must go at once to your chamber and rest.'

'I am a little weary,' she admitted, 'and cold, but I shall be perfectly well once I have warmed myself before the fire.' She smiled up at him, for despite her weariness his concern had lifted her.

'You are not used to this bitter weather after the milder climes of France. We must take care that you do not suffer a chill.'

'I am not prone to chills,' she told him confidently, 'but I thank you for your care of me.' No one had ever cared for her comfort like this, except perhaps long ago her mother.

'I sent word of our coming and your chamber should be ready for you, Alayne—but I would like us to dine together this evening, privately. The feasting to celebrate our return will wait until another night.'

'That would be pleasant, my lord,' Alayne said and hesitated for a moment. 'Shall we dine in my chamber?'

'It is scarce large enough for such a purpose,' Ralph said with a slight frown. 'You have the chamber that belonged to my mother. There is a room between that and the one I have used since…Berenice's death. I moved my things when she was ill and have not used the newer wing from that time.'

So she was not to be given Berenice's chamber. She had wondered if her things would have been moved, but it seemed it was not so. A part of her was glad, for she had found the chamber gloomy and the atmosphere there was depressing, as if the sadness of its previous owner lingered on, but she thought his confession more proof that he could not bear to be reminded of his former wife. But what did he mean about a chamber between her room and his?

'A room between?' Alayne was puzzled. 'I have seen no door.'

'It is a secret entrance by means of a sliding panel,' Ralph said. 'You will find it behind a certain hanging— but I shall show you the trick. It is quite easy once you know, but fear not, it may only be opened from your side. No one could come to you unawares while you slept.'

Alayne flushed, for it had crossed her mind that he might choose to enter her room in that way. After all, he was her husband now. 'Were these rooms used by your parents?'

'They are the best chambers,' Ralph confirmed. 'My father had them built for his own use when he extended from the old castle. When I married I took apartments in the opposite wing, but have been using the two rooms beyond yours as my own for some years now. They are reached by a separate stair, but for convenience sake my mother often left the panel open so that my father could go to her when he chose without using the stairs.'

'I see...' Alayne swallowed hard. For a moment he seemed to be suggesting that she might do the same. She was uncertain all at once, her heart beating faster. What did he expect of her? He had sworn that their marriage would be as she desired it, and she knew that he was deeply affected by his wife's death. The fact that he no longer slept in the room next to the one that had been Berenice's was proof enough of that, though Alayne was uncertain of his reasons. Was it for love of Berenice that he mourned—or was there something more behind his remorse? 'Perhaps one day...'

'Only if you choose,' Ralph assured her, a little frown creasing his brow. 'I hope that we shall be friends and companions, Alayne, and it would be pleasant to come to you that way sometimes—but that is for you to decide.'

Alayne's heart slowed to an easier beat. How could she doubt him when he showed her such consideration, such kindness? No other man would have waited even this long to claim his rights as her husband. To let the wicked lie that had been planted in her mind on her wedding day take root would be foolish.

'I too hope that we shall come to be the dearest of friends,' she told him. As she gazed up at him her senses seemed to swim and she was aware of a strange longing that was turning her limbs to molten honey. He was such a powerful man and she was drawn to him, held by something in his eyes that seemed to promise so much. Her lips parted slightly, her breathing difficult as her heart pounded against her ribcage like an imprisoned bird. It was a feeling so sweet and strange that she felt close to swooning and she swayed towards him, wanting him to hold her as he had once or twice before, to feel his lips on hers. Yet there was still a part of her that held back, a fear of being abused cruelly that made her resist the need deep inside her. She drew away from him. 'With your permission I shall go to my chamber, my lord.'

'You have no need to ask my permission for whatever you choose to do,' Ralph told her. 'You are mistress of my home, Alayne, and may do whatever you choose. It is some years since it was refurbished. You must make changes if you wish, order new chattels and commission hangings for your chamber.'

'None could be as beautiful and fine as those your mother made herself,' Alayne replied. 'I shall endeavour to be as excellent a needlewoman as she was and hope to add to the treasures of your home in time. I would like silks and threads to embroider the comforts that will bring us even more ease, my lord—but I do not wish to make sweeping changes. I am well content with Banewulf as it is.'

'It makes me happy that you are content in my home,' Ralph said and he reached out, letting his fingers trail over her face and throat for a brief moment before withdrawing them. 'I pray that it will always be so.'

'I cannot think that it would ever be otherwise,' Alayne said. 'I feel as if I have at last come home, my lord. Even as a child I was never treated as well as I have been here.'

Ralph inclined his head but said nothing, turning to watch her as she walked away from him. Alayne walked so gracefully, yet with pride. He knew that she feared the intimacy her husband had made hateful to her, but there was courage in her. She had had the presence of mind to warn him of that arrow, which he knew well had been meant to kill him. It was clear that he had made an enemy, and he was saddened by the thought that it might be Berenice's brother.

William had always been a strange lad. He had wept at his sister's wedding, and Berenice had told Ralph that he had begged her not to marry.

'I believe William would keep me always with him if he could,' she had confided in the early days of their courtship. 'He loves me so dearly.'

It had crossed Ralph's mind at one point that perhaps William's love for his sister had been rather too tender, perhaps more the feelings of a man for his lover than a brother for his sister, but he had quashed the thought as unworthy. Berenice was young and innocent when he wed her, and he knew that nothing unlawful had taken place between the brother and sister—yet he had not been able to rid himself of the idea that William's love for her was unhealthy. Their first foolish quarrel had been over William.

But it was time to put the past behind him, Ralph decided as Alayne disappeared from his view. He did not think himself in danger from William, even if the ambush had been of his making, and he would not concern himself with such matters. Whatever the faults of the past, he was wed to a young and lovely woman and he must do his best to make her happy if he could.

Alayne thought of the letter after she had taken off her mantle and wimple, sitting before the fire to brush her hair as Bethel and Louise began to unpack her things. She thought that she would show it to Ralph that night,

so that he could see the handwriting and perhaps he
would know if his late wife's brother had written it.

'Bring me my small coffer,' she told Louise when
asked if there was anything more she required. 'The one
I keep my letters in, please.'

Louise brought it to her and Alayne opened the heavy
lid, looking for the letter, which she had left on the top
of the small pile inside. It was not there. She looked
again, removing all the others in an effort to find the one
she sought, but to no avail. The letter had gone.

'Is something wrong, my lady?' Louise asked.

'There was a letter on the top,' Alayne said with a
frown. 'I cannot find it. I wanted to show it to my lord.'

'Are you sure you put it in this coffer? You could not
have placed it with your jewels for safekeeping?'

'I am sure I put it here, but bring the other one and I
shall look to make sure.' A few moments were enough
to show that there were no letters in the jewel coffer,
which was always locked. Nor had she placed it within
the secret drawer of which only she knew the secret. 'No,
it was in here, right at the top of the pile. I put it there
on the morning of my wedding.'

'On your wedding day?' Bethel said, coming to join
them. 'When I returned to the chamber you were sharing
with the others after watching you wed to Sir Ralph, I
found this coffer opened. I closed it when I began our
packing, but I did not know that something was missing.
Could someone have taken it, my lady?'

'Yes, I think that must be the case,' Alayne said and
a cold shiver ran down her spine. 'It was something I
wanted to show Sir Ralph—but it does not matter.' She
saw the anxious faces of her serving women and shook
her head. 'No, no, I do not suspect either of you. I think
I know who may have taken it.'

'I passed Baron Foulton on the stair,' Bethel said. 'Could it have been him, my lady?'

'I think we shall continue to wonder,' Alayne said, not wanting to confirm her suspicions to her women. 'Leave me now, I would spend a little time alone.'

She frowned over the disappearance of the letter after they had gone. It was not important and yet she had an uncomfortable feeling that it was not the end of Baron Foulton's attempts to drive a wedge between Sir Ralph and his new wife. She prayed that her other suspicions were unfounded and that the man who had fired an arrow at them was merely a robber as her husband claimed. Yet in her heart she did not quite believe that he was as convinced as he appeared to be.

Did he know he had an enemy in Baron Foulton? And why was that? What secret lay behind the hatred William felt for his sister's husband? And why did he blame Ralph for her death?

Alayne had changed into a gown of fine blue wool overlaid with a surcote of silver cloth when Ralph came to her chamber. She had dismissed her women earlier and was sitting by the fire, writing in her journal when he knocked and entered at her behest.

'Were you busy?' he asked, looking at the leather-bound book of vellum that she had laid down. 'Are you casting your accounts, Alayne?'

'No, for I have none at the moment,' she said. 'But I hope you will entrust the household accounts to my charge, my lord. I find figures have a certain fascination and like to see them well kept. You are such a busy man and must have enough to do without such trivial matters. For the moment I was merely writing in my journal. I have letters to prepare and keep a note of my thoughts.'

'I shall be happy to send any letters you write,' Sir Ralph said. 'And if it is not too irksome for you, I should be glad to give you the household accounts. My steward will explain them to you—or I shall do so, if you prefer?'

'I dare say your steward will be of help to me,' Alayne replied. 'I shall ask him for them in a few days. My first task is to make an inventory of the contents of the house, and it was to this purpose that I have set headings in my book.' She held it out so that he might see it and he nodded his approval.

'You have a neat hand, Alayne, but you must not work too hard. I fear Berenice found the accounts too much for her. I scolded her and that was unkind of me. I should have made allowances for her youth. She had been used to William helping her with her lettering and could not manage on her own.'

'I shall not find my duties irksome,' Alayne said. 'I noticed many small things when I was here before our journey to the court that I would like to have set in order, my lord. Your servants are very good, but a house needs a mistress if it is to be properly maintained.'

'You are wiser than Berenice,' he said, a smile hovering on his lips. 'I have always believed that to be busy is to be fulfilled—do you not agree?'

'Yes, I believe you are right,' Alayne said thoughtfully. 'At Poitiers I found the days were sometimes long despite all our pleasures. When I kept house for my—husband, I took solace in my stillroom as well as my accounts.'

'I hope you will not need solace here,' Ralph told her, his gaze intent on her face as he caught the flash of remembered sorrow.

'Oh, no. Here it will be a pleasure to fill my days with caring for your house, my lord.'

'I hope you will sometimes spare a little time to ride with me—or spend time in my company?'

'Yes, most willingly,' Alayne promised with a laugh. Her heart missed a beat as she saw the warmth in his eyes. When he looked at her that way she was almost ready to melt in his arms! 'But I cannot expect you to spend all your time with me, my lord. I know you have many responsibilities and duties.'

Ralph was silent as he remembered. Berenice had sulked because she thought he neglected her for his work. Ralph could not help comparing the two women and seeing the differences. At first he had teased Berenice out of her moods, but then he had grown tired of her pouting and the quarrels had begun.

Berenice's brother had come to Banewulf for a visit. The pair had gone walking in the forest together, staying out late and not returning until nearly dusk. It had been a cool day and Ralph had been anxious for his wife because she was a delicate girl and prone to chills. Indeed, she had taken a chill that day, though she continued to walk out with her brother for every day of his visit. Only after he left did she succumb to her ills, which he had suspected were more feigned than real. Ralph had been angry, blaming William for expecting too much of her and she had been hurt, crying and protesting that he did not love her.

'Do not be so foolish,' Ralph had told her. 'You are my wife. You must know that I care for you.'

'I said love,' Berenice cried. 'William loves me—but you despise me. You have never truly loved me.'

The unfortunate truth was that by this time Ralph had realised his mistake. Berenice was pretty and, as young men will, he had desired her, but he found her too slow, too dull to understand the things he wanted her to know.

Gradually, they had grown apart, and Berenice had taken to spending her time with Christian, Ralph's best friend.

Ralph recalled his thoughts to the present. It was wrong of him to think ill of Berenice! His guilt over her death rose up to haunt him once more, blocking out the beauty of the woman he had now taken to wife, making him turn from her blindly.

'I shall show you the secret panel,' he said to cover the fierce emotion raging within him. He went to lift a hanging, revealing what looked like a solid stone wall at first glance. But when Ralph showed her, Alayne saw that there was a slight indentation in one block, and when he slipped his fingers into the hollow he found a metal lever, which he pressed. To her amazement, a section of the wall slid back and she could see a small chamber beyond, in which a trestle and board had been laid ready with food and wine and candles burned from sconces all about, bringing light and heat.

'We have no hearth here,' Ralph said as he took her hand and led her through the opening. 'But if enough candles are lit it makes the room warm, for it is but small.'

'Large enough for its purpose,' Alayne said and smiled as he held the chair for her. It was one of those that had previously been used for her and Marguerite when they ate supper alone. 'I like this warmth and privacy, my lord.'

'It has been the way for the lord of the manor to dine with his men in the great hall for centuries past,' Ralph said. 'But there are times when it is good to be private—and when we wish for that we shall dine here, Alayne.'

'Oh, yes, I think it is a lovely idea.'

'I have given instructions that we are not to be disturbed this evening. It was expected, for in a way it is our wedding night.'

'Yes…' Alayne felt a little nervous for a moment, but then her fear slid away as he offered her wine and food. There was nothing in his demeanour to make her feel he might suddenly throw himself upon her. Indeed, since they had spoken of his first wife, he seemed to have withdrawn into himself. 'Thank you, I will take a little of the cold fowl and some bread.'

She sipped her wine, watching as he cut himself slices of the roast beef and spiced relish, breaking a large corner of the fresh bread. His mood was easing again, becoming less reserved, and they talked companionably as Ralph told her of his own duties about the estate. He was concerned for his people, for there had been plague in the towns the previous summer and many had died.

'There are too many widows and fatherless children,' he told her. 'The men were journeymen and travelled for their trades. We were lucky that the sickness did not reach our village, but the town was decimated. Many of the craftsmen I have employed here at various times were lost.'

'The plague is a fearful thing,' Alayne agreed. 'When I was a child it visited the village in my father's manor and many were struck down. My old nurse died of it and several of the servants, but though they thought I must have taken it I did not. A wise woman who treated the ills of the village folk told us that some are immune to it and she believed that I was one of them.'

'I have heard that some people are able to go amongst the sick without harm,' Ralph said. 'But it might be that you were not brought into contact with the disease.'

'Oh, yes, I have been, more than once,' Alayne told him. 'It came again the year before I was wed and I helped to tend the people at the manor and in the village. There was little to be done in most cases, but I learned that sometimes there is a way of relieving the symptoms and in a few cases the fever breaks and the sick person is spared.'

'That would be a truly wonderful thing.' Ralph looked at her in admiration. Berenice would never have risked her own life to help a person who carried the plague—like most, she was terrified of catching it, as well she might be. It killed almost all it touched. 'How was this relief achieved—and from whom did you learn the skill?'

'It is a matter of lancing the boils and then treating them with special ointments. I learned it from an Arab physician who had come to France to treat a rich man he had once tended in the Holy Land. I believe his patient died, for he was too late to save him—but many lives were saved in our manor that year. I helped him and he showed me how to make various ointments and cures.'

'That was valuable information, Alayne. To have the power to help others is a wonderful thing.'

'Yes, my lord. I have treated one or two friends since then, but these things must be done carefully for people are suspicious of what they do not understand. Some call it witchcraft.'

Ralph shook his head gravely. 'That is madness and wicked—to turn against a woman who has tried only to save life.'

'If the treatment is successful, the family is grateful and call you an angel, but if the patient should die…the people mutter about the evil eye.'

'Has someone said that of you?'

'My husband said it often when he lay dying,' Alayne said and there was both grief and pity in her eyes. 'He blamed me for his fall down the steps of the tower and, when I tried to help him, he said that I was trying to kill him. Fortunately, there were none to hear him, for the servants would not go near him towards the end. He threw things at them and cursed them if they touched him. I fear his pain was terrible and at the end his mind had gone. He did not always know what he said.'

'Did he say terrible things to you?' Ralph asked softly. He saw the pain in her eyes. 'Forgive me. I should not have asked. Some things are too painful to repeat.'

'They are painful,' Alayne admitted. 'But I think I should like to speak of them to you, my lord. I should like you to understand why…I had turned against marriage.'

Ralph's gaze never wavered as she told her story, leaving nothing out though her cheeks burned as she repeated some of the filth her husband had poured on her incessantly day and night. When she had finished he sat in silence and stared at her as if stunned. She trembled inwardly. Perhaps she had said too much? No decent man could like to hear such things. He might think her brazen and immodest for repeating them.

'It is beyond belief that a man could say such things to his wife,' Ralph said at last. 'To blame you because he could not be a true husband to you was harsh enough, but to use such language in your hearing—to abuse you in so many ways… I am not surprised that you did not wish to marry again.'

'Are you angry with me for not telling you before this? Do you consider me soiled beyond redemption?'

'The wonder of it is that you have retained your innocence and purity,' Ralph said. 'I beg you to forgive me and my fellow men for the way you were treated by this monster who called himself a man and shamed us all.'

'He was not a man, but a monster as you describe him,' Alayne replied and smiled. 'I do not blame you for my husband's cruelty, my lord. I believe you to be a very different man—a man of ideals. Marguerite said you were a perfect knight and I believe she spoke truly.'

Ralph's eyes held laughter, though his expression was grave as he said, 'I believe I am far from the Lady Marguerite's perfect knight, Alayne. I try to live by my vows and treat others as I would wish to be treated by them, though I fear I am but an imperfect knight.'

'An imperfect knight?' Alayne laughed as she saw that he was teasing her and then he smiled and the tension was broken. He rose and took her by the hand, and when she looked up at him he pressed her fingers reassuringly. 'Where are you taking me, my lord?'

'You have not seen my chamber,' he said. 'I wish to show you for there are things I believe you will find of interest. You have some skill at making cures and I also have a little knowledge of these things myself.'

Alayne's curiosity was aroused and she had somehow lost her fear of being alone with him. If they were ever to become man and wife in the full sense, it would be with her consent. She did not fear that he would use his strength to force her and she went with him trustingly.

His chamber was larger than hers and contained several chests and coffers, some of which were locked and bound with iron bands to keep them safe. One of them stood upon a heavy stand, and when Alayne looked at it she saw that it had hinged doors, which opened to reveal rows of little compartments, stacks of small wooden boxes, pewter jars and vessels of earthenware, also a few precious glass vials.

'There are various powders and ingredients used for potions and cures stored here,' Sir Ralph informed her.

'I keep them locked here in my chamber because some of them could kill as easily as cure. My physician asks me when he needs something and I give him the necessary amounts. It is the best way to be sure that no mistakes are made. Now that we are wed, I shall give you the key when I am away.'

'That is a very great trust,' Alayne said feeling honoured by his faith in her. 'But I do not know what all these things are for, my lord. I have only a small knowledge of such things. The Arab physician went away and the things I learned from the wise woman were simple cures that every housewife knows, made from herbs and wild berries.'

'I have a book written by a wise abbot I once befriended; it contains the names of every ingredient I store here, its use and the amount needed to make the cure,' Ralph told her. 'Besides, I do not expect you to dispense them, only to make them available to my physician if he should need them. I shall tell him that in my absence he must apply to you.'

Alayne was looking at the names engraved on the jars, finding that some of them were in Arabic, which she had learned to recognise but not to read, and some in French or English.

'These must be very costly,' she said, looking at him in wonder. 'Does your physician use them for any who are ill?'

'We help those we can,' Ralph replied. 'But as you know, my lady, sometimes it is not possible to help all those who are sick. Life and death is a matter for God and there are those who believe that we should not attempt to meddle in these things.'

'Yes, I know,' she said and a shiver ran through her. 'I thank you for your trust in me, my lord.'

'You have trusted me with your confidence,' Ralph said, 'and I have repaid your trust in kind. If we can learn to trust each other, Alayne, respect and friendship must follow—and perhaps more in time.'

'Yes, perhaps,' she whispered and her throat tightened. There was something in his look at that moment that made her wish he would take her in his arms and carry her to his bed. She knew that unburdening herself to him that night had somehow eased the shame that had lived with her for so long. There was still fear—she knew that it might live with her for always, but it was not as sharp as it had once been. She thought that she might overcome it in his arms—if only he loved her. 'If you will forgive me, my lord, I shall bid you goodnight, for I am a little weary.'

'Yes, of course,' Ralph said. 'Go if you wish, Alayne. I shall never seek to force you to my company, but my door is always open to you. Come to me if you are unhappy or afraid and I will try to ease your mind. Your happiness is my chief concern.'

'You are generous, my lord,' Alayne said and moved towards him impulsively. She reached up to kiss his cheek and then moved back swiftly. 'I wish you a peaceful night.'

'I wish you the same,' Ralph said and watched as she went through the middle chamber into her own. He heard the scraping sound that the panel made as it slid back into place and sighed. 'I pray that you will have a restful night, my lady, but it is certain that I shall not.'

Ralph locked the door of his medicine chest and placed the key in the pouch at his waist, then went to pour himself a glass of wine. He could hear nothing from Alayne's room, for the walls were stout, but he could imagine her moving about, preparing herself for bed, and he fought the mental images of her lying with her hair spread upon the pillows.

She was so beautiful and he wanted to lie with her so badly. It was a burning in his loins that would not be denied, no matter how much he fought it. The longing for her had built slowly in him, at first no more than a whim he had been able to put aside—but that was when they were in France, before he had come to know the real woman.

Alayne was all that he could ever desire in his wife, as wise and caring as she was beautiful. If only he had known her long ago! He might have spared both her and himself a great deal of pain. She had been hurt beyond bearing and he…he carried his guilt with him like a stone about his neck.

Now that he knew the extent of Alayne's sufferings, he could never seek her bed. He had hoped it might happen one evening when they talked, that she might come to feel something for him, but how could she when that brute she had wed had taught her that marriage was filth and sin?

It seemed he must continue to burn for want of her. Yet he could go to her, take her in his arms, kiss her as he had on the eve of Christ's Mass, and she would melt into his arms as she had then. But what if she should not—if she should turn from him in fear and disgust?

Berenice had begun to turn from him, to shudder when he touched her, though she had once been eager enough for his kisses. Towards the end she had seemed to fear him. Yet he had never done her harm, though he had lost his patience with her at times. For that he had done many a penance.

He could not bear it if Alayne were to turn from him

as Berenice had. It would break his heart to see fear and mistrust in her eyes.

No, he would not force himself upon her, no matter how he burned! She was his wife and he would keep his promise to her. He would do all that he could to make her happy, but if their marriage was ever to be a true one, Alayne must give him a sign that she wished it so.

Fool that he was! How could he expect her to offer her love to him when she had suffered such abuse at the hands of her first husband? He must accept that she liked and trusted him, and that must be enough. Despite his failings, which he knew to be all too many, he must strive to be what she thought him—a perfect knight.

Chapter Eight

Alayne was up soon after dawn the next morning. She took a light repast in her chamber and then summoned Mistress Morna Grey to her and found the lady more than willing to help her undertake the task she had set herself.

'I have often thought such an inventory would be useful,' she told Alayne. 'But to begin such a task alone was beyond me. I do not have the authority and none of the serving wenches can write, my lady.'

'We shall make notes as we go about and I shall record everything in my journal,' Alayne told her. 'It may take us some weeks to list all that the house contains, for there must be many rooms that are scarcely ever used.'

'Indeed there are, my lady,' Mistress Grey assured her. 'Some are barely more than an alcove, but used for storage, and I am sure Lady de Banewulf put things away that no one knows of today—I speak of Sir Ralph's mother, you understand. The Lady Berenice never interested herself in such things.' She shook her head and sighed, looking sad. 'In the last weeks she hardly ventured from her chamber at all.'

'That is sad,' Alayne said. 'She was feeling unwell, I suppose.'

'Yes, my lady. Sir Ralph was anxious about her, and at the end he despaired of her. She did not seem as if she wished to get well.'

'I see,' Alayne said. She sensed that the housekeeper was waiting for her to ask more questions but she decided against it, feeling that her curiosity was morbid. Besides, Sir Ralph would tell her anything she needed to know. 'It was very sad, but we must not dwell on the past, Mistress Grey. There is too much to be done.'

'Indeed, you are right, my lady,' the older woman said and her face brightened. 'Where would you wish to begin?'

'I think we shall begin with the linen,' Alayne said. 'The first thing a chatelaine needs to know is the state of the linen chests. Then we shall go on to the pewter and silver and implements. After that we shall visit each chamber in turn to list furniture and other accoutrements. I shall not venture to the armoury, that is properly for my husband and his steward—but all things domestic are my domain.'

'Oh, yes, my lady,' Mistress Grey said. It was clear that her mistress intended to turn the house upside down and shake out all the cobwebs and she was of the opinion that it was more than time. She had done her best since the Lady Berenice died but could not hope to have the authority of Lady de Banewulf. 'And there is the still-room. I believe *there* you will find everything in order.'

There was such a look in Mistress Grey's face at that moment that Alayne guessed it was her pride and joy.

'I see you are fond of your stillroom, Mistress Grey,' she said with a smile. 'Do not fear that I shall interfere too much, but we may be able to help each other. I believe there are always new things to be learned and I have some recipe books amongst my belongings that may be new to you.'

'Oh, yes, my lady,' Mistress Grey said. 'I too believe that there is always something to be learned and I shall be proud to show you my own records.'

Alayne nodded. She felt full of energy and excited to be beginning a new life, which she was sure held much content. This was the kind of household she had always longed to direct, and as for the other side of her life— well, a night spent in peaceful slumber had made her wake refreshed and happy. She had nothing to fear from her husband, and perhaps...perhaps there was something more to be gained.

She could only show him that she was prepared to be a good wife, and hope that one day he would come to love her as she now believed she loved him.

It was bitterly cold that morning, a week after their return to Banewulf. Alayne had wrapped up warmly against the chill and ventured out into the courtyard for some air. Her breath made little whorls on the air and after some turns about the courtyard she decided to go inside and warm herself by the fire in the hall.

'Lady Alayne...' She turned as she heard the voice, stopping so that the man who had spoken could come up to her. She had noticed him once or twice this past week, his eyes watchful as they followed her. And she had known him for the man who had stared at her so oddly at the feast during her first visit to Banewulf. She had asked Ralph who he was and discovered that he was called Master Brendon.

'Good morning, Master Physician,' she said pleasantly. 'I was about to go inside to warm myself by the fire.'

'It is very cold,' Master Brendon replied. 'You are not used to our English weather, lady.'

'No, that is true,' Alayne said. 'But my husband says it will soon pass and I look forward to the spring. It is always the best season of the year, do you not agree?'

'Spring is the season of devilry,' he replied and there was an odd light in his eyes. 'The March hare runs mad and so does the mind of a man and a maid. To go a-maying is to follow the path of the devil and leads to sin. But God sees all and will punish the guilty.'

'Is it so evil for a man and a maid to kiss in the spring?' Alayne asked, her lovely face alight with laughter. 'I believe it is natural, sir, and that God sees and looks kindly on such lovers. It is merely the priests who frown over their innocent folly.'

'You should be careful what you say, lady,' the physician muttered. 'There are some who would say you blaspheme.'

Alayne was silent as she considered her reply, sensing hostility in the other, but even as she hesitated she saw Ralph coming towards them and merely nodded at Master Brendon before going joyfully to meet her husband.

'The cold has made your nose red,' Ralph teased her. He reached out and took her hand. 'Come, let us go in to the fire and drink mulled ale and warm ourselves.'

'Yes, I am cold,' she replied, smiling up at him. 'I shall be glad when the weather changes, my lord.'

She forgot the physician as she went inside with her husband. Master Brendon seemed a strange, cold man, but he was not important. She was happy at Banewulf and she did not intend to let the physician's hostility upset her.

It seemed to Alayne that her life at Banewulf could be a good one and she wanted to make the most of it, to be on good terms with her husband and all his people. Why let the attitude of one man distress her?

Alayne was determined to put the tiny incident out of her mind, but in the days and then weeks that followed, she could not but be aware of the physician's brooding presence in the background. It worried her a little, but for the most part her days were full and happy so that in time it came to seem that she had always lived at Bane-wulf.

It was spring at last! The winter had been a hard one in the countryside about Banewulf, and the snow had lain for some weeks, at first crisp and pure white, but turning in the end to a dirty slush. As the thaw set in the roads became impassable and they saw few visitors at the manor, though one brave messenger did struggle through with letters for Sir Ralph. It was not until late March that Alayne received a letter herself.

She had been to visit her peregrine, Perlita, that morning. Ralph had had the bird brought from France for her with her other belongings, and like its mistress the peregrine was settling well into the life at Banewulf. The letter was brought to her when she returned to the house.

She knew at once that it had come from her father and braced herself for his displeasure. However, he was delighted that she had married a man of rank and wealth and praised her good sense, saying that he hoped she would bring her husband to visit him one day.

'Would you like to visit him, Alayne?' Ralph asked when she showed the letter to him. 'We might cross to France in the summer if it pleases you.'

'It would not please me,' Alayne said. 'I am well content here and do not wish for his company, but if my father wishes to see me he may visit us—with your permission?'

'You need not ask my permission to ask your friends or your father here,' Ralph said and smiled at her in a way that set her heart racing madly. 'You know that I would deny you nothing, my lady.' He took her hand and held it for a moment, playing idly with her fingers.

Alayne experienced a melting sensation inside, a feeling that came to her often when her husband touched her, and it was all that she could do to prevent the moan of desire his caress aroused in her. These past months had taught her that she had nothing to fear and everything to gain from marriage to this man. It was no longer from fear that she held a little of herself in reserve, but pride. She could not beg him to love her and she believed that his heart still belonged to Berenice.

'I shall write to my father and tell him that you have invited him here,' she said, her long lashes veiling her eyes as she fought the sensations swirling inside her. 'I do not wish for his company, but I cannot deny him if he will come.'

'He shall not harm you,' Ralph promised her. 'While I live, all men and women shall treat you with the respect you deserve, Alayne.' His smile was so tender that she felt herself drawn to him and she longed to be in his arms. Surely he must care a little for her or he could not look at her in that way?

'I know that I am safe as your wife,' she said. 'I have complete trust in you, my lord.'

'I am honoured by your trust, Alayne.' There was a gleam of humour in his eyes and she knew he teased her gently as he often did these days.

'My lord…' Alayne drew a deep breath. Would it be immodest in her if she suggested that they might begin to think of making their marriage a true one? She hesitated and then the moment was lost as a servant came into the small chamber where they had chanced to meet while Alayne was busy with some tapestry work. She had set up a frame in what was little more than an alcove, but had a window that caught the morning sun and was therefore light.

'Forgive me,' the page said, faltering as he saw them together. 'I did not wish to intrude, my lord, but I have had word from the village. There is sickness amongst the people and three have already died.'

Sir Ralph frowned, as much at the interruption as the news. 'It cannot be the plague, for that usually strikes when the summer is at its hottest. Do you know what kind of sickness it is?'

'There is fever, my lord, of that I know. I have no other knowledge—except that one of your men seems to have taken it. He fell ill this morning and it was then that we learned of the sickness in the village.'

'You say that one of my men has taken it?'

Ralph did not ask why that should be, for he knew that his men went to the village sometimes when they were not on duty to spend time with wenches who had taken their eye.

'I shall see him myself and the physician shall be consulted as to his symptoms.'

'It was your physician who said you must be told,' the page said. 'He begs that you will come at once, my lord.'

Alayne stood up as he prepared to follow the page. She laid a hand on his arm. 'Will you allow me to come with you, my lord?'

'Not this time,' he replied and smiled at her gently. 'It may be that your services will be needed if the sickness spreads through the house—but I would not have you put yourself needlessly at risk.'

'You risk yourself,' she pointed out.

'One of my men is ill,' he said. 'It is my duty to concern myself, but I shall take no more risk than is necessary, Alayne. Besides, I do not fear a fever. The plague is one thing, these fevers are common from year to year.'

Alayne nodded, removing her hand. She must not detain him, for it was his duty. Had the sick person been one of her women she would have insisted on visiting her.

She returned to her tapestry after Ralph had gone, but was unable to concentrate. It was always disturbing when people were ill, for there was so little that could be done to help them. In many cases Alayne had seen the physicians use cures that were more drastic than the sickness itself, and she believed that their patients often died of the treatment they received rather than the illness. However, it was wiser not to interfere, for the fraternity was jealous of its privileges and women who dabbled too much in medicine could find themselves accused of sorcery and brought before an ecclesiastical court. In these cases the verdict was almost always guilty and the punishment death.

After a while she got up and went out into the courtyard to take a walk in the gardens. Spring flowers were just beginning to poke their heads through the dark earth, though it was not as warm as it had been on the previous day and she shivered, deciding to return to the house.

'It is colder today, is it not?'

Alayne turned as she heard the young squire's voice.

'Yes, much colder,' she said and smiled as he came up to her. She was never alone for long, for Robert came to her whenever he had leisure to spend a few moments with her. 'Have you been training this morning, Master Greaves?'

'Yes, my lady,' he said eagerly. 'My master says that I shall soon be fit to seek my knighthood.'

'That is praise indeed,' Alayne said. 'Sir Ralph's sergeant at arms does not give praise lightly. You must have done well.'

'Yes, I believe he thought so,' Robert said but his smile had dimmed. 'It means that I may have to go away to earn my spurs. Sir Ralph has spoken to his Majesty for me and I may be called to court.'

'That will be an honour for you.'

'Yes…but I shall have to leave Banewulf.'

'Ah…' Alayne understood what he could not say. Sometimes it worried her a little that he was perhaps becoming a little too fond of her, but there was nothing she could do—it would have been cruel to deny him her company. 'All young men must earn their spurs. You will enjoy being at court, Robert. Perhaps one day you may return here—but if the King commands, you must obey him. You have no choice.'

'I shall miss you, my lady.'

'And all your friends,' Alayne said. 'But you will find new ones and forget us in time.'

'I shall never forget you!'

'Pray do not speak so rashly,' Alayne said and frowned. 'You have been my friend, Robert, but could never be more to me.'

He flushed and looked chastened. 'Forgive me. I have said too much. You will not like me any more and forbid me your company.'

'No, I shall not,' Alayne said and laughed. 'But you must promise me not to speak to me this way again.'

'You have my word,' Robert said and then saw Sir
Ralph coming towards them. 'Here comes your husband,
lady.'

'Ralph…' Alayne started urgently towards him. 'The
sick man—you have seen him?'

'One of my best men,' Sir Ralph said and looked anxious. 'He is sweating and has fever, but I do not like the
look of him. I fear that he may die, Alayne.'

'We must pray that your physician can save him, my
lord.'

'Brendon speaks of his fate being in God's hands,' Sir
Ralph said. 'He has given him a physic, but it has not
abated the fever. He was about to bleed him when I left.'

'If he is weak already, can it be a good thing to weaken
him further by loss of blood?'

'I do not know,' Ralph admitted. 'Yet I must trust my
physician—he has been trained in the arts of medicine
and must know more than we can, Alayne.'

'Yes, perhaps,' she said, though in her heart she did
not agree. Yet she knew that she must not interfere. The
Guild of Physicians did not admit women to their broth-
erhood, nor did they approve of women prescribing medicine to the sick. Women were permitted to nurse those
closest to them, but men must always guide them. It was
an unwritten law that she broke at her peril.

'Yes, I am sure that Master Brendon knows best in this
matter,' she replied, her eyes modestly downcast. 'We
must pray that the sickness does not spread through the
manor.'

'God preserve us,' Ralph said and then turned to the
young squire with a smile. 'Good news, Robert. You at
least may be spared the sickness. You are commanded to
court at once.'

'To court?' Excitement leaped in his eyes. 'You have heard so soon?'

'Your reputation goes before you,' Ralph said. 'You may leave with my blessing. A horse and the armour you have worn here is my gift to you. Work hard and follow the laws of chivalry and you shall not shame me, Robert.'

Robert bent the knee before him. 'You have been a generous master, Sir Ralph. You must know that I shall strive to bring honour to my name and yours.'

'You must serve his Majesty now,' Ralph said. 'I shall be pleased to hear of your success—and perhaps one day you may return to us. If the King sees fit to release you.'

Robert got to his feet. For a moment he looked longingly at Alayne, then he turned away with no more than a nod of farewell.

'I believe it is a good thing that Robert was called to serve the King,' Sir Ralph said looking after him thoughtfully. 'He is in love with you, Alayne.'

'I have feared it,' she said and smiled as he turned to look at her. 'Oh, not in that way, my lord. Robert is like you and would never harm a woman he cared for. No, I meant for his sake. Such a love could only ever bring him pain.'

'Because you could not return it?' Ralph's face was strained, a little nerve flicking in his cheek. 'But then, no man could ever win your heart, could they, Alayne?'

She stared at him in surprise, unable to answer as he turned and strode away. Was he angry? Surely there was no reason? Something in his tone had suggested that he was jealous or resentful…but it could not be! He still loved his wife, for why else would he continue to grieve for Berenice? She knew that he did—whenever he spoke of his first wife shadows came to his eyes and he withdrew into himself.

She longed to go after him, but was afraid of making a fool of herself. Supposing she was to offer him her love and be rejected? That would be too painful to be borne.

Alayne hesitated and then it was too late. His steward had come to him and the two men walked off together, deep in conversation.

Returning to the house, Alayne could not rid herself of the feeling that there had been more to her husband's remark than might first be plain.

She was sure he still loved his first wife, but at times she suspected that their marriage had not been happy. She was certain that he blamed himself for Berenice's death.

If only she dare ask him! Alas, she feared rejection too deeply. She had been taught in a hard school and did not wish to risk her husband's displeasure. If he put her away from him the happiness she had known these past months would be lost.

There must be some way she could discover Ralph's true feelings for the lady! As she puzzled over it, an idea came to her. Alayne had listed everything in the house, other than the contents of Berenice's room. Mistress Grey had asked her if she wanted her to do that particular inventory but she had refused, saying that she would do it herself. She had been reluctant to intrude, even to fetch the unfinished tapestry that she had worked on with Marguerite. She decided that she would delay no longer.

It was foolish to be afraid of what she might discover in Berenice's chamber. How could there be anything to distress her? She would list all the important items and then she would look for something that might help her discover the truth.

She was feeling nervous as she made her way down the passage to the room she had last visited when Marguerite was a guest here. Pausing outside, she took a deep breath before lifting the latch.

Alayne shivered, feeling cold as she entered. There was an unpleasant feeling to the room; it had a faint odour and she thought it was musty. She must order a fire lit in here, for it had become damp over the winter months. She began to move around the room, making notes of the furniture and hangings, also the various items of pewter and silver. It was when she opened one of the chests that still contained many of Berenice's things that she saw the small ironbound coffer. It had a domed lid and was beautifully carved on the side panels. She thought it must have been one of Berenice's most precious treasures. Why else would it be hidden away?

Lifting it out, Alayne discovered that it was locked. The clasp was strong and would not give to her even though she tried to pry it open. She would either have to use a knife to force it, which would be a shameful use of such a lovely thing, or find the key.

As yet she had seen no sign of a key. She put the small coffer down and began to search the room again, looking for somewhere that a woman might hide a key, but despite nearly half an hour of searching she could not find it.

She gave up at last. She would take the coffer with her and try to find the secret of its opening. It might be that the key to her own jewel coffer would unlock it. She paused to pick up the tapestry she had worked on with Marguerite, then left the chamber and went back to her own.

It was so much warmer here! Alayne was glad that she had not been given Berenice's chamber, for she would not have been comfortable there. She put the coffer down and laid the tapestry on it, intending to put them away later. She was about to summon her women to help her change her gown when there was a knock at her door.

'Come in,' she said and smiled as it opened and Sir Ralph entered. 'It is good to see you, my lord.'

'I wanted to speak with you, Alayne.' He caught sight of the tapestry and picked it up, frowning over the design. 'You were working on this with the Lady Marguerite. It was Berenice's…'

'Yes…' Alayne faltered as she saw his look. His mouth had gone hard, his eyes cold and distant. 'I thought I would finish it. Marguerite discovered it and thought it would be a shame to waste such fine silk.'

'Yes, it was costly,' he said. 'I dare say it would be a waste. Finish it if it pleases you—but I do not want to see it hanging here.'

'Then I shall not use it,' Alayne said. She felt as if he had struck her a blow. 'I did not know that it would displease you.'

'It does not displease me that you wish to finish it,' Ralph said. 'I merely asked you not to hang it in your chamber. It reminds me of something I would rather forget.'

'Forgive me…'

He was not listening for his gaze had fallen on the coffer. He picked it up and tried to open it, finding as she had that it was locked.

'Do you have the key? Have you seen what is inside this?'

'I imagine it to be letters or something of the kind,' Alayne said, her cheeks warm as she met his stern gaze. He was angry! She had not seen him this angry since they met in France. 'I have not opened it.'

'That is as well since the letters are private,' he said.

'You had no right to remove it, Alayne. You should properly have brought it to my attention.'

'I did not mean to make you angry…' she faltered. 'It was pretty and I thought I might like to use it…' Her speech died as she saw the disbelief in his eyes.

'You were curious,' he said. 'That is the first time you have lied to me, Alayne. Deceit does not become you.'

He picked the coffer up and turned away.

'Forgive me,' she said as he was about to leave.

'Taking the coffer was one thing, but trying to deceive me is another,' he said coldly. His mouth had gone hard and she flinched as though he had struck her. 'I had thought we were friends, Alayne. If you want to know something about Berenice, you should ask me.'

She hung her head, too ashamed to answer him. Tears were trickling down her cheeks as he closed the door behind him. Why could she not have spoken, told him how she felt?

Mistress Grey came to tell Berenice that Sir Ralph had sent his apologies. He was unable to dine with her that evening as he had urgent business. There was to be no supper in the great hall for several of the men had fallen sick of a foul fever.

'Is there anything I can do?' Alayne asked when she heard the news. 'I could perhaps help to nurse the sick.'

'Sir Ralph has given orders that the women who serve you are not to go amongst the sick,' Mistress Grey told her. 'He asks that you remain in your own rooms and do not go down to the hall for a few days lest you take the fever.'

'My lord is considerate,' Alayne replied but inside she was hurting. She felt that she was being punished, because Ralph must know that she would want to help those who had fallen ill. 'I shall of course do as he asks for the moment, but you must tell me if any of the women fall sick, Mistress Grey—for I shall not stand aside if they are suffering. It is my place and my right to see that they are cared for.'

The older woman hesitated, then smiled and nodded. 'I knew you would feel that way,' she said. 'There is a girl who I believe is ill of the same fever. I have not told my lord, but if you—'

'Take me to her,' Alayne said. 'Do not be anxious, Mistress Grey. Sir Ralph shall know nothing of this. It shall be our secret.'

'I do not think the cure Master Brendon uses is helping the men,' the other woman confided as she led her mistress through the house and down a secret stairway to the chamber where many of the women were housed. 'I believe something else might be of more use.'

'You know I have some small knowledge of treating fevers,' Alayne said. 'Of course, should Master Brendon offer a potion we must accept it.'

'Yes, my lady—but we do not need to use it, do we?'

Alayne looked into her eyes and saw that they both understood the need for caution. 'You are wise, Mistress Morna,' she replied, and with the use of her first name they both understood that their relationship had become true friendship. They were allies and friends and would protect each other. 'I have seen a certain bark in my husband's store of medicine that I believe might be of use. He gave me a little when I asked for it as a cure for my headache, and I discovered that it was best distilled. If it seems that it might help her, I can fetch it later.'

They reached the women's chamber unseen by any except a serving wench who bobbed a nervous curtsy. The sick girl was no more than fourteen and lay on her cot, tossing and turning in her agony. Alayne knelt down and touched her face, then turned to look at Morna.

'She is burning up. Far too hot. I think we should take this heavy cover off, Morna, and sponge her. That might cool her.'

'Yes, perhaps,' Morna said doubtfully. 'It may help her.'

'And I believe she has been sick.' Alayne looked at the sour-smelling bile that still lay untended on the floor beside the girl. 'That ought to be washed away lest the sickness is in it. I shall go and fetch that vial I told you of and return.'

'I will sponge her as you suggested,' Morna said. 'Can you find your way here again?'

'Yes, I am certain of it. I shall not be long.'

She left Morna to begin the task of making the sick girl more comfortable and made her way back through the narrow passages, using the little secret stairs that connected the main part of the house to that frequented by the servants. This part of the house was like a warren, Alayne thought, some of the stairs appearing to lead nowhere. Had she not taken careful note on the way there she would have been confused, for it would be easy to be misled by stairs leading to unused turret rooms.

However, she found her own chamber easily enough. The vial was hidden in her coffer in a compartment she had discovered when, as a child, she had been given the pretty box that had once been her mother's. There was a secret catch that only she knew of concealed inside the jewel coffer; she found it easily, opened it and took the tiny vial from the compartment in which she had concealed it, then slipped it into the soft leather pouch she wore at her waist. She returned hurriedly the way she had come, meeting no one in the main part of the house, though she passed two serving women once she had entered the back halls. They smiled at her and bobbed a curtsy then went on, clearly surprised at seeing the lady of the manor in their domain.

When Alayne returned to the women's sleeping quarters, she discovered that the sick girl was lying more peacefully. She took the tiny vial from her pocket and, with Morna's help, placed two drops in the girl's mouth.

'It is quite strong,' she said. 'I shall leave this with you, Morna, but you must remember to use it sparingly. Two drops, but no more than four times during a night and a day.' She placed her hand on the girl's forehead and found it a little cooler. 'I think the sponging helped. She may heat again, but for the moment she is resting.'

'I shall look after her,' Morna said. 'I thank you for helping me, my lady. I would not like Greta to die. She is my cousin and a lovely girl.'

'Then I shall pray for her,' Alayne said. 'I must go back in case I am looked for, but please come to me again if you want to talk about Greta or any other of the women.'

'Yes, my lady. And I will have one of the wenches bring you your meal on a tray. She has not been near the sickness and is sleeping elsewhere for the moment.'

Alayne nodded, understanding that Mistress Grey was doing her best to obey her master's orders in as far as she could. 'We shall say nothing of my visit here,' she said. 'I will come again and bring more medicine if I can.'

Returning to her own chamber, Alayne thought of the precious bark locked in Ralph's cabinet. The key was always kept with him and she thought he might be angry if she asked for more of the bark, for he would know she did not need it for herself. She bit her lip as she wrestled with the problem. If she told him why she needed the bark, he would know that she had disobeyed him, but he would also know that someone had told her of the situation, and Morna Grey might be punished.

Alayne regretted the incident over the coffer from Berenice's chamber. If it had not been for that, she might have asked Ralph for the bark. He would not have been pleased that she had deliberately disobeyed him, but he might have understood that she wanted to help. Now she was afraid to speak. The coldness in his eyes had been so hurtful and she could not bear to see it there again.

Chapter Nine

Alayne did not see her husband for three days. She received an apology for his absence, delivered by Bethel, but felt that there was a growing estrangement between them. It was true that there was much sickness amongst the men and Ralph must be anxious for them, but she would have liked to share his worries with him.

During those three days, Alayne had paid three more visits to Greta and on the last of these she found the young girl very much better. Her fever had broken and she was sitting on the edge of her cot looking pale and drained, but no longer in the grip of the dread sickness.

'Oh, my lady,' she said and looked nervous. 'You should not be here. Mistress Morna has told me how kind—'

'It was no more than any caring person would do,' Alayne told her with a smile. 'I am glad to see you better, but you must not tire yourself. You will feel weak for a few days and should not return to your work until you are stronger.'

'But there are two more girls down with the fever now,' Greta replied. 'Mistress Morna needs my help.'

'Where are they?' Greta pointed to a wooden screen

and Alayne heard a moaning sound from behind it. She was moving to investigate when Morna came bustling into the room. 'Greta tells me there are two more sick?'

'Yes, my lady,' Morna said. 'I still have a little of the cure you gave me for Greta, but it will not last long with two of them in need.'

'You think it helped Greta?'

'I am sure of it. It seemed to ease her pain and the sweating stopped after I bathed her a few times.'

'Continue with the bathing for these two,' Alayne said. 'I shall see if I can obtain a little more of the bark.'

'You must take no risks, my lady.'

'I shall tell my husband I have a headache,' she replied.

After leaving the women's chamber, Alayne returned to her own room. She knew the secret of the sliding panel now and opened it with ease, going through the inner chamber and into her husband's own room. She had hoped she might find him there, but it was not to be.

Alayne looked at the cabinet that contained the bark she needed. It was always kept locked. She knew Ralph would have the key with him and there was no way she could open it without that key, for she did not dare to force the lock. She tugged at it helplessly, but it would not budge and she sighed in frustration. It was so distressing to know that she could help someone, but the way was barred to her.

She would simply have to ask her husband for the medicine, Alayne realised as she went back to her own chamber, leaving the panel in the wall open. Perhaps if Ralph returned to his room and saw that it was open he would come to her. He might be regretting the breach between them, might be ready to listen to her plea.

* * *

Alayne was woken from her sleep by a loud thump. It was dark and she sat up in alarm, wondering what had happened. Then she heard a moaning sound and hastily lit the candle beside her bed. Throwing back the covers, she got out and, carrying her chamberstick, went to investigate the source of the noise.

The light from her candle showed the figure of a man slumped on the floor just inside her chamber. He had come through the secret opening and collapsed. Her heart leaped with fright as she knelt on the floor by his side and saw that his eyes were shut, his face pale in the glow of the candle. When she touched him, she discovered that he was hot and sweating, clearly in the grip of the fever.

She must get him to bed at once—but she could not manage to carry him to his own room alone and she did not want to rouse the servants in the middle of the night. If she did that, his physician would be called and he would be subjected to many of the treatments that had been used on his men. Alayne knew this would include the leeches, which was a form of blood-letting that she hated. She believed it had weakened her first husband when he lay dying, but he had pushed her away when she'd tried to help him and cursed her. From what Alayne knew of the sickness spreading through the castle, her own treatment seemed better than that of Master Brendon and she was inclined to look after her husband herself.

A moan from Ralph told her that he was stirring a little and she bent over him, trying to lift him. His eyelids flicked open and he stared at her; he seemed to know her, his mouth moving as though he wished to form her name.

'Do not try to talk,' she said and smiled, her hand stroking his face. 'I want to get you to bed, but you are heavy for me to lift. Can you help me? I do not want to call the servants at this hour.'

'Alayne, wanted to…' he said, but could not finish. For a moment she thought he had lost consciousness, but then he moaned and made what she could see was a huge effort to struggle into a sitting position. 'My head is swimming…'

'Yes, I know you are faint,' she said. 'I will help you. Please try to get to your feet now, Ralph. Please try, my dearest love.'

He held on to her as she put all her strength into getting him upright and, after some terrifying moments when she thought he would pull her down with him, she managed to get him to his feet. Then, with her arm about his waist, she half-dragged, half-carried him the short distance to her own bed. He was swaying by the time they reached it and Alayne was exhausted by the sheer effort of supporting his weight. She turned him towards the bed and, before she could lower him, he crashed on to it. It was clear that the effort had been too much for him; the fever had gained on him and he was no longer aware of her or what she did.

Alayne managed to manoeuvre him fully on to her bed, and pushed a pillow beneath his head. He was burning hot! She stroked his hair back from his forehead, then fetched water from her jug and poured it into a bowl. She wrung a cloth out in the cool water and bathed his forehead, then she reached beneath his tunic to smooth the cloth over his body, but it was impossible to reach far enough. She was going to have to undress him, but she could not get the tunic off in the normal way. There was no help for it. She must cut it away with her knife.

Alayne worked steadily, cutting the fine material and discarding it piece by piece until it lay in a heap on the floor beside her bed. She then fetched more water, using it to bathe her husband from head to foot. Her hand trembled as she sponged the hard contours of his body, for he was a soldier and honed to the rigours of battle, his muscles hard and taut beneath her hand. His skin was darker than hers, an olive shade, his chest lightly sprinkled with hair. His legs were long, the thighs thickly muscled and powerful, as were his shoulders. She covered his manhood modestly as she worked, for she felt it would be wrong of her to stare at the most private parts of his body while he lay unconscious.

She thought him beautiful as he lay there, his eyes closed, body racked with fever. How much more beautiful might he be when he was his usual powerful self? She imagined him lying close to her, naked as he was now, and felt something stir within her. Then she scolded herself for her immodest thoughts and dried him carefully before covering him with a sheet and a thin blanket.

He seemed more peaceful now, but she knew the fever would heat again. He needed something to help him fight it—the bark from his chest of medicines. His pouch lay with the clothes she had discarded. Alayne hesitated, then bent to pick it up, taking out the key she needed.

Her heart was beating wildly as she hurried into the next chamber and from there into Ralph's bedchamber. It was the work of a moment to find the bark she sought and take enough to make sufficient for her husband's treatment and that of the sick women. Feeling like a thief, she locked the cabinet and went back to her own chamber, where she replaced the key in its usual place.

The bark was ground in a little stone bowl with a heavy pestle. Once it was sufficiently fine, Alayne poured water into the mixture and left it to soak. It would be an hour or two before the healing properties had transferred themselves into the water, but when she returned to the bed she discovered that Ralph was moaning again.

Her potion would not be ready for a while—what could she give him? Ought she to send for the physician after all? Yet she had been told that most of his patients had not recovered. Alayne thought for a moment and then recalled the white powder that her Arab friend had given her. He had told her to use it for victims of the plague, warning her that it was very strong, but she knew it had helped relieve pain in sufferers of that dread disease. Would it help this fever? She could not know, but perhaps if she gave Ralph a very small dose in water it might help.

Alayne took the packet from her jewel coffer, where she had hidden it in a secret compartment to keep it safe. She used only a smallest portion of her precious potion, putting it into a cup with water. The powder swirled in the cup, clinging to the sides. Carrying it to the bed, she took some on a spoon and put it to her husband's lips.

His mouth was closed tightly, but it opened as she pressed the spoon against it and she was able to pour a few drops on to his tongue. He gave no sign of noticing, though she knew it had a horrid taste. Alayne took the cup away to cover it with a cloth. She had made only a small amount of the mixture, for she was not sure it would help with the fever. Besides, she would have her own mixture ready by the time Ralph needed something more. But she would store this in a vial, for it might be useful in the future.

Alayne sat on the bench and watched for any sign from Ralph as the night hours waned and the light began to steal in at her window. He had been restless for a while, but now he seemed more peaceful and he was not moaning or tossing as he had been.

After a while, she got up and went to lay her hand on his brow. He was still hot, but not as much as he had been at the beginning. The white powder her Arab doctor had given her seemed to have had much the same effect as her own remedy, but was perhaps even more powerful. She had thought they must be different, but now she wondered if the powder had somehow been made from the bark by some special process. Her Arab friend was a wise man and knew many secrets that he had not communicated to her.

How she wished that she knew more! Never before had she felt so desperately worried. Ralph seemed better—but would the fever return? She could only watch over him and pray for his safe deliverance.

In the morning she was dressed and ready when the serving wench brought her food and ale. She put her finger to her lips as Louise came in and smiled.

'My lord is not feeling too well,' she said. 'I have been caring for him, but I do not wish it to be known that he has the fever. Ask Mistress Grey to come to me, but tell no one else. Do you understand me, Louise? It is best if no one else knows that he is ill.'

'Oh, my lady,' Louise said. 'Supposing he should die—would you not be blamed for denying him the services of Master Brendon?'

'He will not die,' Alayne said. 'Please do as I ask.'

'Yes, my lady.'

Louise was plainly doubtful. Alayne prayed that she would keep her secret, for she was even more determined that Ralph should not suffer the treatments she believed would do him more harm than good. He was responding to her own nursing, though as yet he seemed still in the grip of the fever for he had not woken.

* * *

When Morna Grey came she saw that her master was in the second stage of the illness, as Greta had been after she had given her some of Alayne's cure and she nodded her approval.

'You are wise to keep this to yourself,' she said. 'It will be difficult to keep the secret, for Master Brendon may look for Sir Ralph.'

'He must be told that my husband is too busy to see him for the moment,' Alayne said. 'I have made more of the cure, Morna, and there is some to spare for your women. How is Greta this morning?'

'A little weak, but much better,' Morna replied. 'She has insisted on nursing the other women since she has recovered from the sickness herself. It is better she should do that than her usual work so I have let her bathe them when they become too heated—but I keep this myself.' She touched the vial Alayne had given her. 'No one else shall know of this, my lady.'

They heard a slight moaning sound from the bed and turned to look. Ralph had his eyes open and was looking at them.

'He has recovered more quickly than the others,' Morna said. 'But he is a strong man.' She went towards the bed, laying her hand upon her master's brow. 'I believe your fever has broken, my lord.'

'I feel like one of the damned,' he muttered and glanced about him. 'How did I get here?'

'You fell on the floor in a daze and I brought you here,' Alayne told him. 'You were feverish, my lord, and I put you to bed.'

'I'm as weak as a mewling kitten,' he said and frowned. 'This is your bed, Alayne.'

'It was easier,' she replied and smiled at him. She stroked his forehead gently, her expression more tender than she knew. 'It was late and I did not want to wake the servants.'

Ralph looked up at her and seemed as if he wanted to say more, but fell back against the pillows, his eyes closing. It was clear that the fever had taken its toll of his strength, even though he had fought it and come through much more quickly than others might.

'I shall go, my lady,' Morna said and went out.

Alayne went back to the bed. She bent over Ralph and found his forehead still a little warm. She was turning away to fetch cooling water when he caught her arm.

'Do not leave me,' he said. 'I wanted to tell you…to apologise for what I said to you the other day. I was harsh with you and I should not have been.'

'It is not necessary, my lord,' she said and smiled. 'You were angry with me and with some right. Let go of me now, for I am going to bathe your forehead and give you a little medicine that I think may help you.'

'I want none of that rubbish Brendon gives my men,' Ralph growled. 'It helps them not at all and may harm them.'

'This is something I made myself from the bark in your chest,' Alayne told him. 'I have found it helps with a headache and fever too.'

He let her go, still clearly feeling the effects of the illness that had felled him the previous night. Alayne brought cool water and soaked her cloth before wringing it out and bathing his forehead.

'That feels good,' he said, and when she gave him the two drops of liquid on a spoon he swallowed it without complaint. 'But that tastes foul, Alayne.'

'I know, but I believe it will ease you. You have been lucky, my lord. Greta was three days before she felt easier.'

'You have been nursing the sick women,' Ralph said and glared at her. 'Did I not give orders that you were to be isolated from the sickness?'

'Sickness will not wait for your pleasure, my lord,' Alayne replied. 'I beg you will not be angry with me. I have disobeyed you, but it hurt me that you would shut me out. I wanted only to help.'

'I never meant to shut you out,' he said huskily. 'I was afraid that you would take the sickness and die. I do not want to lose you, Alayne. I was trying to keep you safe.'

'I should not have wanted to be safe if you had died,' she said. 'And if I had not tried to help Greta and discovered something to ease her, I should not have known what to do for you.'

'Greta has recovered?' He looked at her oddly. 'And last night I thought I would die as five of my men have died—as I might have done. How did you find me?'

'I left the door between our chambers open and heard your cry as you fell,' she said, her heart racing. 'I hoped that you might come. I wanted reconciliation between us and I needed more of the bark from your chest. I have taken some to make this cure, for you and the women. I hope you will forgive me, my lord.'

'It is I who should beg your pardon,' he said. 'When I thought that I might die I realised that you would never know…' He paused and sighed, clearly weary and needing to sleep. 'I feel so weak.'

'What would I never know?'

'That I love you…'

Alayne stared at him. She knew that he had fallen asleep even as he spoke, and she heard the sound of his steady regular breathing, her heart pounding. Did he truly mean what he had just said—or was it the fever talking?

* * *

Ralph made a rapid recovery. By that evening he was able to get out of bed and managed to walk back to his room with a little assistance from Alayne. She placed his arm about her waist, helping him to walk slowly through the middle chamber and into his own. His nearness made her heart race and she felt that he was feeling something similar despite his weakness.

'You should stay here where I can keep watch over you,' she pleaded when he'd announced his intention of returning to his own bed. 'If you were to fall ill again, I should not know.'

'You may leave the way open and come to me if you wish,' Ralph said and there was something in his eyes at that moment that made her heart race. 'But you need to rest—and when I come to your bed it will not be as a mewling kitten.'

'You must sleep and recover,' Alayne told him. She smiled at him shyly, still uncertain despite his declaration of love, though the look in his eyes was making her heart beat wildly. 'But I shall come to reassure myself that you are not ill again in the night.'

'I shall not be ill,' he said. 'I am still weak, but the sickness has gone.'

'You must have been suffering with it for some days,' Alayne said thoughtfully. 'You fought against it while others took to their beds. The fever seems to last for two or three days and then the patient recovers as Greta did.'

'Or dies,' he said, looking sombre. 'Five of my men did not recover, Alayne. How can it be that Greta, who is hardly more than a child, still lives and five strong men died?'

'I do not know, my lord,' she said, avoiding his searching gaze as she helped him into his own bed. He lay back against the pillows, clearly weary from the effort, but then he looked at her once more and she saw the question in his eyes. 'Sickness is strange. It takes some and leaves others; there is no explaining it.'

Ralph looked grave. 'Yet I think Master Brendon's methods may be at fault.'

'I cannot say, for I have no knowledge of such things, my lord.'

'You need not fear to speak out to me,' Ralph said and caught her hand as she would have moved away. 'Surely you know that I would never harm you?'

Alayne hesitated, then realised that this was her chance. 'I do not believe the leeches help such sickness, my lord. I believe they may make the patient weaker if used too often.'

'Brendon said that they would suck the evil spirits from the blood of my men,' Ralph told her. 'I too thought it seemed unnecessary and cruel to bleed men who were already weak from fever, but I thought he knew best. Perhaps I was wrong to trust him. Nothing he did helped them. He had the fires built high to make them sweat— but you used water to cool me and I found it a great relief.'

'Perhaps I was wrong. You may have beaten the fever yourself, my lord, despite anything I did in my ignorance. It is said that some do if they are strong enough.'

'You have seen this fever before?'

'I have seen a similar sickness. I cannot swear that it is the same, for I do not have the knowledge to speak of such matters. I know only that the Arab doctor I told you of before instructed me in the preparation of the bark and its uses. I followed his instructions and it seemed to help both Greta and then you.'

'I believe that your nursing helped me,' Ralph told her, his eyes watching her intently. 'Will you make some more of your cure for me, Alayne? Tomorrow I shall give it to those men who are still sick, if you tell me what to do.'

'I shall go with Mistress Grey to tend them,' Alayne said. 'But first I shall need the key to your chest.'

'I always meant you to have one,' Ralph said. 'Take mine and when I am well again I shall have a second made so that in future you may use whatever you wish.'

'I shall use only those things I understand—but are you sure you wish to trust me to keep the key, my lord?'

Ralph's fingers curled tightly about her hand, and then carried it to his lips, pressing a kiss into the palm. 'I trust you with my heart, Alayne. This key is a mere trifle.'

Alayne's cheeks flamed, but she forced herself to look at him, meeting his eyes as her hand trembled in his. Her heart was racing and her insides seemed to be melting in the heat of the desire his look and his words had lit within her.

'Do you truly love me, my lord?'

'I thought you must have known that long ago?'

'No…' She drew a shuddering breath, knowing that she must speak out now. 'I thought perhaps…' Her courage failed her for a moment, but she gathered it once more and went on, 'Do you not still grieve for Berenice?'

'Ah…' Ralph's eyes seemed to gaze into the distance and for a moment she thought that he had withdrawn from her again, but then he looked at her again and she knew that he was seeing her, his hand holding fast to hers. 'Yes, I grieve, for she was young and innocent, and I blame myself for her death.'

'But why? She died of a fever, did she not?' Alayne held her breath. Would he answer her or would he retreat into that distant place where she could not reach him?

Ralph was silent for a moment, then, 'Berenice was ill

for some weeks after Stefan's birth, and we thought she might die, but her health recovered slowly. Her spirits did not. She was listless and sad and she would not leave her chamber even to walk in the air. I believed she was better, for the physicians all told me so and I had had more than one to visit her during that time. One day I was angry with her. I told her that she ought to go out into the sunshine, that she was wasting her life by sitting always in her chamber. She wept and accused me of unkindness, and the next day she dressed in her best clothes and went out.' He paused and she saw the expression she had come to dread. Such a look of grief and horror was in his eyes that she felt his pain strike her like a physical thing. She reached out her hand to touch his, and he smiled oddly but did not draw away.

'What is it, my lord? What hurts you so much that you cannot bear to think of it?'

Ralph hesitated and his blue eyes darkened with remembered pain. 'Berenice went for a walk as I had bid her, but it was a chilly morning and not as warm as it had been the previous day. I had meant her to go out for a few minutes, just to take the air, hoping it would bring colour to her cheeks and a smile to her lips—but she went further afield and…' He paused, a nerve twitching in his cheek. 'She was gone all day. No one realised until late in the afternoon and when we began to look for her it was almost dark. We searched for and found her at last, but it was too late. She lay on the ground and her body was as cold as ice. We can never be certain, but it was thought by some that she might have taken something to end her life.'

'You do not mean that she deliberately took her own life?' Alayne was horrified. It was a wicked sin to commit such an act and the Church often refused to bury such sinners in holy ground. 'That is a terrible thing…'

'I know what you are thinking, but we let everyone believe that she had died of her illness, which had come back suddenly,' Ralph told her. 'But I have always suspected that Berenice no longer wanted to live and, if that was so, it was my fault. I made her unhappy and she took her life because I had hurt her.'

'How can you believe that? Why do you torture yourself with these thoughts, my lord? You had not beaten her or deprived her of her rights and privileges as your lady?'

'I did not need to. She knew that I did not love her and that hurt her beyond bearing.'

'You did not love her?'

Alayne stared at him in surprise. She had never once thought of such an eventuality. She had believed he grieved because he had loved his wife too well. It was what most believed…what Marguerite and others had told her.

'She was lovely and when I first knew her I desired her.' Ralph spoke of his true feelings for the first time, his words coming slowly as he struggled to find the right ones. 'I have told no one else what I now tell you, Alayne. When I married I was young and did not know that love and desire were very different emotions. Berenice was young and foolish, little more than a child, too delicate and nervous to be wed. I learned very soon that our marriage was a mistake. She was frightened of me and, if I was too urgent in my loving, would cry and beg me to let her rest. I never forced her, but even when she responded to my gentle loving she did not want me in her bed. I tried to be kind and not frighten her, but sometimes I was impatient with her. I expected her to keep accounts and behave as my mother had when I was a child, taking an interest in the manor and its people, but she could not keep the servants in order and she had difficulty in making her letters. My disapproval made her unhappy and then she discovered that she was with child. She drew away from me even further, spending more time with my friend Christian than with me. I suppose I became irritated by her foolish ways and I said something that she thought meant I believed the child was not mine…'

Alayne's gaze never left his face as he faltered to a close. 'Did you think that she had betrayed you with your friend?'

'No…perhaps,' Ralph admitted the truth. 'Yes, there were moments when I wondered. But I had not meant to accuse her of it. I am sometimes abrupt and even you have felt the cut of my tongue. I ask you to forgive me for it and to know that it is merely my way, and not meant to hurt you.

'I knew that Christian loved Berenice. It was in his eyes every time he looked at her, but he was an honourable knight and she swore she loved me. I fought with him after her death, because he told me the child was his. He was angry, devastated by her death, and in his madness he blamed me. In my anger I struck him too hard and he hit his head as he fell. The wound was fatal. When he lay dying in my arms he took back his bitter words and told me that she had never been his—and I believed him.'

'What he said to you as he lay dying was probably true, my lord.'

'Yes, I know it—but I am haunted by his death and hers.'

'You blame yourself, but Berenice and Christian must

also bear responsibility for what happened to them. If there is guilt, it is equally shared.'

That nerve was twitching in Ralph's cheek again. 'You called me a perfect knight, Alayne, but I am far from that. I know myself unworthy and I do not deserve your love, but I wish for it. I have prayed that you might learn to love me one day.'

'Oh, Ralph,' she said and her throat was tight with emotion, tears pricking behind her eyes. 'Do you not know that I have learned to love and trust you?'

He looked at her as a man might if the gates of Heaven stood open before him. 'Can this be true? I thought that you said something the night I was struck down with the fever—but then I believed that I must have dreamed it in my sickness.'

'I called you my dearest love,' she said and laughed softly, her eyes bright with mischief. 'But I thought you were too ill to hear me or I should not have dared to be so bold.'

He looked into her face. 'Have you truly begun to love me?'

'Yes, my lord, most truly.' She leaned towards him, brushing her lips softly over his. 'I do love you. I have been afraid to love, but I cannot help this feeling inside me. It grows stronger all the time, and when I thought you might die I wanted to die with you. You are my husband, Ralph, and I cannot face a world that does not hold you in it. For good or evil the die is cast and I am yours to do with as you will.'

'I promise I shall never harm you, my dearest wife. If I was unkind to Berenice, it was not by intention. I never meant to harm her and I would cut my heart out before I injured you, my love. You must always tell me if I say something to hurt you.'

'I know that you would not hurt me intentionally. At first, when we met at Poitiers, you seemed stern and angry, and I was afraid of you, but now I know you, Ralph.' She veiled her eyes with her long, silky lashes, her heart racing wildly. 'Would you think me immodest if I said that I might like to be your true wife?'

'I should think you perfect,' he replied and she heard the laughter in his voice. He was teasing her again, and she liked it so much! The laughter bubbled up inside her like a spring, making her feel more joyous than she had been for many a year. 'You must know that I have wanted you more than I dare tell you. I was afraid that you would run from me if you guessed my feelings for you.'

'I thought perhaps you might care for me once,' she said. 'But then you were angry with me for taking that coffer and I believed that you still loved Berenice.'

'I was angry because you had not trusted me enough to ask me what you wanted to know.'

'Were there letters in her coffer?'

'From her brother—but nothing that anyone might not read.' Ralph reached out to touch her cheek. 'But why do we talk of Berenice? We should think only of ourselves now, Alayne. I have decided to put the past behind me and grieve no more for something that cannot be changed. I want you to be my true wife and I want to make you happy if I can.'

'You must teach me all the things you want me to know, Ralph,' she said, daring to look at him again. Her heart jerked as she saw the flame of desire in his eyes. 'I do not know how to be a good wife. I fear that I may disappoint you.'

'You could never do that, my love.'

'Then you will be patient and teach me that fine love

I have heard is such exquisite joy? At Poitiers the troubadours sang of it and the courtiers whispered in corners of its beauty.' She blushed as he put back his head and laughed long and merrily. 'You think me wanton to ask such a thing?'

'I was thinking that it would be a pleasure to teach you,' he replied, a wicked smile on his mouth. 'I would fain begin this instant, but I fear that, though my spirit is eager, my body is weak. When I have recovered from the sickness I shall begin to court you, my lady.'

'To court me...' Alayne saw the teasing light in his eyes and her pulses raced madly, heating her cheeks and setting a flame running within her. 'You will be my troubadour, my lover and my husband. Oh, yes, I should like that, my lord. I promise I shall lead you a merry dance before you catch me.'

'Shall you, Alayne? I think that I shall not mind as long as I can chase after you and catch you in the end. I have longed to kiss you and tell you all the things my heart holds, but I feared to distress you. Shall you truly be mine at the last?'

'Yes, but you must win me,' she said, a gurgle of laughter escaping her as the expression in her eyes teased him. She looked so beautiful, so desirable and yet so innocent that Ralph groaned and sighed for his own weakness, the weakness that prevented him from making her his immediately. 'Many tried to win me and failed. Think you that you can succeed, my lord?'

'I shall relish the contest,' he said, feeling the desire course in him, but knowing he was too ill to make love to her. 'But if I am to be well again I must rest. I confess that I am more weary than I had thought. Leave me now, Alayne.' He pressed a key into her hand. 'You have my authority to do as you think fit until I can resume my duties.'

Alayne smiled and kissed his brow. Taking the key, she went to the medicine chest, seeking the bark she needed and removing all that was left of the precious medicine from its container.

'You must order more of this when you are well, Ralph. I think it has many uses and is more helpful than I dreamed. This is the last, but if the fever is on the wane it may be enough.'

'We must pray that it is.'

Ralph lay back against the pillows. Alayne knew that it had exhausted him to speak of Berenice as he had, but at least there were no more secrets between them. She knew the worst and she could not find it in her heart to blame him. Perhaps he had been impatient sometimes, but it was the fault in Berenice that had caused the rift between them. She had been too young to marry and her family should not have permitted it. Now that the truth had been told, the way was clear for Alayne to find happiness with her husband.

She left him sleeping and then returned to her own chamber to prepare her cure.

Once the bark was crushed and left to soak for the required length of time, Alayne sent for Mistress Grey. 'I have my husband's permission to visit the sick,' she told her. 'We shall begin with the women and then go on to the men—if any are still sick?'

'Two are very ill, but a third has recovered,' Morna said. 'He is the first of the men to do so other than Sir Ralph.'

'We shall have more medicine soon,' Alayne said. 'But I have something else that might help.' She went over to her coffer and took out the vial in which she had stored the liquid made from the Arab physician's powder. She slipped it into her pouch. 'We shall visit them all,' she said. 'I would see for myself how they go on.'

'You must be careful,' Morna warned. 'Do not give Master Brendon cause to be jealous of you, my lady.'

'We shall naturally take Master Brendon's advice,' Alayne said. 'But we do not need to follow it unless he is there to watch us.'

In the women's quarters Alayne found that the two who had been sick were recovering; though there was another who had just gone down with the fever. Alayne gave her two drops from her vial and asked Greta to keep her cool if she began to sweat.

When they reached the chamber where the sick men were housed, Alayne discovered that two more had been taken with it. She gave all of those in need two drops of the potion she carried in her pouch, which emptied the tiny vial completely. She and Morna bathed their heated foreheads and shoulders, though they went no further— it would not be modest. And she ordered the young page that had the task of caring for them to let the fire die down. She was just about to leave when Master Brendon arrived.

Alayne found it difficult not to draw away from him. There was an unpleasant sour smell about his person that she disliked and she believed that he never washed his body or his clothes. Like many others he believed that to bathe was to weaken the body.

'I am surprised to see you here, my lady,' the physician said and she sensed the hostility in him. Why did he dislike her? She was sure he did, had felt it from the first. 'I understood Sir Ralph had forbidden it.'

'My lord was tired and is resting,' Alayne replied, lifting her head defiantly, meeting his gaze without fear. 'He asked me to take his place here and I have given the medicine he sent, which you prescribed, sir.' That last was a lie, but she delivered it without flinching, for it would satisfy his vanity.

His eyes narrowed to menacing slits and she sensed that he was barely able to conceal his hatred of her. 'You should properly have left that to me, madam. It was for that purpose I came.'

'I am sure you have much to do, sir. You have been tending these poor men for days. My husband was concerned that you might become ill—and what should we do then? We cannot afford to lose your services.'

'I have a sore throat,' Master Brendon confessed, seeming mollified by her flattery. 'And my head aches. I believe they are the first signs of the sweating sickness. As you seem in command here, perhaps I should rest.'

'I am sure that you should,' Morna Grey said, deciding that she ought to deflect his bile from her mistress. 'For you are sure to be needed, sir. There seems no end to this dread sickness. Come, let me help you to your chamber, for you are dreadfully flushed.'

His cold eyes came to rest on her, narrowed and menacing in a way that made Morna shiver. 'I can manage alone, mistress, but you must call me at once if I am needed. I thought that Sir Ralph seemed a little feverish last evening.'

'Oh, no, he was just tired,' Alayne replied. 'As you must be, good sir. This has taken a heavy toll on you.'

'Indeed, it has been a great burden,' he said. 'Remember to call me if I am needed.'

Both women were silent as he went out, breathing a

sigh of relief when the door was firmly closed behind him.

'I do not wish any ill,' Morna whispered to her mistress. 'But it is my hope that he may be confined to his chamber for some days.'

'We must pray for it,' Alayne said and there was mischief in her eyes. The physician's hatred had been almost a physical thing, so thick and overpowering that it seemed to taint the air. She could not imagine why he should hate her so—she had never done anything to harm him, and yet she had sensed his hostility, even before she was Ralph's wife. What was it about her that had aroused such feelings in the physician?

Chapter Ten

Morna Grey's hope proved well founded. Master Brendon was found prone upon his bed when the page went to wake him the next morning, and was suffering as severe a case of the sickness as any of the men he had tended.

'I shall tend him myself,' Morna said. 'It is better that way, my lady. I fear he already resents you and he might seek to cause you harm one day if he guessed that it was your cures that had helped our sick.'

'Perhaps,' Alayne said, for she had been shocked by the hostility in the physician. 'For the time being we must be glad that he is content to leave the nursing to us.'

Over the next three days Alayne saw all of the men and women she had treated recover. The medicine she had prepared seemed to ease their pain and the sweating was lessened when they were kept cooler. The women seemed to recover more quickly, but the men made good progress. By the fourth day all seemed to be over the fever, though weakened by their illness, and there were no new cases.

'I believe the sickness has run its course,' Morna Grey

said when Alayne told her there was no more medicine. 'If we are lucky, we shall not need more.'

'Have you news of the village?'

'It is not good,' Morna told her. 'I have heard that three men, five women and six children died. Others had the sickness but recovered.'

'Oh, those poor children,' Alayne cried, her heart wrenched with pity. 'Would that we could have helped them.'

'Children often suffer the most from these things,' Morna Grey said, 'and the very old. But does it not seem strange to you that five men died here? In the village it was different, for the men did not die so fast. Here our women lived but our men died.'

'I know what you are thinking,' Alayne replied. 'But you must not speak of this to anyone but me, Morna. Master Brendon would resent any suggestion that his treatment was less helpful than ours.'

'I think he killed them from his ignorance,' Morna muttered and scowled. 'He is not fit to practise the art of medicine. He knows less than any goodwife of healing.'

'Hush!' Alayne was alarmed at her wild talk. 'Master Brendon would make a bad enemy, Morna. If he heard you say such things, he would find a way to harm you.'

'He would be dead if he had been left to treat himself,' Morna said with a snort of disgust. 'It might have been better if we had left him to die alone.'

'No! You must not even think such a thing! You could be taken for an ill wisher,' Alayne said, looking at her anxiously. 'Someone has only to say you have the evil eye and you know what would happen then.'

Morna turned pale. 'They would take me as a witch, torture me and then burn me.'

'My lord would not allow it,' Alayne said. 'Besides, it will not happen—but it is best to be careful, Morna.'

'Yes, I shall be careful, but I know that I may speak my mind to you, my lady.'

'Yes, of course.' Alayne smiled at her. 'We are of like mind in these things, Morna. I think I shall go and rest now. I am weary and want to wash myself and change my clothes.'

'You are not ill?' Morna looked anxious, but Alayne shook her head.

'No, I am quite well, thank you. I do not know why it should be, but I seldom take a fever or even a chill.'

Alayne knew that she had been lucky, as had Mistress Morna, to escape the fever this time, which had been virulent, but she was very tired. Nursing so many had taken its toll of them both. She returned to her chamber and stripped off her soiled linen, washing herself in cool water and her precious scented soap. Feeling very much better, she slipped beneath the covers of her bed and closed her eyes. Within seconds she was sleeping.

Ralph saw her when he came to her chamber some minutes later. Finding her so peacefully asleep, he dropped a kiss on her brow and left a tiny posy of violets beside her on the pillow.

Alayne found his gift when she woke and smiled. She held the posy to her nose, inhaling its sweet perfume. It was a romantic gesture and one she found delightful in her husband. Oh, how different he was to the man she had been forced to marry when she was a mere child! He was such a perfect, gentle knight, despite his denials.

She believed that he was feeling very much better again, restored almost to his usual strength, and she thanked God that he had been spared. Her nursing, and the cures that were known to her through the Arab doctor she had befriended, might have played their part in his recovery. However, she knew that the sickness sometimes waned of its own accord. There had been deaths in the village too, but many had lived. Perhaps Morna Grey was right and the physician had hindered rather than helped their men. Whatever the truth, she would keep an open mind, for it would be foolish to make an enemy of Master Brendon.

After her women had helped her dress, Alayne went in search of her husband. He was in his chamber and had changed his clothes for the evening, wearing a gown of black veluotte heavily embroidered with gold thread over hose of plain black and belted with a chain of gold links studded with jewels.

His attire proclaimed him a man of great wealth and power and she knew he had dressed specially, as if the evening were an important occasion, for he was more normally dressed in soldierly fashion, very little different from his squires. They met as he was about to come through the middle chamber to find her and she could not help thinking how well the short gown suited him; the tight-fitting hose accentuated his powerful thighs, reminding her of his masculine beauty as he lay naked, and sending a little tremor of anticipation through her body. He smiled as he saw her, coming forward to take her hand and kiss it.

'You look beautiful. I hope you have not been working too hard, my love?'

'Mistress Grey did most of the nursing,' Alayne replied. 'We have her to thank that no more of your men are dead, my lord.'

'You are too modest,' he said, his eyes caressing her with a warmth that spread through her like liquid honey.

'But I am grateful to you both. We shall buy material for a new gown for Mistress Grey when we are in London.'

'Oh, yes, I am sure she would like that,' Alayne agreed. 'But we must ask her what colour she would most wish to have. It should be a special gown for feast days.'

'You must do whatever you think right. Perhaps you will buy new gowns for yourself, my love? I want to give you so many things. I cannot wait to take you to London, Alayne. We shall visit the silk merchants and the goldsmiths together and buy their finest wares.'

'Are we not to travel north to your estates?'

'We shall visit London first to replenish our stores. I have given you nothing for months and I owe you my life.' His eyes seemed to burn her with the intensity of the feeling reflected in their depths.

'You gave me violets as I slept. Why did you not wake me?' She looked up at him, feeling the pull of his physical dominance and shivered, but not from fear. Her heart was racing and her lips parted in anticipation as he smiled at her. He took a step nearer, holding her captive with his arresting gaze. She sensed the power and strength of him. Those strong hands could snap her neck if he chose, but he was so gentle when he touched her, so tender. Her stomach clenched with a feeling she was beginning to recognise as desire. She could scarcely breathe as she looked at his mouth, so soft and sensuous at this moment, the tip of her tongue just moistening her lips as the desire spiralled inside her. 'My lord, I...'

'You looked so lovely as you slept,' he said in a voice that was husky with need. 'I wanted to wake you, Alayne. I wanted to kiss you awake, to touch you, caress you as you wakened. I wanted you to hold out your arms to me, to welcome my loving...to be one with you.'

His words had lit a flame in her, curling through her

lower abdomen, sending little darts of desire flashing through her whole body, turning her insides to liquid flame. She bit her lower lip as a soft moan escaped her, and she felt herself melting as the heat began to build within her, possessing her. She breathed deeply, her nipples forming little peaks of need beneath her fine tunic, her mouth slightly parted as he reached out to run his finger over her bottom lip.

'I wish that you had woken me, my lord.'

Ralph took a strand of her hair, letting it slip between his fingers like strands of fine silk, then his fingers trailed her cheek, lingering for a moment at the tender hollow in her throat. She made a little sound of pleasure as she felt the spasm of need deep down inside her. He bent to kiss that tender spot at the base of her throat, circling it with his tongue. Alayne arched her body into his, her breath coming in little panting gasps as she experienced a strange intensive heat that seemed to flame between them, consuming them both.

'I love you,' she whispered, soft lips moist as they parted to receive his kiss. 'My husband…my beloved.'

'You are all I could ever want,' Ralph murmured. 'Compassionate, wise and beautiful. I want you so much.'

'Take me to your bed,' Alayne whispered. She was aching with this strange need that seemed to possess her. 'I want to be yours, Ralph. All of me…yours, your own true wife.'

'Are you sure?' he asked. He was burning for her, his need almost too fierce to be denied, yet he held back. 'I promised to court you, Alayne. You said I must win you.'

'My heart has always been yours. You are the knight I longed for—the man I hoped would love me one day. I believe you have courted me since the day we wed and you have won me, Ralph. I am yours. Do with me as you will.'

'I shall always love you,' Ralph said and then he bent down to sweep her up in his arms. He carried her into his room and set her down on her feet, then bent his knee before her. 'I am not worthy of your love, Alayne, but I do love you, with my heart, my mind and my body.'

With tenderness and kisses Ralph began to disrobe her, lifting her tunic over her head, letting her kirtle fall to the floor at her feet. Alayne, more daring than she would ever have believed she could be, helped to unbuckle the thick leather belt he wore low on his waist and to pull the gown he was wearing over his head so that that too fell discarded to the floor. She reached out to touch his chest, the skin cool and silky to the touch, beneath the skin his muscles were hard and taut, honed to the strength of iron.

'When I bathed you I thought you beautiful,' she said shyly. 'But I did not dare to touch you this way.'

'Touch me now,' he invited. 'You wanted to learn about fine love, Alayne. It begins with a little flirting and then a few kisses stolen in secret and then comes the touching. If we are lucky we shall progress very slowly towards our ultimate pleasure, that passion and pain some believe all important.' He took her face between his hands, kissing her mouth with soft pecking kisses that made her smile, teasing her with his tongue so that she parted her lips for him and he tasted her sweetness.

'You taste of wine and honey,' he murmured huskily.

His kisses were sometimes light, like the brief caress of a butterfly's wing, sometimes teasing so that she laughed and kissed him back, teasing him as he teased her, sometimes so deep and hard that he took her breath away. When he had done with her lips for the moment he kissed her throat, her breasts, circling the nipples with his tongue as he had the hollow in her throat so that they almost ached from pleasure; then, kneeling before her, his mouth and tongue trailed over the curve of her belly, making her flesh pulse with pleasure and her body jerk as the heat mounted within her. Down, down, down to that mound of soft curls.

When she thought that she would swoon for sheer delight, Ralph swept her up in his arms, carrying her to the bed and laying her gently down. He lowered himself to lie beside her, the burn of his flesh next to hers setting her on fire again, make her arch towards him eagerly. He began to caress her with his hand, stroking, exploring, and finding his way into the secret places of her femininity. His kisses covered her entire body, lingering between her thighs, his tongue caressing the sensitive skin there and making her cry out.

'Ralph,' she moaned, panting as the crescendo of pleasure mounted to unbearable heights. 'It feels so good...'

'Does it, my darling?' he murmured and she heard the laughter in his voice, the delight and triumph he felt because he was giving her such pleasure. 'I want you to feel good, Alayne. I want you to want me as I want you.'

'I burn for you,' she breathed. 'Am I wanton, Ralph? Am I wicked to say that I long for more? I want to feel you inside me.'

'My love,' he murmured, his voice cracking with desire. He moved between her legs, which had opened to receive him, and felt the heat and wetness of her as he touched her with his fingers, stroking, caressing. She was whimpering, aching for him as he ached for her, welcoming the hard thrust of him as he entered her. Then he was thrusting deeply, deep into her, breaking the membrane of her virginity as her first husband had tried and failed.

This time Alayne felt none of the revulsion that had so shocked her then. Instead she opened to him as a rosebud to the welcome sun, enfolding him in a hot silken sheath that made him cry out. 'My love…my love!'

The pain of entry was swift and sharp, but she buried her cry in his shoulder and let herself be swept on the tide of his passion to the glory of that wondrous place of which she had only heard. Her whimpers of pleasure grew as she was lifted and tossed on a sea of such exquisite sensation that she abandoned all restraint, letting herself go with him to that paradise she had never known or believed could be hers. The waves of exquisite pleasure washed over her again and again, making her body arch and spasm as she screamed his name, and then she lay quiet in his arms at last, warm and content, the tears slipping down her cheeks.

'Why do you weep? Did I hurt you, my love?'

'You know that you did not. I am just so happy.'

'You shall be happy,' Ralph vowed as he gathered her to him. 'I shall live only for you, my darling wife, to make you happy.'

She smiled as he held her to him. She had feared he would never love her, but now he had taken her to a place that only true lovers ever found and she knew how much she was loved, and she was content.

'Shall we always be as happy as this?' she asked as he stroked her cheek. 'Shall you always want me this way?'

'For my life long,' he promised.

Ralph could not have enough of his wife. It was as if the months of restraint had built such a fire in him that it could not be quenched. He made love to her five times that night and only then did they both sleep, bodies entwined as one, exhausted and satiated by the desires that had raged so fiercely in them both.

When Alayne finally woke the sun was shining and she knew that she had slept later than was her habit. Ralph had left her, but there was a kiss left upon a scrap of parchment on the pillow beside her. She pressed her lips to the symbol of love, feeling her happiness bubble inside. She could hardly believe she was not dreaming— had she really been so thoroughly loved the previous night? Yet she need not ask, for her body still throbbed from his assault on it and her own enthusiastic response. She blushed for shame as she thought of some of the things she had done, for she had learned fast how to give pleasure as well as to receive it. Yet there was no shame in a loving so natural and giving. Ralph had shown her the gates of Paradise and they had gone through them together.

To be this happy! It was more than she had ever dreamed possible and Alayne was singing as she rose and went back to her own chamber, wearing her overgown loosely draped around her.

As if she had been waiting for a sign, Louise appeared with a cup of wine, fresh bread and honey. 'Sir Ralph said we were not to disturb you, my lady. You were so tired after the past few days, and 'tis no wonder. You have done so much to help us all, my lady.'

'I have done very little,' Alayne replied. There was a smile on her lips and she felt dreamy, her thoughts far away. 'It was merely good sense to know that an over-heated body should be cooled, and the potion was one commonly used in my country.' That was not quite the truth, of course, but Alayne felt it best to let the girl believe her medicine was often used in France.

'Everyone is saying that there would have been more deaths if it were not for you and Mistress Grey.'

Alayne came out of her dreaming state and looked at the girl. 'It is best that these things are not spoken of,' she said. 'I am sure that Master Brendon played his part in the recovery of Sir Ralph's men.'

'There is another opinion amongst the men,' Louise went on as if she had not spoken. 'They are saying that Master Brendon is a charlatan and that he should be sent away. They do not trust him to care for them anymore.'

'That is a matter properly for my husband,' Alayne said and frowned. 'It is best that we do not say such things, Louise. Master Brendon may be angry and rightly so. He is an experienced physician and has studied many years.'

'My mother always said that physicians were all charlatans,' Louise said and pulled a wry face as she brought Alayne's gown for her. 'There was an old woman in our village who gave us potions when we needed them and asked us only for a few coppers. My mother always said she had more knowledge in her little finger than the whole Guild of Physicians put together!'

Alayne could not help laughing at her serving woman's vehemence, but she shook her head at her. It was a commonly held opinion, but best not spoken of in the physician's hearing.

'Your mother may be right, Louise, but she could have been beaten for her slander and the wise woman you spoke of was lucky someone did not denounce her as a witch.'

'They did,' Louise said and her mood was suddenly sombre as she recalled the rest of the story. 'I was very young, but I remember Mother saying that it was when a bull died and the village cows could not be served.

Someone accused her of ill wishing the beast and everyone believed it; they would have gone for her and put her to the test had she not run away. She never came back and after that we had no one to treat our ills. My mother said the fools had driven her away and that no one would dare to take her place.'

'Then remember to keep a still tongue,' Alayne warned as she was helped into a dark blue overgown. It had a low waist and draped lovingly about her hips, a girdle of soft leather tied loosely in front. She frowned as she fastened her keys to the girdle. Louise's tale of a woman being accused of witchcraft had chilled her. 'We may think what we please, but it is dangerous to speak too openly.'

'Yes, my lady, I shall remember,' Louise said. She understood what her mistress was telling her. However, she knew that everyone at the manor was talking about how the men had all died until Lady Alayne and Mistress Grey had begun to nurse them, and how strange it was that all the women had lived.

The men could not speak highly enough of their mistress, for not all ladies of her station would have risked their own lives to help others. The whispers were circulating. It was said that she bore a charmed life and never became ill, that she had gone amongst sufferers of the plague in France and remained untouched. It was also said that she had the healing touch, and some believed she could work miracles, though others dismissed that as nonsense.

They were grateful to her and the word sorcery was never spoken, though some might have thought it, but for the men and women she had helped she was an angel and they adored her.

Yet in their midst the serpent watched and hissed his displeasure as he heard the whispers, waiting for his chance to strike at the woman who tormented his dreams and turned his days sour.

The spring had truly come now, Alayne thought, as she picked bluebells and primroses in the manor gardens that morning, holding them to her nose to inhale their fresh perfume. On the morrow they were to set out on their journey to the north, stopping for a few days to break their journey and buy much-needed goods in the walled city that had been named Londinium by the Romans.

Alayne and Morna Grey had been busy for days making lists of stores that were required to replenish those depleted by the long winter past. The shelves in the still-room were almost bare of preserves and the simple cures that they had made themselves from herbs and berries, and fresh ingredients must be purchased from the merchants in town if they were to be replenished.

'You are so busy that I hardly see you,' Ralph had complained the previous evening, but it was said with an approving smile. He had brought her a letter lately come from her father, yet another apology that he could not find the time to visit them, with promises for a certain visit in the future. Alayne put the letter aside and smiled at her husband. She did not mind that her father made his excuses, for she was happier than she had ever been with this man who was now her husband in every way. They were together every evening and every night, sometimes in company with their retainers and friends, but often alone in their private rooms. It was a charmed existence, their loving passionate and frequent, and their friendship ever deepening so that they were often aware of each other's thoughts without words needing to be spoken.

'We are blessed, my love,' Ralph had said to her as he bent his head to place a kiss on the nape of her neck as she sat busy with her stitchery. 'Such happiness as this is not often found in marriage.'

'I know,' she replied and turned to lift her face for his kisses. 'We have both been unhappy and this content is doubly precious to us both, Ralph. I pray that nothing will come to spoil it.'

'What should spoil it?' he asked, a teasing smile on his lips. 'We love and trust each other. Surely nothing can come between us?'

'Not from ourselves,' she agreed. 'But I cannot help feeling that we are too happy. Can anyone know perfect content for long, Ralph?'

'You must not let yourself have foolish thoughts,' he said with a frown. 'They are merely superstition, unless—I have not done something to distress you?'

'No, of course not,' she said quickly. 'You are everything I could ever want, my husband.'

'Then what worries you, Alayne? Do not shake your head, for I know something does.'

She hesitated, then took a deep breath. 'It is Master Brendon, Ralph. He has disliked me since the sickness came here. He has heard those foolish rumours about me, that I have the healing touch, and I can see the hostility in his eyes when he looks at me.'

'I fear the men no longer trust him. Has he been rude to you, Alayne? I will not have anyone I retain show you disrespect.' His expression was fierce, angry.

'He is not disrespectful,' she said. 'But I feel that he dislikes me.'

'You must not fear him,' Ralph said. 'He cannot harm

you, my love. I would dismiss him if he dared to raise a hand against you and he knows it. He would not easily find as good a place again if I dismissed him from my service.'

'I do not ask that,' she said and a cold shiver ran down her spine. 'But if I should ever be ill, I would not want him to attend me.'

'I shall think about taking another physician into my service,' Ralph promised. 'But I think you are anxious for nothing, my love. Master Brendon knows his place.'

'Yes, of course,' Alayne replied and smiled. 'I shall not think about it again.'

She had tried to avoid the physician as much as she could, but that morning as she turned to go into the house with her posy of flowers she saw him coming towards her.

'I see you gather flowers, madam,' he said, his manner chillingly hostile. 'Do you use them in your potions?'

'Flowers have many uses, sir,' Alayne replied carefully. 'All good chatelaines know that. I make only simples, and lotions for my skin.'

His eyes were narrowed, cold and accusing as he stared at her. 'I have heard otherwise, madam.'

'Then you have heard foolish tales, sir.'

'In some villages you would be named as a witch.'

His vicious tone made Alayne gasp, but she recovered swiftly.

'Many women have been falsely accused of such things,' she said. 'But there must be some proof. Have any told you that I have harmed them?'

She saw the anger in his face and knew that it was because she was loved and revered by her people that he had spoken so viciously. He suspected her of sorcery, for his mind was filled with the prejudices of many of his ilk, but he had no proof.

'You think yourself so clever, madam,' he muttered. 'But one day you will make a mistake and when you do—'

'Are you threatening me, sir?' Alayne raised her head proudly. 'I believe I must remind you to remember your place. Sir Ralph is master here and I am his wife. He would not be pleased if he heard that you had threatened me.'

Master Brendon's face went white and then red as he fought to control his fury. She was so beautiful and there was always a haunting perfume about her. He could smell it now and it inflamed his senses, making him feel forbidden desires. He had wanted her the moment he saw her, but she was his lord's wife and not for him. Not only could he never have her, never taste the honey of her womanhood, he knew that she despised him.

If he did not need this place so badly, he would throw her to the ground and rape her, he thought, his guts churning with the mixture of the hate and desire that coursed through him. She was a witch! She must be a witch, for no other woman had ever made him burn this way.

He turned away abruptly as she continued to look at him, fearing that she had put a spell on him. Was it not enough that he was continually tortured by his desire for her—did she want to destroy him as well?

Alayne stood staring after him as he retreated. She had won a battle, but she knew the war between them would continue. He was jealous of her and he would find a way to harm her if he could.

Alayne knew that she ought to beg Ralph to send him away. He would do it if she asked him, and yet she believed that that would be the worst thing she could do. While the physician remained here, his hatred was contained by his observance to his master. If that restraint no longer held him back, what might he do?

Alayne shivered despite the warmth of the sun. She walked quickly into the house. Master Brendon was not to accompany them on their travels so she would be free of his oppressive presence for some months. She breathed deeply, fighting her fear that the physician represented a danger to her, a danger to her happiness.

She would not let his shadow fall across her, she decided. Ralph loved her and that was all she cared for.

They spent some days in London, visiting the various merchants at their warehouses along the banks of the river. Long lists of their needs were presented to the spice merchants, for in the heat of summer when it was difficult to keep meat fresh for longer than a few hours it must be prepared with salt and spices to make it palatable.

She also bought silks and materials for her embroidery, lengths of cloth both for herself and her women, who, she had decided, should all have new gowns since her lord was so generous as to give her his purse and tell her to spend whatever she wished.

Ralph came with her to the silk merchants—he said that she would not buy enough for herself if he did not, and he chose several lengths of good wool, rich silks and damasks in bright colours that he said would do homage to her beauty.

They commissioned shoes from the finest makers to be collected when they returned later in the year—most of the other goods were to be sent in Sir Ralph's own wagons to his manor at Banewulf. But the visit to the best goldsmith in the city was one that Alayne would not forget.

The little house was stoutly built of stone but dark inside, for its owner kept it shuttered even during the day, and with good reason. He was a Jew and feared that his goods might be stolen, for his kind was not liked, perhaps because many of them were so very wealthy. Yet Ralph told Alayne that much of the gold the man stored in his strongroom was held for wealthy nobles, placed with him to be invested in ventures that made money for the merchant's customers.

'But then why is he so afraid?'

'Because he is also a money lender,' Ralph told her. 'His customers come to him when they need help, but he charges high interest on the money he lends and the people who borrow from him do not like to repay it when the time comes.'

'Then why do they borrow from him?'

'Because only the Jews will lend money.'

Alayne nodded, but she did not really understand. For herself she found the little man eager to please, but when she saw the merchandise he brought out to show them she understood why he was so happy to serve them.

Precious jewels that sparkled in the light of candles flashed from a cloth of dark blue. Gold chains so heavy that she would find them oppressive and rings the like of which she had never seen.

'Choose whatever you wish,' Ralph told her, smiling in amusement as she hesitated, uncertain of their price. She did not want him to part with too much money for such things.

'I like pearls best,' she said after spending some time in deliberation. 'This pendant set with pearls and turquoise is very pretty, my lord. I think I should like that.'

'Very well, we shall have that,' Ralph said and the merchant looked disappointed, for it was one of the cheaper of his goods. 'But we shall also have this string of pearls, this gold chain and this pearl-and-turquoise ring to go with your locket.'

The merchant was all smiles again. Clearly Ralph had chosen some of the most expensive things. Alayne made a sound of protest, but she knew better than to try and dissuade her husband in the matter. He had already heaped costly gifts upon her and she could only smile and thank him.

'You shall thank me properly later,' he whispered to her as the merchant went to put his other treasures away. 'I shall expect to receive my present this night, my love.'

Alayne blushed as she saw the heat of his look, but the familiar churning began inside her and she whispered back that what she had in mind would be as much a gift for her as him. Ralph laughed, amused by her wicked sally, and they left the merchant's house in high good humour with themselves.

Alayne paid her dues in full that night, making Ralph lie back while she kissed and tasted him as he had taught her, her tongue flicking at his throbbing manhood until he cried out that he could bear no more and thrust her beneath him in the bed. His loving was fierce and swift that night, bringing them both to a shuddering climax, but after they had rested he loved her tenderly and they slept entwined in each other's arms.

Afterwards, when she knew she was to have a child, Alayne often wondered if it was at that moment of their fiercest loving that she had conceived.

Chapter Eleven

The journey north to Ralph's other manor, which had come to him through his mother's family, was made at a leisurely pace, the weather fine enough to make it pleasant enough to linger as they went. In Nottingham they stayed with Ralph's cousins, who were also kinsmen to Marguerite and her father, and it was there that they learned of her coming marriage to Baron de Froissart.

'I hoped that we should see you,' Marguerite said. 'I wrote to you to tell you of my happiness, but I think perhaps you had already left Banewulf before the letter arrived.'

'We had not received it when we left,' Alayne told her as they embraced. 'You know that I am happy for you, Marguerite. Shall you like being a soldier's wife?'

'I should be happy anywhere with Pierre,' she replied and blushed. 'I think he cares for me a little, Alayne. He has learned to forget you.'

'I think perhaps he always cared for you in his heart,' Alayne told her. 'I shall hope that perhaps one day you will find the time to stay with us at Banewulf?'

'Perhaps,' Marguerite said and smiled at her. 'I have

no need to ask if you are happy, Alayne. I can see it in your eyes.'

'Yes, I am very happy,' Alayne said. 'And I am sure you will be too, Marguerite.'

Marguerite nodded and then she frowned. 'I do not know if this means anything now,' she said hesitantly. 'But Pierre told me that he believes he saw de Bracey at Nottingham fair one day.'

'Here?' Alayne was surprised. 'What does he do here, I wonder? I did not know that he had manors in England.'

'Pierre thinks he hopes to win favour at King Henry's court since he has been banned from Poitiers.'

'I suppose that he might,' Alayne said doubtfully. 'But do you think that his Majesty would receive him if he knew the truth—that he had behaved shamefully, betraying the laws of chivalry?'

Marguerite shrugged. 'I do not know—and we waste time in speaking of him. I am not interested in de Bracey or his wishes. I told you only because Pierre thought I should warn you.'

'The baron is not staying with you?'

'He is busy for the moment,' Marguerite replied. 'The outlaws he pursues are nearly routed. By the summer he will have more time to spend with me and then we shall be married.'

Alayne nodded, remembering the day that an arrow had been fired at them from the forest as they made their way back to Banewulf. Both she and Ralph had assumed that it was either robbers or someone sent by Berenice's brother—but supposing someone else had been behind that attack? Supposing it had been de Bracey who fired that arrow, hoping to kill the man he must blame for his disgrace? Alayne shivered at the possibility of such a man planning his revenge on them.

She must remember to tell Ralph what Marguerite had told her.

* * *

Ralph laughed away her fears as she had suspected he might.

'I do not fear de Bracey or any that send a fool to do work they are afraid to do themselves,' Ralph murmured as he held her close in their bed and stroked the satin arch of her back. 'Besides, though he may be in England now, I doubt he was here at the time of the attack. He would have been some months recovering from his wound.'

Alayne did not press the point. She did not believe it was important, for they never travelled without a large escort and were unlikely to be taken by a surprise attack. Ralph was even more alert since the attempt on his life, and his men kept a careful watch over them.

They stayed a few days with Marguerite and then travelled on to Ralph's manor, some twenty leagues further north. The weather was not quite as warm as it had been at Banewulf when they set out, but the countryside looked beautiful, the hills green with spring grass and the trees bursting into bud. Sheep grazed on the hills; they were a source of much of the wealth that made England's nobles so powerful, for English wool was the best quality and much sought after.

Alayne was conscious of a deep happiness within her, though it was not until they had been at the manor of Thane for some weeks that she knew for sure that she was to have her husband's child.

She had waited to be sure before speaking of it to Ralph, and was a little hesitant, for she knew that he both longed for and feared to have another child. It would be a great happiness to them both, but he remembered Berenice's fear of giving birth and the way she had withdrawn into herself for weeks before her child was born.

They had been to a fair when Alayne decided it was time to tell him of her condition. He had bought her ribbons and a silver trinket from the peddlers and they were laughing as they walked home across the meadows towards the house, which was a simple country manor and not a great house and fortress like Banewulf.

'I like your mother's home,' she told Ralph as they lingered in the sun and he bent to pick a buttercup for her. He tickled her face with it and she laughed and ran away from him, but she did not run fast and he soon caught her. 'It has been a happy time for us here, my lord. I shall be sorry to leave.'

'You would not like it so well in winter,' he said and pulled her close to kiss her. 'But we shall stay longer if you wish, my love.'

'Perhaps it is best that we leave as you had arranged,' Alayne replied with a blush. 'I think it might become uncomfortable for me to ride in a few months' time— and you will want your son to be born at home.'

'My son…' Ralph stared at her for a moment, seeming stunned, and then he smiled and reached out to grasp her hand. 'Is it so, my love? Are you carrying my child?'

'Yes, my lord,' she replied a little shyly, for the warmth in his eyes made her blush. 'I have thought for a while that it might be so, but I wanted to be sure before I told you. I have not seen my womanly flow for two months and I asked Brother Harding's advice. He said that I had all the signs of being with child.'

'You do not mind?' He looked at her anxiously. 'You are not afraid of what it entails?'

'No, Ralph, I am not afraid. I ask only that you will not allow Master Brendon to attend my couching.'

'You have my word,' Ralph said and looked thoughtful. 'I have spoken to Brother Harding and he has agreed to come to us at Banewulf for a while. I believe you like him, do you not?'

'I trust him,' Alayne said. 'He is a simple man, a kind man, and does not claim to know a cure for many ailments. He has worked in the dispensary at the Abbey here for many years, but he uses only the things that you and I know of and is humble in his opinions.'

'Then he shall come with us and advise your women if need be,' Ralph said. 'You must promise to take care of yourself now, Alayne. You should rest more.'

'And you must not make so much fuss over me,' she retorted. 'Brother Harding has told me that it is good for me to take exercise and do all the things I feel able to do.'

'Or has he fallen under your spell and told you what you wish to hear?' Ralph teased, his eyes tender with love. 'I know that you have all my men eating from your dainty hand, wife. It has come to pass that I hardly know whether they serve you or me.'

Alayne laughed as he teased her, for he knew well enough that her heart was his, as was her mind and body. They were together as often as his duties permitted, and she often rode out with him as he visited his people and inspected land and the tiny cottages in which most lived. The peoples of Thane and Banewulf were tied to their lord and owed him service, which was paid in so many days working for him on his land. He was their feudal lord and had complete authority over them, including many rights that were unfair and unjust. However, Ralph took his duties seriously and was a just lord, forfeiting many seigniorial rights that he believed were cruel and wrong.

'I expect obedience and loyalty from those who serve me,' he had told her as she remarked on how happy his people seemed. She had noticed the way the men and women sang as they worked, whether it was on their lord's land or their own strips, which they held from him and by his bounty. 'But what you expect you must also give, Alayne. My people know that I look after them in times of trouble, and if there is food in my barns and the winter is hard it will be shared with them.'

'You are loyal to each other,' she said, 'and that is the way it should be—in this as in marriage.'

Ralph's care of her made her happy, and she saw that same happiness reflected in the people around her. It had not been thus in her first husband's manor. There the peasants had been sullen and withdrawn, serving their lord reluctantly. It seemed to Alayne that her life was being lived within a circle of warmth and love, and there were times when she thought that it was too wonderful to continue.

It was high summer when they returned to Banewulf, stopping for three days in London to buy things that Alayne might need for the child, also medicines that Ralph had ordered for his stores. He had taken Brother Harding's advice and purchased various herbs and barks that could be used in medicines that might be beneficial to a woman in the advanced stages of child bearing.

Ralph had watched over Alayne's progress despite her warning that he must not fuss over her, fearing that he would see the signs of withdrawal and fear in her eyes. However, they were if anything brighter than before. She seemed to glow with health, her skin warmed to a clear gold by the sun as she roamed the meadows behind Thane, her laughter lifting his spirits whenever he felt the fear worm inside him—the fear that he might lose her. She was so beautiful, so enchanting, that he believed he would find life impossible without her now.

'Is it a sin to feel such happiness in a woman?' he had asked of Brother Harding once when they talked of an evening. He had come to like the gentle monk, who had been attending the people of Thane for many years, and to respect him.

'Ah, that is a question men have asked since time began and will continue to ask until it ends, my lord,' the brother said with a twinkle in his eyes. 'If you were me and given to God's service it could be considered so, but in your own case I think you may be forgiven. You are the lady's husband and she is both beautiful and pure of heart. There are many that would change places with you, Sir Ralph.'

Ralph smiled—he knew that the monk had a certain fondness for Alayne, though he was not the kind who would seek more of her. Gentle, dedicated to the care of the sick, and to God, Brother Harding was one of the few men Ralph would trust, and he had more than one reason for asking him to return to Banewulf with them.

Alayne was not privy to all her husband's thoughts in this matter, though she was aware of his care for her, the loving watch he kept over her, and it warmed her. She was happy to return to her home, for the months away had helped her to forget her fear of Master Brendon, and she had begun to think it mostly imagination on her part.

She knew nothing of the interview that took place between Master Brendon and Ralph on their return, nor that the arrival of Brother Harding, who, despite his gentle manner and soft voice, was underneath a man of iron, had aroused even more bitterness in the heart of her enemy.

Watching the way the monk smiled at Alayne and the readiness of her laughter at his often witty comments, the resentment festered deep in Master Brendon's heart, waiting to boil over.

It was well that Alayne was cocooned in her happiness and did not notice the evil looks and smouldering glances that came her way. As the weeks passed, she began to think more and more of the child growing within her. Her thoughts were pleasant and she smiled all the time, greeting her people as she walked about the manor, accepting their good wishes and the small gifts they brought her.

Everyone was touched by the happiness that seemed to shine out of her, for it was like a glow that warmed them, letting them share in her magical joy. She was beautiful, young and enchanting, and most of the men who served Ralph would have given their lives for her.

Alayne and Mistress Grey spent many pleasant hours together embroidering the tiny garments she would need.

'This shawl was your lord's,' Morna said, bringing her a package one cold day in December. The wool was as soft as gossamer and very fine. 'It was put away a long time ago and I do not think we listed it when we made our inventory.'

'No, I am sure we did not,' Alayne said, stroking the fine material thoughtfully with her fingertips. 'Thank you for thinking of it for me. I shall want a gown for my son's christening—you did not find anything suitable with the shawl?'

'There are other things in the chest,' Morna replied. 'It

is put away in one of the turret rooms and difficult to
find, that is why we missed it before. You must not tire
yourself by looking. I will have one of the men bring it
down another day. There is, after all, plenty of time, my
lady.' She smiled at her mistress, but did not say that
they could not yet be certain the child would be a boy
and Alayne would naturally want to save the gown for
her first son.

Alayne sighed after the older woman left her. She was
beginning to weary of sitting for long hours. Everyone
told her that she should rest more, but she preferred to
be busy. Discarding her needlework, she decided to go
in search of the christening gown herself. She knew exactly where to look, for Mistress Grey had told her where
the chests were stored.

She climbed the twisting stairs to the turret room, taking her time so that she would not tire herself and worry
her husband. She knew that he did worry about her and
suspected that it was because Berenice had been so ill
after the birth of her child. But Alayne did not feel ill
and she was not tired, only weary of being unable to do
all the things she enjoyed.

The room was very tiny, an odd shape, and at the top
of a short flight of stairs in the older part of the house,
where it adjoined the keep. The air was musty and it felt
cold, making Alayne shiver as she went in. There were
several old chests taking up most of the space inside and
the room looked as if it had been neglected for a long
time. She did not much care for the atmosphere here.
These chests had been forgotten because no one ever
bothered to come here.

She opened them one by one, discovering that they
contained mostly old clothes that must have belonged to
a long-ago lady of the manor and were partially destroyed

by the moths. It was useless to keep such things, Alayne thought. She would instruct the servants to throw these clothes away.

She found the gown she was looking for in the last chest. Carefully wrapped in silk and lavender to keep it fresh, it was a beautiful garment and had been embroidered with such skill that she knew it was the one she sought. Ralph's mother had been such an expert needlewoman. Her work was finer than anything Alayne could produce and she smiled as she took it out and held it up to the light. It had been preserved beautifully, unlike the clothes that had fallen prey to the moths. Yes, it had been worth looking for, she decided, and got to her feet to return to her chamber.

At the head of the stairs, her head seemed to spin and she clutched at the wall to steady herself. She had been taken with a feeling of faintness once or twice recently and she knew that it would pass in a moment if she simply waited.

After a few moments her head cleared and she walked down the first flight of stairs and along the passageway towards her own part of the house. The light had faded while she was in the turret room and the tapers had not yet been lit. When she reached the turning that led from the older part of the house it was quite dark and she paused for a moment to get her bearing. Suddenly she heard a sound, but even as she turned to see what was behind her, something hit her a glancing blow on the side of the head and she fell.

'My head...' Alayne muttered as her eyes flickered and she opened them to see someone bending over her with a lighted candle. 'Something hit my head.'

'You turned dizzy and fell, my lady,' Morna told her

and put the candle down on the stool beside the bed. 'It was fortunate that I had come in search of you or you might have lain there all night.'

'No, something hit me,' Alayne said as the mist began to clear from her head and she was able to focus again. 'It is true that I had been dizzy earlier, but I was feeling quite well when I fell. Something—or someone—hit me.'

'I found you at the bottom of the turret stairs,' Morna Grey said and frowned. 'Sir Ralph was anxious when you could not be found and then I remembered you asking about the christening gown.'

'I went to fetch it,' Alayne agreed. 'But it was not at the foot of those stairs that I fell. I had walked most of the way back here and was leaving the older part of the house when something struck me.'

Morna shook her head and looked anxious. 'Why would anyone do that, my lady? Why would they carry you back to the turret and leave you there?'

'To make it look like an accident,' Alayne replied and sat up. She touched the back of her head where it felt sore. 'Did my head bleed?'

'Yes. Brother Harding came to tend you, and he said it looked as if you might have hit your head as you fell.'

'Then it must have been made to look that way, for I did not fall.'

Her manner was so certain, so positive, that Morna was convinced and looked shocked. 'Who would do such a thing?'

'There is only one person who hates me,' Alayne said. 'I believe it must have been Master Brendon. Yet I cannot believe that he would dare to try and harm me.'

'If you had not been found…' Morna shuddered. 'I dare not think what might have happened, my lady. It is very cold in the older part of the house and you might have died had you lain there for long.'

'Yet it would have looked like an accident,' Alayne said. 'Even if I had not died, I might have lost my child…' She clutched at Morna's arm as the fear gripped her. 'Pray tell me it is not so! I have not lost my baby?'

'No, no, my lady, rest you easy. Sir Ralph was also anxious that no harm had come to the child,' Morna told her. 'Though his first concern was for you. But there was no bleeding and Brother Harding told us that he thought no real harm had been done.'

'Then we must thank God for it,' Alayne said and crossed herself.

'You should tell Sir Ralph if you were struck,' Morna said, looking over her shoulder as if she feared they might be overheard. 'If you were struck by Master Brendon…'

'I know that someone struck me,' Alayne said and frowned. 'But I cannot prove it was Master Brendon. If I told my lord that I believed it was the physician, he would be angry and dismiss the man—and that might be dangerous.' The physician could do much harm if he were to spread pernicious lies about her in the countryside.

'It is dangerous for you if he remains here. Next time he might kill you.'

'I do not believe he would dare,' Alayne said. 'Not while he stays here under my lord's jurisdiction. I think this was meant to look like an accident. He must have hoped I would not remember what happened. Or perhaps he simply meant it as a warning. I think we should keep this to ourselves for the time being, Morna.'

'If that is your wish,' Morna said, though she still looked doubtful.

'For the moment. I would prefer to have proof before making my accusation.' She smiled at her friend. 'Please, would you ask my lord to come to me now?'

Alayne closed her eyes as Morna left her. Her head was aching, but she could think and remember clearly. She had heard a sound just before she was struck, and there was a smell…a smell she knew well and disliked. She was almost certain that it was the physician who had struck her, but she could not be sure of his intention. Had he meant to kill her—or simply to frighten her?

'Alayne! You frightened us all, you foolish girl!'

Alayne opened her eyes and smiled as Ralph came to her. He sat on the edge of her bed, reaching for her hand and gripping it tightly.

'It was unfortunate,' she told him. 'Nothing more. You must not worry about me so much, my lord. I am quite strong.'

'But you could have died. You could have lost the child.'

'Yes…' Alayne was shocked by his expression, which revealed his devastation at the idea of losing his child. 'I am sorry, Ralph. I did not mean to fall and worry you.'

'Have I not warned you to take care?' His expression was stern and despite the love between them she was hurt by it. 'It was foolish of you to go alone to that part of the house. That stair was worn and broken; it was no wonder that you fell. Why must you always take risks, Alayne? It is not sensible in your condition.'

'Please forgive me. I believe no real harm has been done to the child or me.'

'That is not the point—' he began and then stopped as he saw her face. 'No, no, I am not angry, just anxious, Alayne. I do not want to lose you, my love.'

'Well, you have not,' she said and smiled, but there

was still a tiny pinpoint of hurt inside her. Was the child so important to him? Did it mean more than she did to him? He had refrained from her bed for some weeks now—did that mean he had begun to tire of her or was she merely fretful because of her condition?

'You will promise me to take care in future?' he said. 'I have just received word from the King, Alayne. I am bidden to court and that means I shall be away from you for some weeks.' He frowned as he looked down at her. 'I do not want to leave you at such a time, but I cannot refuse an order from Henry. I am truly sorry for it, Alayne. You must know that I would not leave if the choice were mine?'

'Yes, of course you must go,' she said, though it hurt her that he would go at such a time. 'I know that you cannot disobey the King. I shall be perfectly safe, my lord.'

'No more visits to the turret room?'

'No, I shall take the greatest care not to have another fall.'

'Do not look at me like that, Alayne. It is for your sake that I worry. Please believe me, I feel this parting as much as you.'

'Yes, my lord.' She lifted her face for his kiss, but that foolish hurt inside her would not be banished. 'I pray you return as soon as his Majesty will release you.'

'I shall be here for the child's birth,' Ralph said and stood up. He was frowning as he looked down at her. 'Promise me you will take care of yourself, my love— and do not hesitate to send for me if you are ill. I shall come at once if you need me.'

'I shall not be ill, Ralph. I have Brother Harding and my women to care for me. You must take care on your journey—and do not be anxious for me.'

'You know that you will be always in my thoughts,' he said and bent to kiss her forehead. 'I must leave at first light, Alayne. I shall not wake you, for Brother Harding says that you should be left to sleep—the best cure for an upset like this is rest, according to our good friend.'

'My thoughts go with you,' Alayne said and smiled as he left her, turning once more at the opening in the wall between their rooms to look at her.

'Close this in the morning,' he told her. 'It is better that no one else should be able to come this way, lest you are taken unawares. I ask you to take the greatest care while I am away, Alayne. Think carefully before you do anything and take no risks.'

'Yes, my lord, I shall remember,' she said. 'God be with you.'

'And with you, my love.'

Alayne closed her eyes when he had left her. It was very foolish of her to be upset by his scolding tone. She knew that he loved her and yet she could not help feeling hurt. He had every right to scold her for risking the life of his unborn child—except that she had done nothing wrong.

Perhaps she ought to have told him the truth. She knew that he would have instantly dismissed Master Brendon if he suspected that it was he who had struck Alayne from behind, and perhaps it would have been better if he had. Yet if the physician was an enemy, she felt it better to have him near rather than hiding in the shadows.

Brother Harding advised Alayne to stay in bed and rest for a few days after her fall. She decided it was best to accept his kindly concern for her, because like everyone else he believed that she had probably turned faint on the turret stair and was lucky to have escaped real harm.

Morna Grey visited her every day, spending some hours sitting with her, as did Louise and Bethel. They gossiped about the life of the manor and told her stories, and they helped her choose her silks for the delicate work she was embroidering for her child, but still the time passed slowly and she was relieved when she was at last permitted to get up again.

The first time she went out for a walk it was a cold frosty day and more than a week after Ralph had left for London, and she had wrapped up well against the bitter wind. It was as she stood looking across to the open downs, wishing that she might be riding there with Ralph, that she heard the sounds of horses arriving and looked round, her heart racing as she hoped it might be her husband returning. She had missed him so dreadfully and wanted the reassurance of knowing he was nearby.

A small party of horsemen was dismounting in the courtyard, and she felt a small knot of unease in her stomach as she saw that it was the Baron William Foulton. Why had Berenice's brother come to visit unannounced? She was sure Ralph had not been informed of his intention or he would have warned her of it.

Alayne went reluctantly to meet the baron. It was her duty as chatelaine to greet him and make him welcome in Ralph's absence, but she did not trust him.

'I fear you have come when my husband is from home,' she told the baron after she had bid him welcome. 'We keep early hours at Banewulf for the moment, sir, and can offer only poor entertainment.'

'I came to see you,' William Foulton replied, and his eyes seemed to hold a strange glitter that chilled her. 'I shall not stay long in this accursed place. Word reached me that you were with child and that you had recently had an accident...and I felt it my duty to come to you.'

'I do not understand you...' Alayne sensed a strange excitement in him that made her uneasy. 'If you were concerned for my health you need not have been. I am quite well, as you see, sir. A simple inquiry would have sufficed. You might have saved yourself the journey if that were all.'

'You do not understand,' William replied. He reached out to grip her arm, steering her to a quiet corner of the courtyard where he could be certain they were not over-heard. 'I do not want you to be murdered as my sister was, Lady Alayne. It was for this reason that I came to you while *he* was away...'

'Do you speak of my husband, sir?' Alayne shivered as the chill trickled down her spine. 'What can you mean?'

'I believe that Berenice was murdered, either by her husband or by someone employed by him on his behalf.'

'No! That is a lie,' Alayne cried, feeling the sickness swirl inside her. For a moment her head seemed to swim and she felt faint. 'How dare you say such wicked things of Sir Ralph?'

'Berenice wrote to me just before she died,' William told her, that strange light in his eyes once more. 'She told me that her husband did not love her and would be glad if she were dead. I had three letters from her that were written in fear of her life. She begged me to come to her before it was too late—but I was from home and did not receive them until she was dead.'

'No! She was ill...wandering in her mind.'

'That is what *he* would have you believe,' William muttered. 'He was tired of her and he made her so unhappy that she became ill—and in the end she drank whatever it was they gave her that ended her life.'

'What do you mean?'

'It was his physician that gave her the medicine she took,' William said. 'She said it made her feel worse and in the end it killed her. I believe it was poison and that Ralph ordered it to be given to her.'

'No, no, how can you say that?' Alayne cried, shocked by the bitterness that poured out of him. 'Ralph is a good, gentle knight. He has grieved terribly for Berenice and would never have done such a thing. You are mistaken if you believe that he knew aught of this.'

'He appears to be generous and kind,' William muttered. 'But beneath that smile there is a man of iron. He will not suffer fools lightly and my poor sister was too young and sweet for him. He was tired of her and wanted to be free so that he could marry again.'

She shivered, the coldness seeping into her. She could not, would not, believe that Ralph had killed his first wife, or that he might wish her dead—but the fact remained that someone had tried to harm her, Alayne. Could it be that Ralph had tired of her? She closed her eyes for a moment, fighting the doubts that came to torment her. But no, she would not let this man's poison turn her against the husband she loved. It was not Ralph who had struck her from behind. He loved her, even if he thought her foolish for falling down that turret stair. Besides, she knew he was not the evil monster this man claimed. He had not wanted Berenice dead.

She raised her head, looking at him proudly. 'If you believe that, tell me—why did he not marry for so many years?'

'He wanted a rich wife,' William said. 'And he was afraid that the truth of Berenice's death would come to light if he took another bride too soon. You were an heiress worthy of his pride, and that is why he married you. Yet even you mean nothing to him, for he is cold and unfeeling as my poor sister learned to her cost.'

'You speak falsely,' Alayne said. 'Your sister was ill and you mourn her death. Your mind has turned with grief. You should not spread such wicked lies. If Sir Ralph knew—'

'He would have me murdered too,' William said and smiled oddly. 'As if I would care for that now my sweet Berenice is dead. I have lived only to take my revenge on him and now it is within my grasp.'

'What do you mean?' Alayne was gripped with fear. 'Do you mean to harm him?'

'The sooner he is dead the better for you, lady,' William said. He turned as if to go, but she caught at his arm. 'I have done what I can to warn you. I go now to the King to present my evidence as witness before his Majesty. If I succeed, you may be safe—but take care what you do in the meantime, for your life is in danger.'

'You cannot go just like that,' Alayne cried, but he broke away from her. His wild look and manner shocked her, and the accusations he had made filled her with a strange dread. 'You have lied to me, sir. I know it! Your accusations are as base as they are false.'

'Be warned, you are in danger,' William said and the look he gave her as he grasped his horse's reins sent a thrill of fear through her. 'Trust no one, even those you think your friends.'

Alayne watched as the baron and his party cantered out of the courtyard, then turned towards the house. She was feeling sick and her head was swimming as she fought the faintness that swept over her.

Taking a deep breath, she paused to let the faintness

pass. It was nothing and had happened before. She had merely been shocked by William Foulton's bitter accusations against her husband. She would not let his wicked lies upset her. He had tried once before to destroy her happiness, leaving that letter for her on the day of her wedding, and now he had come to her when Ralph was away, spreading more lies that were meant to wound her.

'Are you faint, my lady?'

Brother Harding had approached her and was looking at her anxiously. She shook her head, forcing a smile as his eyes continued to assess her.

'It was nothing, good brother,' she said. 'A momentary faintness that soon passes. I shall be better in a moment.'

'It has happened before?' His eyes narrowed. 'Are you taking anything for it?'

'I take only the medicine that you made for me.'

'Perhaps it was not suitable,' he said. 'Send it back to me and I will give you something else that will make you feel better.'

Alayne stared at him for a moment, and the baron's words echoed in her mind. He had warned her to trust no one, saying that Berenice had died because of a medicine that was prescribed for her at Ralph's behest.

No, no, she would not let the baron's lies make her turn against all those she trusted. Ralph loved her. There was no reason why he should want to be rid of her—or of Berenice. She believed William Foulton was so eaten up by jealousy and hatred that his mind had been affected, and she would not listen to the ravings of such a man.

'I am sure it is not your medicine,' she told the monk and gave him one of her enchanting smiles. 'It is nothing very terrible—a little faintness, no more.'

'Yet you fell the other day, Lady Alayne.'

'No, I did not fall,' she said and raised her eyes to his. It seemed important that she should speak out, that he at least should know the truth. 'I was struck from behind and, while I lay senseless, carried to the foot of the stair so that it seemed I had fallen.'

'In God's name, who would do such a thing?' he asked and his gaze narrowed. 'Why have you said nothing of this before, my lady? Sir Ralph did not know this.'

'No, I did not want to worry him before he left,' Alayne said and bit her lip as she wondered if she had done right to speak even now. 'He was bidden to the King and might have been tempted to disobey if he had known. Besides, I may be mistaken—perhaps I did fall…'

'No, I do not think you are mistaken,' the monk said. 'You must be very careful, my lady. I shall do what I can to protect you, but with my lord away…'

'I shall not go anywhere alone,' Alayne replied. 'But I cannot think my life is in danger, for he might have killed me then had he so wished.'

'Do you suspect someone, my lady?'

Alayne hesitated, then shook her head. 'I have no proof and will make no accusations without it, sir.'

'You are wise to keep a still tongue, but I think I have no need to warn you of a certain person within this house.'

Alayne stared at him, the coldness seeping into her flesh, making her shiver. 'What do you mean?'

'I would say only that you should be careful what medicines you take, my lady. My own are simple and cannot hurt you but…'

'You think that…' Alayne was pale as she saw the expression in the monk's eyes. 'I take only what you give me.'

'In future I shall give you only enough for each day,' he replied. 'For even that might be tampered with, sweet lady. I do not like this faintness. It was such faintness that began the Lady Berenice's illness, I am told.'

Alayne closed her eyes for a moment. Was it possible that William Foulton had not been lying—that his sister had been poisoned by the medicine she was taking?

'I shall take my medicine from your own hand and no other,' she told Brother Harding. 'And I thank you for your care of me. Now I shall return to my chamber and rest for a while.'

Alayne's mind was whirling in confusion as she made her way slowly back to her own rooms. Was it possible that Berenice had been in fear of her life? Was that why she had been afraid to leave her chamber after the birth of her child—and whom did she fear?

Was it her husband, as William Foulton believed—or had there been someone else? A jealous, evil man who had wanted her dead, perhaps? Or was the truth more simple than that? Could it be that the medicines prescribed for Berenice by Master Brendon had made her ill and thereby caused her death?

Alayne was suddenly sure that Master Brendon had played some part in the death of Ralph's first wife, but how could she find proof? Ralph had taken the coffer containing Berenice's letters and said there was nothing secret in them.

Yet it had been hidden away and there must have been a reason for that, thought Alayne, as she went back into the house. Was it possible that Ralph had missed something?

Oh, where was he? And why had she heard nothing from him? She had looked for a letter every day since he left, but nothing had come. Was he still angry with her? Was that the reason he had not written to her?

Chapter Twelve

Ralph had left Banewulf with mixed feelings. The King's message had seemed odd, couched as it was in formal terms, its very nature a command rather than a request for his company. Had it been otherwise, he would not have thought of leaving Alayne at such a time, when she was so near to the birth of their child.

He was puzzled by the King's sudden command and had made all haste to him in London, wondering what could have brought about this urgent summons. Feeling weary and travel-stained, his hose stiff with the mud of the roads, Ralph and his small party dismounted in the courtyard. Suddenly, the King's personal guards surrounded him, the officer in charge announcing that he was under arrest.

'Under arrest?' Ralph stared at the officer in bewilderment. 'I do not understand. Pray tell me of what I am accused?'

'You are charged with the murder of your late wife, the lady Berenice,' the guard replied, his gaze studiously avoiding Ralph's as if he found his duty unpleasant.

'Nonsense!' Ralph replied angrily. 'By whose word am I charged?'

'It is not for me to say, sir,' the guard replied. 'I am commanded by the King to arrest you and it is my duty to do as he orders.'

'Pray conduct me to his Majesty at once!'

'The King will see you when he is ready.' The officer turned to his men and barked an order: 'Take him to the chamber that has been prepared for him. He is to remain there and speak to no one until he is sent for.'

Ralph knew it was useless to struggle. His men were looking anxious, ready to try to fight their way out of this trap, but he shook his head at them.

'If it is the King's command, then I must submit, for I will not raise my hand against his Majesty,' he said. 'But one of you must ride back to Banewulf and let them know what has happened here.' He glanced at the captain of the guard. 'It is permitted that my man leaves to inform my steward of what has occurred?'

'His Majesty said that no one was to leave. Forgive me, sir, but your men are also under arrest.'

Ralph nodded, knowing that there was little he could do unless he would make himself a traitor to the king he served.

'Then we shall obey,' he said. 'I must pray that Henry will listen to my side of the story.'

'You will be granted a hearing,' the guard told him. 'His Majesty awaits the coming of Baron Foulton and then your case will be heard.'

Ralph frowned and inclined his head, making no further reply. He had known for some time that William hated him, blaming him for Berenice's death. And he did bear some part of the blame for her death, for he believed that his neglect had caused her to be unhappy. Had William accused him earlier, he might not have tried to defend himself against the charge, but now he had so much to live for.

A nerve flicked in his throat as he realised why William Foulton had chosen this time to strike against him. His love for his sister had been unnaturally fond and his grief had turned his mind. He knew that Ralph had found happiness with another woman, and was determined to destroy that if he could.

Yet Henry was just and would surely listen to both arguments. Ralph had no proof that he was innocent, but William Foulton could have none that he was guilty. There was but one way that Ralph might prove his innocence according to the laws of chivalry—and that was a trial by combat.

William was not his equal in such a trial of strength, of course, and it would be his right to choose a champion to fight in his stead—and it would be a fight to the death. Yet who would be willing to take up such a challenge? It could only be someone who hated him…

Why did not Ralph write to her? Alayne paced the floor of her chamber in agitation. Three weeks had passed since he left for London and she had heard nothing of him. Even Master Grey was concerned that no letter had come from his lord in all this time.

'It is not like Sir Ralph not to send word,' Master Grey told his daughter. 'I do not like this, Morna. He would not stay away at such a time unless he was forced.'

'Pray say nothing of your fear to my lady,' his daughter begged, 'she is anxious enough as it is.'

Alayne's anxiety was not only for her husband. She had noticed the physician staring at her in an odd way of late and his brooding presence made her nervous. Perhaps it was because Ralph was absent, but he seemed more menacing. Sometimes the brooding expression in his eyes was so intense that it brought shivers to her spine. Supposing Ralph did not return before she gave birth to the child? She would be vulnerable and—but she would not let herself be afraid.

Alayne had become more and more convinced in her own mind that Master Brendon had in some way caused Berenice's illness, and that she had known it—had perhaps meant to expose him. Perhaps he had killed her because he feared what she might say.

Was she wandering in her mind? Alayne almost doubted her own sanity, for her thoughts seemed wild and impossible, yet she felt that she was right—but how could she prove it?

There must be proof of Master Brendon's guilt in the Lady Berenice's coffer. She had not liked to look, thinking it best to wait for Ralph's return, because he had been so angry with her the first time—but supposing he returned too late? If she was right, the physician had somehow got away with one murder—what could prevent him from doing it again?

Perhaps she could find the key and open the coffer… Once again her mind shied away from the thought, because she feared Ralph's anger and she ought not to pry into another lady's privacy. But if there was some clue…something that would tell them why Berenice had died…it was surely her duty to find it.

Alayne lifted her head, a look of determination in her eyes as she decided that she could delay no longer. If she could give Ralph proof of the physician's guilt on his return, he could send Master Brendon away with just cause.

'Ah, there you are, my lady,' Morna Grey said, coming in as she was about to open the secret panel that led into

Ralph's bedchamber. 'You look tired, mistress. You should try to sleep. My lord bid me make sure you took enough rest while he was gone. You should not do too much or the child may come too soon.'

'I thank you for your care of me,' Alayne said, impatient for her to be gone. 'It is good to know that I have a friend in you, Morna. Leave me now and I shall try to sleep for a while.'

After the other woman had gone, Alayne went back to the wall and sought out the lever to open the panel, her heart beating faster than normal, her palms damp with sweat. She felt guilt at what she was about to do, but was determined to put an end to the worry that had hung over her like a brooding shadow of late.

'I do so wish you were here, Ralph,' she murmured. 'If only I could tell you what I fear…'

Her pulses were racing with a mixture of guilt and anticipation as she entered Ralph's bedchamber. He had been so angry with her for taking Berenice's coffer the first time. If he knew what she was doing now he would think it shameful, and yet she could not rest easily in her mind. The fear that Master Brendon would harm her if he could had taken root in her mind and would not be dismissed.

The small coffer that Alayne had discovered in Lady Berenice's chamber was standing in a recess in the thick stone wall and other things had been carelessly placed in front of it, almost as though Ralph had wanted to put it out of his sight. Alayne's hands trembled as she picked it up and carried it to the bed. She had no right to pry into the Lady Berenice's things, but if she did not try to find proof of the physician's treachery she would be haunted by her fears.

She tried the top of the domed coffer and discovered

that it opened easily. The lock had been forced, which seemed unfortunate, but Ralph had clearly been determined to discover the contents. Inside were several letters, which Alayne removed. Ralph had clearly read them, so they were unlikely to tell her anything. What she was looking for was something hidden. She held the coffer up and gave it a little shake. It rattled and yet appeared to be empty. It was as she had suspected—there was a secret compartment, just as she had in her own jewel coffer. Ralph had not thought to look further than the letters or he might have discovered what was hidden there.

She began to feel around the inside of the wooden box, her fingers encountering what seemed merely a slight bump in the smooth surface. A little thrill went through her as she hesitated, then took a deep breath and pressed hard. Again as expected, a tiny compartment sprang out at the bottom. It was just such a drawer as she had found in the coffer that she had been given as a child. She trembled as she took out what had been hidden, discovering that there was a tiny glass vial containing a dark liquid, also a letter addressed to William Foulton.

Now that she had found Berenice's secrets, Alayne hesitated uncertainly. Her heart was thumping and her mouth felt dry with fear. Did she have the right to read that letter? Perhaps she ought to wait and tell Ralph of her suspicions when he returned? Yet if Brendon was truly evil, to delay could prove dangerous.

Alayne closed the secret compartment and replaced the coffer in the alcove before she returned to her own chamber. She closed the secret panel, her mind wrestling with the problem of what to do about her discovery. Ralph might be angry with her for prying, but she needed to know the truth.

She must not falter now! Opening the vial, she sniffed at its contents. The smell was strong and unpleasant, but not one she recognised, so she replaced the stopper carefully. Taking a deep breath, she broke the seal of the letter and began to read what Berenice had written.

It was addressed to, 'My dearest brother,' and went on:

I have told you before that Ralph no longer loves me, William. Now I have cause to believe that he wishes me dead. He suspects that the child is not his, though I have sworn my innocence. I have not committed adultery, but he has turned from me. Today his physician came to me again with another vile potion he says I must take if I am to be well. I promised I would, but I did not take it. Later I gave a little to one of the yard cats in a piece of meat. My maid told me that it was sick and died horribly soon after. William, I beg you to come to me for I fear for my life.

The letter fluttered from Alayne's fingers. She shivered as the horror seized her mind. The shadows seemed to close in about Alayne and she felt sickness in her throat. In her own words Berenice had seemed to accuse her husband of wanting her to die. She had obviously been in fear—and soon after this letter was written she had died, seemingly by her own hand. But supposing she had died for a very different reason? No, it could not be! For a moment the room seemed to spin about Alayne and she thought that she would faint—but she must not give way. She must think!

If Berenice had sent other letters of a similar nature to her brother, it was no wonder that he believed Ralph guilty of her murder. Yet as Alayne forced herself to reread the words Berenice had written, it seemed clear that no thought of murder had been in her mind until she was given this last potion. Before that she had merely accused her husband of not loving her, of being unkind.

Alayne paced the room in agitation, her thoughts whirling in horror and confusion. To many this letter would seem to be proof of Ralph's guilt. He did not love his wife and he suspected her of having betrayed him with his friend Christian. It followed that he might want to be rid of Berenice. Yet he believed that Berenice had taken something to end her life because he had made her unhappy, and because of that he was ridden with guilt. That was surely not the behaviour of a guilty man—was it?

No, no, it could not be!

Alayne dismissed the suspicion as unworthy almost at once. Ralph might be impatient sometimes, even harsh, but he was not a murderer. Yet the questions remained unanswered, like creeping shadows of evil in her mind, bearing down on her so that she found it difficult to breathe.

Had Berenice taken the potion herself? Alayne questioned. From the terms of her letter, it was clear that Berenice had been suspicious of the physician—had deliberately not taken the medicine he had given her.

Why had she not taken it? Only one answer came to mind. It must surely mean that Berenice believed other potions he had given her had made her ill—were perhaps the cause of her sickness in the weeks after her child's birth.

Supposing someone had forced Berenice to swallow the poison that had killed her? But why would anyone do a thing like that? Who would have the necessary knowledge? The finger of suspicion seemed to point at Master Brendon—but why should he want to kill his master's wife? Alayne was puzzled. She paced about her chamber in agitation, worrying at the problem like a terrier at a bone. Surely the physician had nothing to gain from Berenice's death, unless…

'May God forgive him!'

Alayne cried out as the truth came to her in a blinding flash. It was so simple after all. Master Brendon was not what he claimed to be. His cures had not helped the men who had fallen sick of that fever—indeed, they had seemed to make them worse, as Lady Berenice had discovered to her cost. The potions he had made for her had prolonged her sickness, making her ill. He had made them too strong! Alayne knew from her Arab friend that it was important to use the right measure of certain ingredients, for they could kill as easily as they cured if wrongly used. Lady Berenice had given some of her potion to a cat and it had died. Alayne had wondered why the physician should want his master's wife to die, but now she saw it clearly.

'Of course!' she cried as paced the floor. 'He made a mistake because he did not know what he was doing—he is a charlatan!'

Master Brendon had not intended the lady to die—at least, not at first, not until she told him that she believed his potions were making her ill. When she discovered the effect the latest one had on the cat and threatened to tell her husband, he had known he would be discovered. He would have been disgraced, punished, perhaps imprisoned for his crimes. Who could tell how many had died because of his imposture?

'He must have been afraid of what would happen to him if Ralph discovered he had been lying to him, cheating him,' Alayne murmured as she unravelled the puzzle in her mind. 'He holds his position here under false pretences.'

Why had she not guessed it sooner? She knew little of the art of medicine, but her simple cures had helped the men and women who were struck down with fever—Master Brendon's patients had died. No one would have thought it unusual if Alayne had not been able to save those she tended. The physician had been able to get away with his wickedness for years because so many died of their illnesses that no one had thought to blame the physician.

'It all fits…' Alayne said to herself and stopped her pacing. 'Now I know why he hates me so. He killed Berenice to save himself and now he thinks I shall unmask him!'

A shiver ran through Alayne as in her mind she saw what must have happened that fateful day. Ralph had told Berenice she must go out more so she had gone for a long walk, away from the house and the people who might have protected her. She went alone because she wanted to think…because she was afraid that her husband might have ordered the physician to poison her.

Master Brendon had seen her go. He had followed her and when they were far enough away that he could be certain of not being seen, he had caught hold of her and forced her to swallow something similar to the potion that had killed the cat. Perhaps they had quarrelled first. She might have threatened to expose him.

He must have feared that he would be seized and punished, but Ralph had taken the blame for his wife's death, accepting that she had killed herself because he had made her unhappy. Master Brendon could not have expected to be so fortunate, and must have lived ever since in a state of uneasy anticipation that his guilt might one day be discovered.

He was an impostor! He clearly knew enough to appear knowledgeable, but in fact he was a cheat and a liar, pretending to have studied at the medical schools of Rome and Verona.

Certain that she had solved the mystery, Alayne hid the vial and letter in her own coffer. She had never trusted Master Brendon and she knew that he hated her. She had not been sure why, but now she believed she had the answer. He was afraid that she had some small knowledge of medicine and would unmask him as a charlatan. But it had not occurred to her to doubt his position before this. She had merely thought him to be a creature of his profession, for others of his ilk often failed to save their patients. Indeed, more died of their ailments than recovered, and such things were accepted as the will of God.

But now she knew him for what he was, she could not allow such a man to continue to treat their people. As soon as Ralph returned she would speak to him, tell him what she discovered, and what she believed. She prayed he would come soon. Her time was near now and she would rather Master Brendon was sent away before she was brought to bed of her child.

Alayne decided she would go in search of Brother Harding and confide her suspicions in him. He would advise her what to do for the best, whether or not she should ask Master Grey to dismiss the physician immediately, but even as she started towards the door she felt the pain strike at her belly and clutched herself. Her child was coming!

'No...' she whispered, fear sweeping over her as she swayed. 'It is too soon. Please, not yet...'

Alayne bent double as the pain ripped through her. It hurt so much that she did not know how she could bear it. She staggered towards the door, wrenching it open and calling for help.

'My lady…' Morna Grey came running as she saw her. 'I was on my way to tell you that— Oh, my lady, is the child coming?'

'Help me,' Alayne gasped. 'Help me, Morna. I am in such pain.'

'You will always do too much,' Morna scolded, putting an arm about her as she helped her towards the bed. 'But I shall not scold. Mayhap the child is ready to come and we miscalculated the time of its birth.'

Alayne shook her head. She was certain in her own mind when her child had been conceived and she knew it was almost three weeks too early. It was the shock of discovering the truth about Master Brendon's evil deeds that had brought her pains on. She should have waited until Ralph came home, she thought tearfully. It was her fault. He would be so upset if she lost the child and he might not love her anymore.

'It is my fault,' she whispered to Morna. 'If my child dies…'

'Nonsense!' Morna scolded. 'The child will not die and nor shall you, my lady. It is not the first time a babe has come early and sometimes it is better that way. You have grown large these past weeks and to carry full term might have proved too much for you.'

Alayne tried to smile at her, but another pain ripped through her and she almost collapsed on to the bed. She smothered her cry of agony as she gazed up at Morna.

'We must send word to my husband, Morna. He must know the child is on its way.'

'He shall know,' Morna replied and frowned. 'As soon

as he returns.' In her opinion it was better that Sir Ralph could not come to his wife at this time. Men were not welcome in the birthing chamber. She turned as Bethel came into the room. 'Go down and tell my father that Lady Alayne is in labour, Bethel. And tell the servants that I shall need hot water and linen brought here by and by.'

Turning back to Alayne, she bent over her and smoothed her forehead gently as she said, 'Try not to fight the pain, my lady. I shall help you and it is not the first child I have seen into the world. You must push when the pains come faster and take deep breaths to ease yourself—and scream if it helps.'

Alayne gripped her hands as the pain came again. She did not scream that time, but later, as the night wore on and still the child did not come, she could no longer hold back her screams of agony.

'I must go to her,' Ralph said as he heard the terrible scream from Alayne's chamber. Having arrived to the sound of his wife's screaming, he was desperate to see her. He had been gripped by a premonition as he made his way home, afraid that something terrible might have befallen his wife, and now he was filled with fear for her. 'I must be with her in her ordeal.'

'No, my lord.' His steward laid a restraining hand on his arm. 'It is not fitting. My daughter and her other women are with her. They will do all they can for her. You would only be in the way.'

'But if she dies…' Ralph was torn by his fear and grief. 'I cannot bear to lose her…'

He glanced up as someone came into the ante-chamber in which they sat and, seeing that it was Brother Harding, he jumped to his feet.

'What news, sir?'

'She grows weaker by the hour, my lord,' the monk said with a frown. 'I believe that I must help her to give birth, but that means the child may be damaged. It is your choice, Sir Ralph—risk damage to the child or allow your wife's agony to go on.'

'Then my wife must come first—' Ralph began, to be rudely interrupted by an intervention from Master Brendon, who had followed the monk into the small chamber.

'If she had taken the potions I made for her, this would not have happened,' he muttered, glaring jealously at the monk. 'If he uses the instruments on your child, its skull will be crushed, my lord. Let me give the Lady Alayne something and she may give birth without the need for such instruments.'

Ralph stared at him uncertainly. He was not sure that he trusted Master Brendon and Alayne had begged him not to let the physician near her. Yet he would save both his child and his wife if it were possible.

'I think—' he began, then another terrible scream rent the air. He glanced upward in the direction of the sound and moved towards the door that would take him to the stair leading to her chamber. 'Both of you—come with me. Alayne must be saved at all costs…'

'My lord…' the steward protested, but Ralph was not to be stopped.

He ran up the stairs, followed by both Brother Harding and Master Brendon. Pray God that it was not too late to save Alayne! But even as he reached the door of her chamber it was thrown wide and Bethel appeared in the opening, tears streaming down her face.

'My wife…' Ralph's heart caught with fear as he saw her tears. 'Is she…?' He could hardly go on for the crushing sensation in his chest. How could he bear it if she died?

'Lady Alayne has suffered greatly, but she is alive and will recover,' Bethel told him with a smile and now he saw that her tears were those of joy. 'And you have a fine son, my lord. He is a little small, but he has all his fingers and toes and he is breathing.' As if to prove her point, there was a lusty cry from the bedchamber. 'There—he makes himself known.'

'I would see him,' Ralph said. 'And my wife…'

Morna Grey came to the door, barring his passage. 'My lady is too weak to see you now, sir,' she told him. 'Bethel will bring your son to you in a little. I pray you let my mistress rest. It would disturb her too much to see you, for she needs to sleep and recover from her ordeal.'

'Then I shall see her later,' Ralph said and suddenly he was smiling. Alayne had come through her ordeal, and he must curb his impatience for her sake. 'Tell her that I love her and thank her for the gift of my son.'

He turned away to be greeted by the congratulations of his steward and Brother Harding. In his delight at the news, he did not notice the scowl on Master Brendon's face as he slunk off, unnoticed and ignored.

'Do you feel better, my lady?' Bethel asked as Alayne smiled a little wearily at her. 'You have slept for some hours. I did not want to wake you, but the child is hungry. The wetnurse has been sent for, but she has not yet arrived.'

'I shall nurse my child myself,' Alayne replied and pushed herself up against the pillows to receive the babe in her arms. She glanced down at the child's head and saw the dark fluff of hair, stroking it tenderly with her fingertips as she put him to her breast. 'I have a son,' she murmured, more to herself than the serving girl. 'His father will be pleased, I think.'

'Sir Ralph is delighted with his son,' Bethel told her. 'I took the child to show him while you slept. He has ordered a feast for the people this evening and food is to be sent to the village in celebration of the birth.'

'My husband has ordered a celebration?' Alayne stared at her. 'When did he return to Banewulf?'

'Yesterday even',' Bethel replied. 'An hour or so after you began your labour.'

He had been here when she was in such terrible pain, but he had not come to see her.

Alayne felt the hurt sear her and closed her eyes, fighting the tears that threatened to overwhelm her. Ralph was delighted with his son, but he had not come to her. That must mean he did not truly care for her.

'Are you ill, my lady?' Bethel asked as she saw a tear slide down Alayne's pale cheek. 'Should I fetch Mistress Grey to you?'

'No, I am merely tired,' Alayne replied. She kissed the top of her child's head as he suckled at her breast. She must not let this hurt her or destroy her delight in the babe. It was natural that a man would love his son—but she wished that he had spared a moment for her, and her heart ached with the knowledge that he had not bothered.

After a while the child slept and Bethel took him from her, laying him in his cot. Alayne lay back against her pillows, closing her eyes once more. She was still tired after her ordeal, but she longed for Ralph to come to her. Yet she was too proud to ask. If he loved her as she had believed, then he would have come before this.

'Leave me now, Bethel,' she told the girl. 'I would rest a little. You may come to me in an hour or so.'

'Yes, my lady.'

Bethel bobbed a curtsy and left her to sleep. As she was going down the stairs she met her master coming up. He looked at her eagerly.

'Is your lady awake at last, Bethel?'

'She was for a while, my lord. She fed the babe, but then she said she was tired and bid me leave her to sleep for an hour or so.'

'Is she unwell?' Ralph asked, suddenly anxious. He took hold of the wench's arm, his fingers biting into her flesh. 'Are you hiding something from me?'

'No, my lord. The Lady Alayne is merely weary. Your son caused her much pain.'

Ralph's grip intensified, but when she winced he let her go and apologised. 'Did your mistress not ask for me?'

'She said that you would be pleased with your son, but when I told her that you had ordered feasting she seemed surprised…' Bethel faltered as he frowned at her. 'I think she was just too weary to care, my lord.'

'Then I must let her rest a little longer,' Ralph said and turned away to his own apartments.

His expression was harsh as he went into his bedchamber. Alayne had seemed to withdraw from him a little in the last weeks of her confinement and now she was too weary to see him. He had a terrible fear that she was turning against him as Berenice had after the birth of their son. What would she think when she knew that he had been accused of murdering his first wife, that he had been forced to kill a man to prove his innocence?

Ralph felt a bitter taste in his mouth as he remembered the moment when he had taken the life of Baron Foulton's champion, the feeling of self-revulsion that had swept over him as he was acclaimed the victor by all those who watched. He had been given no choice, but to take life wantonly caused him nothing but pain. Perhaps he was being punished for his sins, perhaps Alayne had turned from him because he did not match her picture of a perfect knight.

Pray God that he was not going to lose Alayne…

Chapter Thirteen

It was late in the evening when Alayne stirred and, opening her eyes, found Ralph staring down at her. His expression was remote, almost withdrawn, and she felt the familiar ache in her breast begin again. He had come to see her, but now there seemed to be a barrier between them.

She pushed herself up against the pillows and smiled at him. She would not show her hurt, for perhaps she was making too much of his tardiness in visiting her, being too sensitive because of her weakness.

'Are you rested now, my lady?' Ralph asked in a polite tone. The angles of his lean face seemed carved in stone, his eyes flinty as they gazed at her unwaveringly. It seemed that all the love and laughter between them had never been and they were back at the beginning. Why was he angry with her? 'They told me you were very tired and I did not want to disturb you. Forgive me if I woke you.'

'You did not wake me,' she said and held out her hand to him. 'I was weary after my ordeal, but I am rested now. You have seen your son. What shall we call him?'

'Whatever pleases you, Alayne.' A little pulse flicked

in his cheek, betraying the emotion he was holding inside.

'I thought we might call him Ralph after you?'

'Why not Alain after his mother?' The child should not bear the name of so tainted a knight.

'No, not after me, for he would be teased by his friends,' she said. 'What was your father's name, Ralph?'

'Sir Guy de Banewulf.'

'Yes, I like that,' she said. 'We shall call our son Guy, if it pleases you, my lord.'

'I would please you, Alayne. We shall call him Guy if you wish it, as his second name, but he shall also be named for his mother. Alain de Banewulf. I think he will be proud to bear such a name, my love.'

She saw that he was set on it and smiled. 'Then it is settled,' she said. 'Did your business with the King go well?'

'You are not well enough to trouble yourself about such matters.'

'I pray you tell me, my lord. I have been anxious. I felt that you were in some trouble… I wondered if some ill had befallen you?'

'You were aware of it?' Ralph frowned and sat on the edge of the bed. 'I was called to court to account for Berenice's death,' he said, his eyes never leaving her face. 'Her brother accused me of murder, though he had no proof other than a few letters from Berenice accusing me of unkindness to her. But I could offer no proof that his accusations were lies. His Majesty decided that it should be settled by a trial of arms…'

'Of arms!' Alayne stared at him, her heart catching in her throat. 'You had to fight to prove your innocence?' He nodded, his expression severe. 'But who did you fight? Baron Foulton could never hope to beat you in such a trial.'

'No,' Ralph replied, his mouth thinning to a hard line as he struggled to keep a hold on his emotions. 'To make the contest fair, he was allowed to call upon a champion.'

'But who…?' Alayne felt a tingle at the base of her spine. 'He came here, you know, to warn me that I might be in danger, and to tell me that he was going to accuse you of his sister's murder.'

'I know. He told me after I defeated his champion. He was angry that he had lost and that I was held innocent. So furious that he tried to stab me in the back when I turned away. He was arrested by Henry's guards and dragged off screaming his hatred. He will languish in the King's dungeons until Henry sees fit to release him.'

'The poor man,' Alayne said. 'I do not think he knew what he did, my lord. His love and grief had turned him half-mad.'

It was the same as had happened at the court of Queen Eleanor with de Bracey, and yet it was not the same, for William had been out of his mind with grief, while de Bracey had known exactly what he intended.

'Yes, you are right,' Ralph said. 'I bear him no malice, Alayne, and I asked Henry for clemency for him, but it was not granted. His Majesty was angry that he had not accepted the verdict of his court.'

'You defeated his champion—but you have not told me…' Her eyes widened as she saw something in his eyes and instinct warned her of what he would say. Now it had all become very clear. 'Was it Renaldo de Bracey? Marguerite told me he was in England. Yes, of course it must have been. He hated you as much as William Foulton and the two of them plotted to destroy you…that is why Berenice's brother chose this moment to move against you. Only someone who hated you would accept such a challenge. Did they plan it between them—that, if de Bracey failed, William would stab you in the back?'

Ralph shook his head, but Alayne sensed that it was in his mind.

'Whatever was said between them, de Bracey will plot no more,' Ralph said and his eyes narrowed to icy slits. 'It was a fight to the death, Alayne. I had no choice. I had to kill or be killed—to die tainted with the sin of murder upon me.'

'The fight was not of your making,' Alayne told him and reached out to take his hand. Now she understood that brooding expression in his face. He was not angry with her, but torn by guilt at what had been forced upon him. His strong fingers curled about hers in a grip that was almost painful. 'You should not blame yourself either for his death or Baron Foulton's imprisonment. These things were not of your making.'

'You do not turn from me in disgust?'

'How could I? I know what this has cost you, my lord. Yet you have done only what was demanded of you, following the custom. Such things are cruel, but cannot be helped. You were innocent of that foul crime and your innocence is proved beyond doubt.'

'It is past and must be forgotten,' Ralph said, and carrying her hand to his lips he kissed it. The ice had gone from his eyes now as he gazed down at her, driven away by the warmth of love. 'I am only distressed that I was not here with you. What happened to make you give birth early, Alayne? Did you have another fall?'

'No, I did not fall,' she replied and took a deep breath. Now was surely the time for what must be said between them. 'But I do have something important to tell you—'

She was interrupted as the door of her chamber opened

and Morna came in, carrying the child, who was crying lustily.

'Oh, forgive me, my lord,' Morna said as she saw Ralph sitting on the bed. 'But it is time for the babe's feed.'

'Then I shall leave you to your task, my love,' Ralph said and smiled as he bent to place a kiss on Alayne's brow. 'Nothing must come before the needs of that young fellow.'

He was laughing as he said it and Alayne smiled as she took the child and held it to her breast. It was natural that Ralph should think his son all important. Sons were what a man needed to inherit his estate and keep his house strong, and now he had two of them, her own, and Stefan by his first wife. She knew that her husband had a deep love for Stefan, and only his strong sense of duty had forced him to send him away for his training as a future knight. Yes, both his sons were very important to Ralph, but that did not mean he did not care for her a little. She had been foolish to let his neglect hurt her. Men had other duties and women could not expect too much of their time.

She was feeling more content as she nursed her son, enjoying the feel of his small fist against her as he sucked greedily. She had been lucky, for there was nothing feeble about him, and it might have been otherwise. So many children did not live beyond their first few months and she had feared her son might be a weakling for having been born too soon.

Morna was fussing about the room, tidying it and setting it to rights. Alayne had been foolish to let herself be hurt by Ralph's seeming neglect. It was clear that he still cared for her, even if not as much as she had once thought.

* * *

Three weeks passed before they would allow Alayne to leave her bed, even though she declared herself well long before that time. She was cosseted and fussed over, and Ralph came to see her twice a day, sitting with her for a little while in the mornings and the evenings. He brought her gifts for herself and for the child, but seemed to keep a distance between them, which Alayne found disturbing. She had thought they understood each other, but something seemed still to trouble him. Surely he could not still be brooding about what had happened in London?

She wanted to tell him about her discovery, but as the days passed and he seemed almost a stranger to her, she found it more and more difficult. She was safe enough in her chamber, for the physician was not allowed to visit her, and Brother Harding came only once to make certain that she was recovering well.

Not until she had been blessed by the priest and finally allowed to leave her chamber was she considered cleansed and ready to be in company again. It was a beautiful morning in January, the sun shining despite an overnight frost on the ground when Alayne was at last able to venture out into the air again.

It was such a delight and a pleasure to be outside once more, almost a month after she had been brought to bed of her child. She had passed the nursing of her babe to a woman from the village, who had weaned her own child and was still full of rich milk. Alayne's own milk had not proved enough for her son, and though she still suckled him occasionally he was now in the hands of his nurse and seemed to be thriving.

Lost in her thoughts, Alayne was unaware that she was being watched. It was only when someone called out a greeting to her that she stopped and turned to glance back.

'Robert,' she cried gladly as she saw the young man walking swiftly towards her. 'How good it is to see you again.' She held out both her hands to him. 'When did you arrive and what brought you to Banewulf?'

'I came to see Sir Ralph and tell him that I have won my spurs,' Robert replied, a look of pride in his eyes as he grasped her hands. 'The King has sent me to the west, where I am to hold a castle for him on the border with Wales. The Welshmen are troublesome creatures and we must always be on our guard against them. But his Majesty gave me his permission to stop here and visit with you a few days, my lady.' His smile caressed her. 'They tell me you have a fine son?'

'Yes, indeed,' she said. 'He was born a little early, but he thrives and we thank God for him.'

'And for your recovery,' Sir Robert said, looking at her with such open adoration that she blushed to see it. 'You are even more beautiful than before, my lady.'

'Oh, no, you flatter me,' Alayne replied and cast down her eyes. She knew that she had not yet lost all the plumpness that carrying a child had brought to her, though she was gradually regaining her slender figure.

'No, I do not flatter you,' Robert said huskily. 'You are wed to another and can never be more to me than a friend—but I adore you and shall do so all my life. No other woman can ever be as much to me.'

'You must not say such things to me,' Alayne said, withdrawing her hands from his. 'You promised you would not.'

'I shall not see you again for a long time,' Robert said. 'I wanted you to know of my love, lady—and to know that if ever you should need me, I am yours to command.'

'Please…' she said and smiled gently. 'I know you mean no harm, but if your words were overheard they might be misconstrued by others.'

'Forgive me,' he said and bowed to her. 'I would bring no harm to you, my lady. I have always known you were above me.'

'May God keep you safe, sir,' Alayne whispered as the young man walked away. It was a dangerous place he was being sent to, for the Welshmen were barbarians by repute and fierce fighters, and she knew that the young knight might be killed in his service for the King.

Turning back towards the house, Alayne stopped short as she saw the physician coming towards her. A shiver of apprehension ran down her spine. She would have avoided him if she could, but it was not possible, and she knew they must meet again one day. Her head went up and she looked at him proudly, determined not to show fear.

'I see that you have ventured out at last, Lady Alayne,' Master Brendon said, his eyes narrowed with malice as he gazed at her. 'It did not take long for Sir Robert to seek you out. I dare say he wanted to ask about the child…'

The menace in his voice made Alayne gasp, for its inference was plain. He was hinting that she had had an affair with Robert Greaves before he left for court.

'I think you forget yourself, sir,' she said and tried to go past him. He moved to stop her, catching her arm and gripping her, half-turning her so that they were brought close together. 'Pray let me go, sir.'

'Not until I have finished with you, you whore,' he muttered and there was hatred in his eyes. 'I know you for what you are—an enchantress, robbing men of the power of their will, making them your slaves…'

'You are foolish, sir. I do not know what you mean.'

'You have bewitched that young fool as you bewitched Sir Ralph,' he muttered angrily. 'You cast your spells over all men and make them your slaves, but I know you for what you are. What would Sir Ralph say if he knew that the son you bore was not his, but—?'

'How dare you!' Alayne broke free of his grasp and, as he lunged at her again, she hit out, catching him with a blow to the side of his head. 'You are a false liar, sir. Everything you do and say is a lie. I know you for what you are—a cheat and a charlatan. You killed our men when they lay sick because you did not know how to treat them. You made the Lady Berenice ill because the potions you made for her were too strong—and one of them poisoned a cat. She was going to expose you for what you were, wasn't she? She told you that the day she died…' Brendon's face had gone as white as a sheet and suddenly she knew that she was not mistaken, had not imagined his evil. It was all true. 'So you killed her. You came upon her alone as she walked and you forced her to take that evil potion that killed her.'

'You witch!' Brendon cried, beside himself with fury and fear. 'You cannot know! Unless you used the powers of darkness to conjure her spirit from the shades…' He was shaking, his face white, spittle on his lips as he launched himself at her. His hands were at her throat, closing hard as he attempted to squeeze the breath from her. 'You shall not betray me. You are a witch and shall die for your evil!'

Alayne was fighting for her life. She struggled to push him off, but he was too strong for her and she found it almost impossible to break his grip on her throat. She could not breathe. Her mind was going blank, the blackness crowding in on her as she felt herself falling…falling into a pit. She was dying. She knew that nothing could save her. Master Brendon would have his way after all.

Alayne was falling into the pit. There was nothing but blackness and the pain in her chest as those strong hands squeezed the breath from her, crushing her throat. She knew that she was dying—then she heard a great shouting and the sound of running feet, as from a distance. She could see nothing, for there was a mist before her eyes, but she heard voices and sensed a struggle around her, and then those terrible hands were torn away from her and she went staggering back, falling to the ground in a faint.

'Kill him!' someone cried, but the words were indistinct and she did not know who spoke them. 'Strike him down, Sir Robert.'

'No!' another voice spoke with authority. 'He must be tried and punished in the proper way.'

'She is a witch!' Brendon cried out. 'She bewitched me as she has all of you. She is a witch and should be put to the test…she cast a spell on me and made me attack her.'

'Take him away. I shall deal with him later.'

Alayne's eyes flickered open as someone bent over her and she saw Ralph's face as through a haze. He touched her face, stroking her hair, and she thought she saw tears on his cheeks as he lifted her gently in his arms. She lay against his chest, half-swooning, only half-aware of what was happening, but knowing that she was safe at last.

'Forgive me,' he whispered as he held her close, carrying her into the house. 'Forgive me that I let that madman stay here—where he could harm you. It is my fault.'

Alayne could not answer him. Her throat was too sore

for her to form the words and her head was still swimming.

'Ralph…' she tried to say, but it was a husky whisper that made no sense.

'Do not try to talk, my love,' he said and his expression seemed carved of stone. 'I shall never forgive myself for what has been done to you. Never…'

Alayne closed her eyes, tears slipping from beneath her lashes as she was carried up to her chamber and laid on the bed. Morna came fussing round, but as Ralph would have turned away she found the strength to grip his arm.

'Stay…' she whispered hoarsely. 'Please.'

'She must rest, my lord—' Morna began, but Alayne clutched at him and he sat down on the bed beside her. 'My lord?'

'Leave her to me, Mistress Grey,' Ralph said. 'I know you mean well, but she needs me here and I shall stay.'

'As you wish, my lord.'

Alayne smiled weakly as the woman went out and Ralph sat with her on the bed. He got up and she tried to catch his hand, but he smiled at her. 'I go only to bring you a little honey wine and water, my love. It is in the middle chamber and may ease your throat.'

Alayne watched as he opened the secret panel, disappeared through it and then came back to her, bearing a pewter goblet.

'Drink a little of this…just a few sips, my dearest.'

Alayne obeyed, then lay back and gazed up at him from her pillows. He bent over her, smoothing her hair back from her face and placing a finger to her lips as she would have tried to speak.

'Hush, my love,' he said. 'Rest your throat and do not try to speak. You will feel better in a little, but it will hurt you to talk too soon.'

She smiled and held out her hand. He took it and then turned it up to kiss the palm, his tenderness so sweet to her that the hurt was eased.

'I should have dismissed the man long ago,' he said, and his face was drawn, made pale by the fear and emotion raging within him. 'It was my fault that he was here, Alayne. Forgive me…'

She shook her head and pointed to her coffer. 'Please…' she whispered and he got up to fetch it for her.

'What is it, Alayne?' He was puzzled by her obvious distress. 'What do you want me to know?'

When he brought the coffer to her she opened the secret compartment and took the vial and Berenice's letter out, giving it to him.

'You want me to read this?' She nodded and Ralph opened the letter. He read swiftly and she saw him frown, then he looked at her. 'When did you find this?'

'You were away…' she said and swallowed a little more of her wine. 'I wanted to…tell you.'

'Yes, I believe you meant to just after the child was born, but we were interrupted by the needs of our son. Yet you could have told me afterwards?' His frown deepened. 'You could not bring yourself to do it? No, let me guess,' he said as she would have spoken. 'I have been a little distant with you, perhaps?' She gave a little nod, her cheeks flushed. 'Then I was at fault, Alayne. I was afraid that if I tried to show my affections too openly you might be frightened of me—as Berenice was. I was afraid that your suffering might have made you fear being my wife. I did not want to force attentions on you, to make you fear me.'

'No…' Alayne croaked, each word a tortured whisper.

that must be spoken. 'I do not fear your love. And Berenice was ill, not afraid of you. *His* cures made her ill.'

'Yes, I see that now,' he said, looking thoughtful. 'Yet she believed that I might have ordered him to give her potions that made her ill. She thought that I might want her dead.'

'She was foolish and ill. Forgive her, my lord.'

'Yes, she was ill, and I was at fault for not understanding that, but her death was not my sin, but another's,' Ralph said. 'You do not know how you have eased my mind. But the past has gone, we must let it go.' He bent to kiss Alayne softly on the lips. 'Some would think me guilty, having read this letter—but you did not?'

'No!' She gripped his hand as hard as she could. 'They could not believe…not if…not if they…'

'Loved me?' he said and smiled a little oddly. 'Do you still love me, Alayne? I had thought of late you might have begun to wish that you had not married me?'

'No!' she cried loudly and then choked. She drank some more of her wine to ease her sore throat. 'You were cross with me for falling—before you went away. I thought…' She paused and sipped her wine, choking a little in her agitation. He bent his head to hush her with a kiss.

'And you thought I no longer loved you?' Ralph smiled and shook his head at her. 'My foolish one. Do you not know how much I adore you? When Brother Harding told me I must choose between you and possible damage to my son, I knew that there was only one choice I could make. He wanted to use the instruments and I feared for our son, for they might have damaged him, but when you screamed in such pain I told them they must save you. Thank God you had managed the task alone, my brave darling. I wanted to come to you at once, but they told me you were weary.'

'Not too weary to see you,' she said and put a hand to her throat. 'It hurts…'

'You must rest, my dearest love. We shall talk again later. Close your eyes and sleep. I shall not leave you.'

'Stay?' Alayne croaked. 'Lay beside me.'

'Yes, I shall stay with you,' he said and lay down, gathering her to him so that she nestled into the crook of his arms and rested her head against his chest. 'You are safe now, my love. He shall not hurt you again.'

Alayne closed her eyes. The wine he had given her was strong and it was making her relax, the warmth of Ralph's body lulling her to sleep. He held her until she was deep in sleep, then he gently slipped from the bed and pulled a fur rug over her to keep her warm.

'God watch over you, my love,' he whispered and went quietly from the room. 'There is something I must do…' He would return to her once the deed was done.

It was morning when Alayne woke again. She felt the weight of Ralph's body close to hers, and turned to him, moving closer so that she could feel the warmth of his breath on her face.

'You are awake, my love?' he asked and smiled down at her, kissing her brow as she gazed up at him, still flushed by sleep.

'Yes. I feel much better,' she said as he leaned on one elbow to look down at her and she saw the anxiety in his face. 'I believe the honey and wine did my throat good, my lord—and it made me sleep.'

'There was also a little something to ease you in the wine,' Ralph said. 'Since Berenice's death I have set myself to learning of these things. I wanted to understand as much as I could and, though I do not consider myself a physician, I have a little skill. Brother Harding and I have talked much of what is known to help in certain illnesses. I think we shall do without the services of a physician for the time being, Alayne. Brother Harding must return to the Abbey, but he says that he knows of a good man who might take up the position here.'

'Then Master Brendon has gone?'

'Yes, he has gone,' Ralph said and there was harshness in his voice, his eyes hard and unforgiving. Alayne could not repress the shiver that went through her, but she would not question. Justice was for her lord to dispense and not the business of women. 'He will not trouble us again.'

'I thank God for it,' she said and hid her face against his shoulder. 'I knew that he hated me. He thought me a witch, Ralph. If he could, he would have had me put to the fire. He said terrible things to me and I struck him. It was then that he attacked me.'

'I have been told that he had muttered such things to others,' Ralph said, his mouth hard and cold as he thought of the punishment meted out to Master Brendon. It had been harsh and given by the combined judgement of the court he had convened, not by his own decision. Beaten, deprived of his tongue, and cast out into the forest with nothing but what he wore, Brendon would most likely fall prey to the hungry wolves that roamed there. 'He will not speak his lies again, Alayne.'

'Do not tell me more,' she whispered. 'Let us speak of happier things, my lord. When shall our son be christened?'

'In a few weeks, when you are truly well again, my beloved.'

'I am well now,' she whispered and snuggled closer to

his warmth, reaching up to kiss him on the mouth. 'I have missed you, my lord. It seems an age since we were together like this…in our bed…'

Ralph chuckled and kissed her hungrily. 'You *are* a temptress, my angel. You know well enough why I dare not come to your bed before this. You suffered greatly at Alain's birth and needed time to heal. I have been hard put to it to keep my distance, my sweet enchantress, for to look at you is to desire you.'

'The bleeding has stopped now,' she said, her cheeks warm as she looked at him. 'And I have been blessed— there is nothing more to keep us apart, my lord.'

'Do you truly feel ready to let me love you again?' he asked, looking into her face in wonder. He stroked her cheek, kissing her softly on the mouth, lingering sweetly, tenderly, almost in wonder, as if he could not quite believe that she wanted him to make love to her. 'Your ordeal has not made you fear the union between a man and woman?'

'I had much pain,' Alayne agreed with a little smile on her lips. She reached up to touch his cheek, trailing her fingertips over the contours of his face. Such a harsh face at times, but at others soft with love. 'But I believe it is often so the first time a woman gives birth. It may not be so bad again—and if I should suffer next time, it will soon be over. It is forgotten now, my lord, and I would not have you fear to touch me. I am strong and healthy and, if God blesses us, I shall bear more sons.'

'I have two sons and care not if I have another,' Ralph told her as he brought his lips down to kiss hers, teasing her with little flicking kisses that sent a wave of pleasure through her. 'You are my dearest love, and above all I care for you. Without you, my life would have little meaning.'

'As mine would have none without your love,' Alayne replied. 'You are my love, my perfect knight...'

Ralph chuckled deep in his throat as he reached out and drew her close to him, the desire raging between them so that an unquenchable fire was lit—a fire that not even time would dim.

'My sweet enchantress,' he murmured huskily. 'I am a very imperfect knight, but I shall strive to be all that you could wish. We may quarrel sometimes, I may seem stern or harsh to you, for I have an uncertain temper at times, but know this, my love—I shall love you all my life and mayhap beyond. My work may take me away from you, life may hurt us as it will from time to time, but nothing can diminish what is in my heart.'

Alayne smiled at him, her heart filled with tender emotion as she saw that he was in earnest. She had been a fool to doubt his love even for a moment and would do so no more. 'And that, my lord, is all that any woman can ask,' she said and kissed him.

And after that there was no more need for words.

* * * * *

2 FREE

BOOKS AND A SURPRISE GIFT!

We would like to take this opportunity to thank you for reading this Mills & Boon® book by offering you the chance to take TWO more specially selected titles from the Historical Romance™ series absolutely FREE! We're also making this offer to introduce you to the benefits of the Reader Service™—

- ★ **FREE home delivery**
- ★ **FREE gifts and competitions**
- ★ **FREE monthly Newsletter**
- ★ **Exclusive Reader Service offers**
- ★ **Books available before they're in the shops**

Accepting these FREE books and gift places you under no obligation to buy, you may cancel at any time, even after receiving your free shipment. Simply complete your details below and return the entire page to the address below. You don't even need a stamp!

YES! Please send me 2 free Historical Romance books and a surprise gift. I understand that unless you hear from me, I will receive 4 superb new titles every month for just £3.65 each, postage and packing free. I am under no obligation to purchase any books and may cancel my subscription at any time. The free books and gift will be mine to keep in any case.

H5ZED

Ms/Mrs/Miss/Mr ....Initials ....
BLOCK CAPITALS PLEASE

Surname ....

Address ....

....

....Postcode ....

Send this whole page to:
UK: FREEPOST CN81, Croydon, CR9 3WZ

Offer valid in UK only and is not available to current Reader service subscribers to this series. Overseas and Eire please write for details. We reserve the right to refuse an application and applicants must be aged 18 years or over. Only one application per household. Terms and prices subject to change without notice. Offer expires 31st July 2005. As a result of this application, you may receive offers from Harlequin Mills & Boon and other carefully selected companies. If you would prefer not to share in this opportunity please write to The Data Manager. PO Box 676, Richmond, TW9 1WU.

Mills & Boon® is a registered trademark owned by Harlequin Mills & Boon Limited.
Historical Romance™ is being used as a trademark. The Reader Service™ is being used as a trademark.